DEATH IN THE DIAMOND LANE

PETE O'DONNELL

Death in the Diamond Lane

Library of Congress Control Number: 2019913598

Print: 978-1-7333261-0-0
ePUB: 978-1-7333261-1-7
MOBI: 978-1-7333261-2-4

For Louise -
for everything.

Prologue

Using hindsight to predict your future is like taking a suppository to change a tire. As late as last week, I was leading a nice unremarkable existence when the fruits of actions taken years ago by someone I'd never heard of pulled me into a sequence of events I couldn't have imagined, let alone seen coming. I'm not complaining. But it's still someone else's story.

June 1968 - Four kilometers west of U.S. Army Headquarters - 10th Special Forces Group - 1st Battalion - Bad Tölz, West Germany

Facing the mirror in the locked bathroom of a quiet Esso station, Staff Sergeant Raymond Doubletree pulled a scraggly blond wig on over his own close-cropped black hair and adjusted oversized rose-tinted sunglasses to better cover his face. Wearing a torn Army jacket, loose-fitting drawstring pants, and huarache sandals, he gently slung a large rucksack covered with daisy decals, peace sign patches, and an upside-down American flag onto his back. After six years of service in the field on an A-Team, he could throw the one hundred pound-plus load around the way a beach-goer might toss a towel over wet shoulders. He then re-read the note for the last time.

Dear Ray,

We simply cannot go on together and you must never contact me again.
The love we shared in the past is now irretrievably gone.
Please believe me, that as hard as this is for both of us, it is for the best.

Please please get the help that you need that I can't give you.

Take care always.

Beth

Doubletree kissed the note and folded it back into its envelope. He added another folded sheet of his own titled *Last Will and Testament* and re-sealed it with Beth's letter. He scrawled RETURN TO SENDER across the front in thick black ink, walked out past the drowsy cashier, and dropped the envelope into a yellow mailbox just outside the front door.

He'd figured the note would be coming. He'd braced himself for it. But the pain had been as sharp in its own way as that from the copper-jacketed 7.62x39 mm rounds that had bounced around his lung and liver four years ago. He was alive today only because of the sacrifice of the Montagnards, who, after losing eight of their own in saving him, had since been abandoned despite American assurances of support.

The young Green Beret had been quickly medevaced out of Vietnam and laid up for six months before reassignment to Western Europe, where he'd faced the Soviet bear in its own backyard.

Team members of Green Light were all volunteers who had cleared the highest hurdles in the U.S. military. The sixty-six fully-qualified carriers served worldwide and were screened four times a year for any imaginable threat to mission success.

As the Soviet Union and Warsaw Pact powers enjoyed a troubling conventional advantage over the United States and NATO, it became a hushed doctrine at the Pentagon that any overt aggression toward Western Europe would be met asymmetrically with tactically-deployed low-yield atomic explosives. Each Green Light detail was tasked with infiltrating enemy territory, locating a pre-designated target, and detonating a 1-kiloton weapon designed to cause crippling blast damage to key infrastructure and immobilizing radiation trauma to East Bloc forces. The SADM (Special Atomic Demolition Munition) or "backpack nuke", resembled a beer drinker's pony keg in size and shape, and was designed to be hauled to its target by a single combatant on foot, on skis, underwater, or by parachute. Carrying the bomb became known as "camping for keeps".

Raymond Doubletree served with uneventful distinction through two rotations in Green Light. Sometime after his 27th birthday he began to show subtle signs of what military physicians would later call Post Traumatic Stress Disorder. While there was no direct dishonor in this diagnosis, he was nonetheless medically discharged against his wishes following his last tour.

Shortly thereafter, the scattered remains of Major Kirk Devine, M.D., the psychiatrist attached to the 1st Battalion, were discovered in a minefield on the western margin of the Fulda Gap. This was a curious end to a promising clinical practice and Army career now marred by the unlikely but also undisprovable suggestion of cooperation with the East German Stasi. Doubletree had, in addition, gone to great pains to jaggedly sever the tip of his own left ring finger, and leave it and its identifying print whorls stuck to a loop of razor wire near an empty, cylindrical green canvas cover that had been cleanly stripped of its contents. The Army CID investigation would conclude that either Devine and Doubletree had conspired to provide a SADM to the East Germans, or that one had tried unsuccessfully to stop the other's treachery. Either way, officially, both were now victims of a tragic but all-too-common tank rollover, and there was nothing to confirm or deny about losing a nuke to the side that already had too many to count.

Doubletree drew little attention during his journey by freighter across the Atlantic and then rail across the better part of the United States. He'd added a prop guitar to his look and was met only with disinterest at Customs and Immigration checkpoints and undisguised disdain from an older generation already so over last Summer of Love.

He paid cash for a used 250cc Yamaha dirt bike off a lot in Gallup, New Mexico and throttled his way through tribal lands across the northeast corner of Arizona and finally into a desolate southern sliver of Utah. His single-wide mobile home was set under a humble grove of two limp tamarisk trees alongside a seasonal creek whose water ran year-round just a few feet below the summer-dry gravel bed. His grid was his own, with water from underground and propane for most everything else, and his cupboards were larded with enough canned and dried food to last for years.

He'd had a good chuckle when passing the old Hopi village, imagining the sputtering of the tribal council and the Bureau of Indian Affairs if they ever found out what this wandering Navajo was carrying in his backpack. The smoke from all those peace pipes would be visible from space.

The morning after his homecoming he set out once again, this time on foot. He rucked the SADM up a narrow wash that all-but-disappeared into a shoulder-width slot canyon two ridges north of his trailer. After an hour of climbing and scrambling he'd gone less than one-half mile as the crow flies. He pushed his way through the branches of a short piñon tree that hid the opening to an old mineshaft and turned on his flashlight.

He entered what amounted to a hole in the wall on hands and knees until rounding a bend that served to block most daylight from the entrance. There he could stand fully upright as he ventured further into the rock. After about 200 meters, the slant-shaft ended abruptly: this had been an exploratory tunnel dug in vain and deserted for decades.

While designed to be carried until shortly before detonation, an unattended SADM was shielded by its own casing to withstand any environmental damage it might sustain for up to three years. Doubletree would be leaving again in less than three months, or at the end of Vietnam's rainy season, when he planned to present the weapon to the Montagnard tribesmen who had saved his life. Whether they traded it for greater American protection or employed it directly against the Viet Cong would be strictly their call. In the meantime, they were getting hammered merely for occupying a long-ignored stretch of the Central Highlands they'd called their own since the 8th century. They reminded Doubletree of the early Navajo. Both were stand-up people who'd taken it on the chin for too long.

Sergeant Doubletree opened the backpack, dialed in the combination to access the control panel, and reconfirmed that he'd disconnected the two leads from the weapon's basic mechanical timer, which had been originally devised to foil electronic pulse countermeasures. He reset the lock, zipped the warhead cask back into its pack, leaned it up against the rough-hewn rock wall, and alighted from the one-way tunnel.

The towering cumulonimbus clouds of an earlier-than-expected Utah monsoon were already roiling as Doubletree crossed the ridge atop the canyon. When the lightning bolt entered below his clavicle, the current found the three copper-clad bullet fragments remaining inside his torso, sparking the gaps like the discharge of a Tesla coil. He was dead before the thunder.

Three years later, after the desert had reduced Raymond Doubletree to his mineral constituents, another, even more elemental breakdown was underway beneath the earth's surface. An endangered rodent, a subspecies of the Mexican vole, had finally gnawed its way through the rough canvas and ripstop nylon of the cylindrical backpack hidden deep in the mineshaft. Eventually the fiberglass housing protecting the firing mechanism also yielded to tooth and nail. An afternoon of nibbling at the red insulation around the fuse-set on the SADM exposed two twists of copper wire. The unclad ends made contact, completed a simple circuit, and initiated the device. Best mouse trap ever.

Navajo and Hopi on reservation lands to the south and Mormon ranchers to the north would feel only a sharp but short jolt preceding a louder-than-usual thunderclap in a clear sky. The regional USGS seismograph recorded an uncommonly shallow earthquake measuring 5.3 on the Richter scale. Dismissed as a calibration error, the common cover story for the needle spike from a nearby slammed door, no one took more than a fleeting notice of the reading. The mineshaft contained what would have developed into a small mushroom cloud and the daylight absorbed the visible flash. The only eyewitnesses were a pair of raptors in flight whose retinas were singed to blindness.

It would take a year for the background radiation to bleed off. But life did re-emerge phoenix-like in the remote canyon. And though she didn't yet know it, the lone beneficiary of the estate of Staff Sergeant Raymond Doubletree was now the richest person on earth.

Chapter 1

Present Day - San Francisco Peninsula, California, USA
3:55 am

The 2011 Town Car I drive, the last model-year true passenger coach Lincoln would make, crunches around the gravel oval in front of Mrs. E. J. DeLong's stone-turreted estate. My boss thinks Mrs. DeLong must be a widow, but no information of any kind can be found about her or her family anywhere on the world wide web: not on its indexed surface with polite company - not in its dark underbelly where souls are sold. Somewhere between 60 and 70 years old, a few inches taller than five feet, pale-skinned, rail-thin, and with professionally colored and managed hair, she always accessorizes a different Chanel suit with the same red Hermès scarf. Around here, where fashion designers sell a lot more phone covers than actual clothes, her refinement is out of the ordinary.

She opens the rear passenger door on her own like always and slides across so she's right behind me. Like always I place her single piece of luggage in the trunk and shut the door she's left ajar. Thirty-five minutes, give or take at this hour, to San Francisco International Airport (SFO), a trip we've been making together once a week for more than four years now.

The pickup and return leg really makes it twice a week. We see a lot of each other. God knows why I got the nod.

"Morning."

A reply never comes. Tips are rarer still.

I haven't a clue what this woman does, or whom she sees once she touches down in Salt Lake City. But it's probably not Latter Day Saints-related as she always smells slightly of stale coffee. She's a nervous flyer and it gets worse at the first distant sound of a jet engine. There's no rustling of clothes, folding of tissue, sipping of water, or fiddling with anything electronic. It's her breathing. It gets even quieter than when we started out. Sometimes I lean back slightly to make sure I'm not driving a hearse.

At the private jet terminal, I present her bag to her on the curb, handle scoped out to the hilt, and she smiles and nods without a word. (The smile showed up at about the one-year mark.) Then she slips past without a sound on mysteriously-muffled high heels. The effect creeps me out every Tuesday morning, and I wonder if all this time she's been bringing her husband home to Utah in pieces.

On to arrivals and a pre-dawn pickup: Sanjay Singh, another regular, 180 degrees removed. A Silicon Valley venture guy, with a brown complexion, prematurely gray hair, and just a hint of an East Indian accent. He's talking before he's even within earshot. He talks as I open the door, through its closing, while I'm putting his bag in the trunk, as I resume driving. More often than not he'll be on his cell, with only a tiny earpiece visible, speaking rapidly into an unseen microphone. Sometimes he'll banter directly with me without beginning, middle, or end. It's like walking in late to a documentary about fire ants narrated by a Punjabi racetrack announcer, and then leaving halfway through the next scene. You're not sure who the players are, what's happening, or even if you're in the right theater.

"...but there's not going to be any 'R' in the 'ROI' because our user base isn't bright enough to two-hand their own sippy cups let alone be left alone to configure their own IUD-hotspots. Sex and Wi-Fi - meet Death and Taxes. Call an audible on wearables, re-brand our foosball table a *time machine,* and license the technology to H-P. The all-in-one printer/copier/scanner/fax/team builder. Pivot solved. Namaste."

"Mr. Singh, welcome back. Going home or to the office?"

"Hi Bill. The office please. How's business?"

"No complaints. Thanks. Good trip?"

"AustinBostonAustin. All bumpy flights. Or maybe early Parkinson's. I dunno. This founder kid wants me to join his *theme camp* on some dry lake bed over Labor Day. I am way-way too dial-up for that deal. The last Burning Man I attended was my grampy on the banks of the Ganges. Not that he's really *dead*, mind you. Just stored to the *cloud*. At least *he's* in a better place. Unlike all our secure customer data which is now on some thumb drive in Nigeria."

As the sun came up Singh got out and I pulled away from the curb in front of the two-story office building housing Varanasi Ventures, one of Silicon Valley's marquee firms. This was the high-octane end of Sand Hill Road, the "billion-dollar exit" off Interstate 280, where tech ambition and risk capital bat lashes and flash feathers. Once in a while the two fall headlong for each other and make out famously.

More often, these infatuations lead to unhappy returns. But the fact that overall yields to limited partners have been fairly disappointing over the last decade or so has done little to dampen the ardor of the institutional investors and wealthy individuals who park their dreams with the sages of Sand Hill. It's sort of like Powerball for smart people. And there's nothing like a plumped up IPO to raise your IQ.

Chapter 2

Had an hour to kill before my next airport arrival, a first-time customer, one Glenn Fletcher coming in from JFK. I headed up to the cell phone lot at SFO, reclined the Lincoln's driver seat, and caught a few winks. My phone's alarm alerted me when the plane landed and I tapped out a text to the new client off the info on the email reservation and waited for his reply. We agreed on a curbside pickup, I gave him my plate number, and he and his carry-on were in the back seat in less than fifteen minutes. His destination was the Four Seasons Hotel in Palo Alto.

Glenn Fletcher was one of those people who doesn't look anything like their names might suggest. No Celt or WASP here, it seemed to me. He was compactly-built, with olive skin, bushy brows and moustache, and incongruously high Slavic-esque cheekbones. Somehow his face didn't quite add up. It was as if several sketch artist depictions of different features had been overlaid with little thought to the whole. The parts just didn't go together somehow, and it was a little unsettling.

"Your plane made good time. Tailwinds from your last storm back East?"

"Probably, yeah. Some parts of Long Island are still without power. It's gettin' old."

"I bet."

"How long you been drivin' for a living?"

"Four years and change."

"Whatcha do before?"

"Different stuff. Unremarkable mostly. Went to grad school, but nobody's hiring anthropologists at the moment."

"Oh the Humanities. Must be frustrating."

"Yeah. You know. You do what you have to. And everybody gave me fair warning about the job prospects."

"You still looking?"

"Got a few CV's around. Might luck out and get another post-doc, but those're usually hand-to-mouth."

"Coeds and office hours. What's not to like?"

"Ramen noodles don't agree with me anymore at my age."

Fletcher chuckled and continued.

"Are you married? Kids?"

"Both prospects a little too expensive at the moment. Someday."

I dropped him off under the hotel's glass awning adjacent to Highway 101, or "Bayshore" as we natives still like to call it to mark our territory and confuse the carpetbaggers, a group loosely defined as anyone who showed up after electrons replaced apricots as the area's principal commodity. The geographical fact is that there's really no such place as The Silicon Valley. It's less a location than a notion whose technological fruit happens to ripen disproportionately within a space roughly circumscribed by the greater Santa Clara Valley, once one of the most productive patches of farmland on the planet. As annoying as it may be to some of us who sprang from this soil, today around here, apps grow on trees and apples come from Chile. And nostalgia just takes up too much RAM. Even if my faithful steed will too soon fade into memory.

The Lincoln Town Car, cousin to the venerable Ford Crown "Vic" - once the go-to vehicle of most law enforcement agencies and taxicab fleets throughout the U.S. - is the AK-47 of livery. The ubiquitous Russian assault rifle also lacks fine lines, fit, and finish but is rumored to be able to shoot rusty roofing nails through its bulky barrel in a pinch. The same sort of durability goes for the ultra-reliable Town Car. Carefully maintained, the engine and transmission will last more than half a million miles while delivering better than twenty miles per gallon using regular gas in a car that weighs almost 5000 pounds, has an enormous trunk, and can carry four adult passengers plus a driver in comfort. Yet Lincoln seems to have shut down the assembly line for good. Somewhere six feet under, Henry Ford took himself for a spin.

Chapter 3

Glenn Fletcher had requested a return ride to SFO shortly before noon. These types of touch-and-go business trips have become more and more common. If the scarcity of one's time is a metric of relative importance, then less must mean more. Leisure is for amateurs. Someone could be gaining on you.

Driving to the airport at this hour was a relative breeze traffic-wise. And passengers frequently reflect the more relaxed road conditions. Some prefer to ruminate quietly, others might strike up a conversation, most hop right on the phone or internet. Hardly anyone anymore reads a physical newspaper. They're getting as rare as direct eye contact. Fletcher brought an unopened *Wall Street Journal* into the car and looked right at me. His candor seemed a little practiced, but I like to give everybody the benefit of the doubt.

"Hey, Doc."

Not even my own mother on the very occasion of my earning a PhD had addressed me like that. There was something about this guy.

"Hello again."

"How long to SFO?"

"Right now the GPS is saying twenty-four minutes. But they don't make one just yet that can predict what might happen once we're underway."

"What's your gut?"

"Around that. Barring a wreck or unannounced road construction."

"Fair enough. You're a local, right?"

"Yeah. Right nearby. How 'bout you?"

"Pittsburgh, PA. Originally, anyway."

"My second favorite team, after the Giants."

"How'd you get to be a Pirates fan from way out here?"

I thought I'd check his bona fides.

"Roberto Clemente. Saddest day of my childhood was when they found him in the wreckage of that plane."

Fletcher paused ever-so-slightly.

"Yeah. That was a real low point in the Burg. Let me tell ya."

He waited a moment before continuing.

"You must have some interesting stories to tell after your time behind the wheel. Trying not to overhear other people's conversations when they're on the phone and whatnot."

"Some people talk like you're not even there. Most everybody's like that after you've driven 'em a few times."

"Any good dirt? Juicy stuff?"

"The clients we drive are pretty much all business."

"Then you're in on some big deals as they go down, I bet."

"I've heard a few here and there."

"Don't be modest."

"You know. Sure. If I'd had the money or the inclination I could've made a buck or two."

"But isn't that inside information? Wouldn't that be illegal?"

"Like I said, 'If I'd had the inclination'..."

"..or money. You said that too."

"I've never acted or traded on anything. Look, if a driver wants to keep his job, you can count on his discretion. But there's no legal expectation of confidence, like attorney-client privilege. And nobody yet has asked me to sign a NDA."

"So you've considered it enough to maybe run it by a lawyer."

"I only know enough to know when I should take the Fifth. Like right about now."

Fletcher chuckled.

The rest of the trip went quietly and I pulled up to the curb outside American Airlines departures. Glenn Fletcher started to get out of the car.

"Well, nice meeting ya, Doc."

"Safe travels."

"And you've still got my credit card information?"

"Yessir. We'll email you your receipt."

"And the gratuity's included?"

"Yup. Thank you."

I noticed his unopened newspaper on the center armrest.

"Don't forget your paper."

"Keep it. Who knows? You might find it interesting. Oh.."

He held the door open and smiled without warmth.

"..and you know as well as I do that Clemente's body was never found. And I'm pretty sure that was all well before your time."

He closed the door firmly and we both also knew he'd just eaten my lunch without chewing. I picked up the newspaper to throw it into the curbside recycling bin and noticed the thin rubber band holding a sealed white envelope under the fold. Inside was $5000 in one hundred dollar bills. The block lettering on the Post-it note covering Ben Franklin's face on top of the stack read: THANKS FOR LISTENING.

Chapter 4

I parked the Town Car in the hourly lot and hoofed it into the terminal. The TSA line was long and slow and smelled of ripe socks and resignation. Fletcher, not likely to be stuck with the great unwashed, had no doubt already been ushered through to the gate, leveraging one of the several leapfrog amenities available to the elite business traveler. No self-respecting captain of commerce risks scuffed Cole Haans and plantar warts if he can afford not to.

I reached Fletcher on his cellphone. He agreed to meet me on my side of the security gate and appeared less than five minutes after we'd hung up. He was rolling his carry-on behind him. I didn't wait to hand him back the money.

"It's all there. All 5K."

"Then you counted it."

"Look, I'm not at all clear with what you were going for with that, but I'm not your guy."

He placed the opened envelope in the inside breast pocket of his coat without so much as a glance at its contents.

"I'm sorry. That was clumsy of me. Can I buy you a cup of coffee?"

"You'll miss your flight and I'll be late for my next passenger."

"Next time then."

As I watched him retreat in the direction of his plane, my belly of smug virtue turned sour at the thought of how far five thousand dollars might have gone in my strapped financial state. I hadn't even asked him what the money was for exactly. I just figured that whatever strings were attached included me eavesdropping on some of my higher-profile clients for his benefit. But was I indignant because he'd insulted my integrity or because he'd low-balled the opening offer?

While rooting around in my conscience on my way back to short-term parking, I bumped right into another limo driver getting out of my vehicle. It was a she, which was obvious when she turned around and stood up to her full five feet, eight inches. A firm, forty-something brunette knockout with bright green eyes and an unlined caramel complexion, she could cause a four-car pileup in a three-piece suit.

"Is this one yours? I am so sorry. It was open.."

It's funny how quickly the likelihood of that occurrence became greater under her gaze.

I saw a similar Town Car nearby.

"Maybe that one's yours?"

"Yeah. Yeah. That looks more like it. Thanks."

She pressed the electronic fob on her key. Her car's doors thumped open.

"Throw a stick and hit a dozen black Lincolns in this lot. Are you new to this?"

"First day on my own."

For my benefit she tapped the laminated name badge clipped to her shirt pocket.

"Good outfit", I said.

She looked down skeptically at her work uniform.

"I meant your company there. Victory Coach. Good reputation. But the suit suits you too."

She blushed and readjusted her name badge, and in the process snapped off a press-on painted fingernail which flew past my nose. Lifting up the badge had given me a glimpse of the outline of her left nipple which showed prominently through her dress shirt. She quickly and modestly straightened her name plate and necktie.

"Lara Fratelli...I'm Bill Feeney."

She looked puzzled.

"It's on your name tag."

We shook hands and she rolled her eyes at herself.

"Again, I'm really sorry."

"Hang in there. It gets easier. See you around?"

Gleaming white teeth appeared in a megawatt smile. The small cleft in her chin was joined by two button-shaped dimples in the middle of her cheeks.

She definitely finished well.

"I'd know your car anywhere..."

Chapter 5

Driven to a pleasant distraction by the eminently attractive and seemingly absent-minded Lara Fratelli left me motoring right past my freeway exit. I had to loop back to gain access to Moffett Federal Airfield, a former Naval Air Station and home to the locally-iconic Hangar One, a colossal structure which once housed dirigibles flown briefly in the 1930's.

After passing through security I headed out onto the tarmac to await the arrival of a Boeing 767, commonly configured to carry more than 200 airline passengers. I parked next to an unoccupied Tesla S, its faint green halo almost visible over the hood. It seemed to have arrived by its own free will and I really didn't know whether it had driven itself or some unseen minion had just left it and scurried away. The big plane rolled up, two landing agents in Parsec polo shirts wheeled a staircase into position by the forward exit door, and out stepped a total of two people. My guy, the CEO, climbed into the back of the Lincoln as the agents put his golf bag in the trunk. Meanwhile the founder slid into the rear passenger seat of the electric sedan, which pulled away in silence. Hear no evil.

We arrived at Arun Agrawal's Atherton digs, a walled-in acre of lawn surrounding stacks of concrete and glass cubes accented with hardwood siding. It was a masterpiece of manly architecture with an almost aggressive embargo against anything remotely feminine or welcoming. This suited the widely-feared and newly-divorced titan, whose front door lacked a bell or knocker and probably required all visitors to loudly clang their testicles to announce themselves. The estate did, however, have a front gate keypad and I punched in the access code from the driver's seat. Agrawal always acted surprised either that I'd remembered it or that he'd shown the lapse in judgment in giving it to me in the first place. Ours was a shaky trust built on mutual suspicion. I would clearly have been cast as "help" in the old country and he had made the mistake of needing my help with a particularly heavy bag after one overseas trip. Before he could shoo me back out to the blacktop I'd gotten a chilling glimpse of his nightstand reading: *The Architecture of Albert Speer* (picture book) and *We Don't All Use Fenugreek - The Spice That Almost Cost Me The National Spelling Bee* (his autobiography in well-eared paperback). Today, as then, he nodded at me warily as I drove away.

I tanked up the Town Car at El Guanaco, an independent gas station with low prices and Mexican hot chocolate. There by the pumps I tried a quick background search of Mr. Glenn Fletcher via smartphone. He'd implied that he was a native of Pittsburgh, I inferred that he might today live on Long Island, and from all appearances he'd been flying in and out of New York's JFK. When everything came up blank, I looked at the billing address on the credit card he'd provided: 7750 K Street NW, Washington, D.C. I was only slightly familiar with the layout of D.C. and even less so of its inner workings, but more than once I'd watched the Sunday morning TV pundits lambaste loathsome lobbyists for "pimping the Potomac" from their offices along K Street. Sure enough, number 7750 housed Crenshaw & Turner, a lobbying firm registered with both Houses of the U.S. Congress.

Chapter 6

My next four passenger pickups, all short point-to-point transfers, yielded the following disparate information: approximately 30% of all published peer-reviewed findings in the health sciences contain intentionally false or fabricated results (from the CEO of a biotech company), 90% of all the digital information in human history has been collected in the past two years (senior computer scientist at a big data company), the largest installed customer base of a multi-player online gaming platform which encourages participants to purchase virtual clothing for their avatars is women age 18-35 living in sartorially-repressed Arab states (board member of said gaming company and Stanford University lecturer), and the retail sales of chewing gum have dropped by more than 25% due to widespread smartphone distraction at checkout counters where most impulse purchases are made (marketing director of major consumer products company). The fifth passenger, who spoke little English and what I think was Mandarin into his phone, had limited his interests to $400 bottles of California pinot noir from a biodynamic winery on Skyline Boulevard in the Santa Cruz Mountains and officially licensed San Jose Sharks memorabilia from their home ice at the SAP Center. He wanted to drive through In-and-Out and eat his Double-Double in the car before I dropped him off at the Chinese Consul General's residence in San Francisco.

All five clients were fairly chatty either with me or with someone on the phone, or some combination of both. Come to think of it, they all must've been burning up the 4G as each asked for the location of the 12 volt DC receptacle and three for a connecting cord.

(We do our best to please, and have most Parsec and Cameo-compatible chargers and cables available right in the cabin.)

I think I kept it cordial, but all afternoon I was preoccupied with another question: what did a major Washington lobbying firm want with my clients? Were they all targets of opportunity or was Fletcher (if that was his real name) only interested in a specific someone? My hunch was that anything even potentially lucrative would be coveted regardless of the source. Eavesdropping for insider info seemed a natural fit for a Wall Street black op. But didn't political buttonholers and influence peddlers serve a different kind of constituency?

On my way up to Aquatic Park for an evening swim, my boss texted to tell me that Glenn Fletcher's credit card had been declined, his phone had likely been a prepaid disposable, and Crenshaw & Turner had never heard of him.

Chapter 7

The South Side Rowing Club has been around for well over a century and wears its age like a battered square schooner run aground on the beach just north of Fisherman's Wharf. It encourages rowing and swimming on and in San Francisco Bay and handball and horseplay in and around the clubhouse. Members are by-and-large warm, gregarious, and slightly nuts. It's a place that honors its colorful history but doesn't stand on formality. Bores and the bored need not apply.

After a brief, bracing dip in the bay, I tried warming up in the club sauna. In a far corner sat a wee, wrinkled Irish guy looking like a piece of wet brisket in a bath towel. In deep black ink were the letters "DNR" tattooed across his chest. On his left shoulder were four red Rising Suns covered with black X's, confirmed kills from his days as a Marine raider in WWII. Finbar, a lifelong Leatherneck believed to be more than 100 years old, was a fixture in the club hotbox.

A tall man on wooden crutches pulled open the door and entered. Carl Frost, in his early fifties, was a former special agent of the FBI, and one of the club's fastest open water swimmers, holding records for both the Alcatraz and Golden Gate crossings. He continued to improve his times despite missing the better part of his right leg. A few years previous he'd been a liaison to the Russian FSB in Vladivostok on a six-month assignment. Out jogging, he had plunged into a utility access point in the street. The black market for cast iron was so robust at the time in Russia's Pacific Far East that manhole covers were routinely stolen for scrap value. His fall had been gruesome; his leg had been trapped in the metal rungs of the ladder below street level, and after rescue, repatriation, and months of excruciating pain, he'd elected amputation. He was a never-look-back kind of guy, refused a desk job with the Bureau, cut his expenses, and retired to a life of swimming in San Francisco Bay and volunteering for the American Red Cross. Like everybody else in the club, he looked out for Finbar. He handed the old mascot a small paper cup of cold water and spoke to him in a loud voice.

"Fin...how's life?"

"Nasty, brutish, and no end in sight."

"And how did it go at the DMV?"

"They told me next time wear a bigger towel."

"They didn't renew your license, did they?"

Silence. I chimed in.

"Fin...did you make an appointment to see the eye doctor?"

"I don't trust doctors."

"Me neither. But I can take you if you change your mind," offered Carl.

"I can see fine. The thing in the galley was a one-time flub. That's all."

"Hey, peeing in the Mister Coffee could've happened to anyone."

"...switching to tea's probably healthier anyway."

Fin seemed satisfied.

"Are we havin' fish sticks again?"

"Suppose so. It's Wednesday. Want us to save you a place?"

"Thanks."

♦♦♦

Later, over dinner in the club mess at a picnic table with Finbar, I told Carl about my run-in with "Glenn Fletcher". After listening without interruption, he weighed in.

"Strictly speaking, it doesn't sound like any laws were broken. Even stiffing you on the fare could be construed innocently. He'd just claim that the consulting fee you declined was also intended to cover the cost of the ride. That said, the guy's trouble."

"A shady figure", croaked a slightly perkier Finbar.

"Do you suspect he was casting a wide net or is there someone you drive who might be of particular interest?," Carl inquired, as he adjusted the fit of the prosthesis under his pants leg.

"I'm thinking more opportunist on a fishing expedition. Many of our passengers fit a target profile: successful, well-connected, and quite a few of 'em a lot less guarded than they ought to be. Somehow he got ahold of our client list...which wouldn't be all that tough. Most of our business is referred from one admin to another."

"Any other drivers you know been similarly solicited?"

"Of the several I've asked so far, none."

Fin patiently blew the heat off his chowder.

"Did you work any insider trading cases when you were with the Bureau?", I asked the former G-Man. He nodded.

"Early on in my career. One of my classmates from Quantico way-back-when now heads up the financial fraud unit alongside the SEC. It's still all show horse stuff: make examples of a few crooked big shots, trot 'em out before the cameras, and try to shame off the wannabees. Walkin' perps is as old as Eliot Ness, but a lot of the stigma has been lost over the years. For some people today, a mugshot's just a selfie with subtitles."

Carl paused and then continued.

"Your guy showed his hand early. He wasted no time trying to cultivate you. His opening move was purely transactional. It points to someone in a hurry. And old school. For all you hear about the egghead quants devising more and more complex algorithms to tweak their trades, there's still no advantage like having a flesh-and-blood insider."

"Should I be worried?"

"About Glenn Fletcher? Probably. About the feds? There's no nice way to say this, but like a colleague at Scotland Yard once put it, you'd be known as 'bagging the Corgi'. You're low-level game. Maybe the Queen rubs your ears. If they really thought you could lead them to the palace, they'd run you through the wringer. But you haven't done anything, and insider trading can be a bitch to prove. If today I overheard Fin inside the locker room talking to his fellow board member about an imminent acquisition, and I parlayed that information into a tidy market return for myself, prosecutors working in the same office would disagree about whether I was a criminal or just in the right place at the right time."

Carl removed a phablet from his gym bag and turned it on. Fin looked at it like a woodchuck might regard the Periodic Table.

"If you see this Fletcher again, you're gonna need some leverage. Here's a contact I've still got inside the Bureau. Special Agent Janet Farr. Don't sweat the introductions. Just let me know before you call so I can give her a heads-up."

Chapter 8

Interstate 280 between San Francisco and San Jose immodestly bills itself as the "World's Most Beautiful Freeway". In the day it offers expansive views of SF Bay, the inland slope of the coastal range, and several links in a chain of pristine, drinking water-filled reservoirs which hold Sierra snowmelt piped from 167 miles away. Much of the land surrounding its midsection has remained undeveloped watershed, protected in perpetuity, thanks to decades of hard-fought open space advocacy. Once the weekday commute winds down and the sun disappears, there are stretches of asphalt where your single set of headlights may be the only source of illumination for miles. The road which earlier carried more than ten thousand vehicles per hour abruptly returns to the wild.

Mrs. DeLong was snoring gently but unevenly in the back of the Lincoln. This had been a whirlwind trip for her, as typically she would spend a few days in Utah before coming home. As well, her return flight had been delayed and finally arrived just after 10 pm. Still, I had never known her to fall asleep in the car. Nor had I ever seen her in anything but high heels. Tonight, with the predictable Chanel suit, she wore a pair of white running shoes. Perhaps owing to unfamiliar footwear, she'd appeared a bit unsteady at the curb at SFO, and had actually let me take her elbow to assist her into the back seat. Another first to be sure. Bodily contact had been previously unthinkable. I now probably knew more about her than her doctor.

My mind returned to the earlier conversation with Carl Frost. He'd urged me to draw up a list of all the passengers I'd driven over the past few months, with particular emphasis on regular or repeat customers. Without thinking very hard I could count at least four recent backseat eavesdrops which might have reaped insider rewards from the unwary:

- a startup CEO who'd negotiated the acquisition of his company by a publicly-held network security giant on a conference call which fixed the date of final escrow,
- a private equity investor who discussed the poaching of a Chief Technology Officer with multiple patents to his name from a portfolio company to a competitor,
- a VC on the board of the segment-leading video-on-demand company who was informed of a pending exclusive distribution deal for the entire film library of a major Hollywood studio, and
- a hedge fund analyst who revealed the unencouraging results of a midsize pharma's flagship chemotherapeutic agent after preliminary human trials.

This didn't even include the young investment banker with chronically loose lips or the management consultant's humble-brag to her former "B-School" classmate about the specific vulnerabilities of the federal government's bidding and procurement process for military satellites.

Still, even with advance intelligence, it would take a certain level of sophistication to determine which stock (the acquirer or the acquired) could be relied upon to go up and which one down, where best to peg a short position, or even when to execute a trade. But often enough the little birdie told you just what you needed to know.

Carl also advised me to scan the reports posted regularly online and in the financial sections of most big-city newspapers which detail the public disclosures of permissible sales of equities by insiders. The volume of activity on all securities exchanges is so vast and the process so digitally accelerated that the SEC/FBI rarely took the time to leverage the subpoena powers of the U.S. Attorney except in the cases of glaringly enormous transactions or those made by individuals already under suspicion/investigation. Like the Unabomber, whose own brother turned him in when the posse's trail had gone cold, an awful lot of dodgy deals on Wall Street come gift-wrapped to the feds. Jealousy becomes indignance, which then buffs itself a coat of concerned citizenship. The authorities simply must be alerted.

♦♦♦

I smelled a skunk. The four-legged kind. Saw it too, out of the corner of my eye. Just a quick flash of white, which at first looked like a lane stripe peeling itself off the roadbed and wriggling toward the shoulder. Then came the cliched thud of you-know-who being struck by the undercarriage of the car. I winced, but thankfully hadn't had time to swerve. A rollover at this speed would likely cause grievous injury or worse to the soft-skinned humans inside.

There followed a sickening flapping noise from the right rear wheel well, succeeded by the sound of my passenger flinching herself awake with a shallow pant. The low-level horror that was happening between the Lincoln and the tarmac was only a few layers of sheet metal away from Mrs. DeLong's right leg. She cleared her throat repeatedly but remained mute. Yet the message couldn't be any plainer: "Deal with this. *Now*."

I pulled off at the next exit and stopped on a broad section of dark shoulder, pushed on the hazard lights, put the car in park, turned off the engine, and grabbed the flashlight from the glovebox. The flapping noise seemed to have stopped. But as I got out of the car and walked back around the trunk the sounds of distress took on a whole different tone. From somewhere between the tire and the axle came a clamor I'd never heard before: a cross between a wheeze and a hiss that roiled the gut and slowed my approach. And, of course, there was the smell. Consider the aroma of rancid patchouli oil mixed with diesel exhaust, and then imagine the bouquet of a colicky musk ox after a rain. It was fear, and blood, and excrement all hitting my nostrils in combination as the stricken animal's fight or flight reflexes duked it out just behind the rear quarter panel of the Lincoln. I threw up all over my necktie when I remembered my high school chemistry teacher explaining how all odors were particulate.

I pulled off my tie, opened the cavernous trunk, and located the tire iron. The death throes continued from almost directly under where I'd left Mrs. DeLong sitting. Ironically, she had never before, to my recollection, sat where she did tonight, typically preferring the left side seat. But in her fatigue she hadn't bothered to slide over. I was guessing that behind the tinted windows she'd by now be occupying her customary spot, as far from the caterwauling as possible.

I leaned over and shined the flashlight above and behind the tire. Writhing and seething was a mangled mass of black, white, and red. I tried to carefully dislodge - pry, really - the skunk from the steel undercarriage. It was embedded in, more than impaled by the metal, but still managed the moxie to snap and claw furiously at my probes with the tire tool. At one point, the iron was jerked from my hand and clanked to the asphalt. I picked it up and angled the beveled end between the wheel strut and the frame and managed to free the better part of the animal, but not without leaving a good chunk stuck behind. It squirmed toward me like an angry toupée, lifted what was left of its tail, and sprayed me as it breathed its last. *Braveheart* reincarnated.

Not to split hairs, but I found out that skunk spray is really more of a directed stream, which in this case hit me squarely in the chest with the force and accuracy of a well-aimed, big-bore squirt gun. I rolled around on the ground next to what remained of the dead critter until my eyes stopped watering. The dry heaves would be with me for a while.

While ripping off my shirt I staggered to the front passenger door and grabbed as many single-serve drinking water bottles as I could from the center console, flushed my eyes, and emptied the rest over the front of my torso. I used a chamois cloth from the door's side pocket to dab my eyelids, dry my face, and wipe myself down. Out of some rote sense of decorum I put my suit jacket on over my bare skin. By now I'd depleted all the front seat water and needed some to drink. The back seat always had a ready stash.

I knocked politely on the rear window and then pulled the door open. Mrs. DeLong's lifeless, gray body flopped halfway out of the car.

I knew I should've looked harder at STEM.

◆◆◆

Grace under pressure. Grace under pressure. Grace under pressure.

Maybe if I kept repeating it?

I slid Mrs. DeLong out onto the ground, rolled her onto her back, and checked for a pulse. Nothing. We had a portable AED somewhere under the front seat which I hadn't laid eyes on since my first day of training almost five years ago. I scrambled into the cabin, rifled through the small case under the driver's seat, cast aside a couple of road flares, and grabbed the defibrillator. I snatched my cell phone from the dashboard holder, dialed 911, and, feeling more and more like the boatman on the River Styx, knelt down next to a rapidly cooling client. Her mouth hung open, her limbs were slack, and her eyes had rolled back in their sockets.

"911 emergency."

"I'm a limo driver stopped just off southbound 280 on the shoulder of the Edgewood Road exit ramp. My passenger has no pulse. Please send help. Gotta go."

I turned on the speakerphone setting, put my mobile down on the gravel, and left the line open. I could hear the dispatcher say something, couldn't make out exactly what, and opened the AED. Holding the flashlight in my mouth was not going to work, so I ran back, grabbed and ignited a flare from the emergency kit and placed it on the ground nearby.

Now the hard part. I removed Mrs. DeLong's scarf, tore open her blouse, pulled off her bra, and placed the conductive pads on the upper right and lower left quadrants of her torso as in the diagram under the AED's plastic cover. I pushed the button to start the device. Nothing. I waited a few seconds and tried it again, this time holding the button down. Again nothing. A third time and still no light came on, no beep sounded, no robotic voice instructed me that the unit was self-charging and searching for a shockable heart rhythm, like we'd observed in our four-hour training course. It had to be the battery.

I remembered that there was an adapter for the device in the kit in the car. As I pushed off the ground to get to my feet my hand slipped on a slick trail of gore. Wiping what I could off on my jacket, I retrieved the adapter from the cabin and plugged it into one of the receptacles in the back seat armrest of the car.

Nothing.

I tried another outlet.

Nothing.

The dispatcher's faint voice continued to trill unintelligibly. My phone was dying along with my passenger.

I tried the AED in every 12 volt plug I could reach in the back seat.

Nothing. Nothing. Nothing.

OK. OK. OK. Compressions to breaths. Compressions to breaths. I think I remembered it was 30 to 2. I knelt to one side of her body, tilted her head back, pinched off her nostrils, covered her mouth with mine, and blew in two rescue breaths. Her chest rose, so her airway was open. I felt for and found the notch at the bottom of her sternum, positioned my hands, and started in.

The loud crunching began immediately. I could feel her ribs snapping under the heel of my hand; the sharp, broken ends threatening to break through her skin and maybe my own as well. I kept up a steady pace, timed my retches, and tried to ignore the now-squishy sound accompanying each compression on Mrs. DeLong's naked chest. Every few cycles I'd check for a pulse without success and resume CPR.

It seemed like months had passed by the time the scene was flooded by the lights from a CHP cruiser. The officer hurried to my side. He was squawking something into the radio speaker attached to his shoulder.

"How long has she been down?"

I finally figured he was addressing me.

"Don't....know....exactly."

After another cycle of compressions, the trooper took over, and I was able to dedicate myself to giving breaths. It was a few minutes before the paramedics arrived. With great speed they removed the leads I'd placed earlier on Mrs. DeLong's torso and replaced them with their own. A computer-generated voice pierced the quiet.

"Analyzing....Analyzing...Pulse detected...Pulse detected...*No* shock advised...*No* shock advised."

We backed away slightly from the victim as both disbelieving paramedics checked manually for signs of life.

"Yeah. We got a pulse."

"Confirmed."

"Sweet. Nice work, man. This practically never happens."

"She still may not make it. But now at least she's got a shot."

They fit a rescue mask over her nose and mouth and continued ventilating her lungs by squeezing a breathing bag.

As the cop reached over to shake my hand he slowly surveyed the scene. His fingers closed just before contact was made.

The sizzling red light from the flare cast an eerie glow over a dead polecat and its entrails lying next to an unconscious old lady with her breasts exposed. This shirtless white male in an unbuttoned suit jacket, looking like a doughy understudy from a Chippendale's farm club, appeared to be covered in blood and bits of fur.

One of the paramedics called it.

"Dude...looks like somebody forgot their safe word."

Chapter 9

After narrowly convincing the state trooper that no roadside voodoo had occurred, I was escorted to the ER at Stanford University Medical Center, where the paramedics had taken Mrs. DeLong. As far as personal effects, she had carried only clothes, a tortoise-shell comb and matching sunglasses, a small LED flashlight, a tiny prescription vial of nitroglycerin tablets, and about $2500 in cash. There was no cell phone, or any contact information of any kind in her handbag or pockets. Jane Doe had nothing on her.

A gravel-voiced nurse resembling LBJ with bosoms and bangs glared in my direction and loudly noted the patient's conspicuous lack of jewelry just as a young resident interrupted to ask if Mrs. DeLong had any known medication allergies. I called and woke my boss, who provided a home phone from the customer file. The doctor tried her number, reached only an answering machine, and left a short, urgent message to contact the hospital. After allaying my concern about possible exposure to rabies, the ER team insisted I take a complimentary supply of skunk-off solution and practically pushed me out the door while giving assurances that my nearly-late passenger had been stabilized in the ICU.

I'd parked in a dark space under the branches of a large oak tree in the hospital lot. As I sat behind the wheel, out of the corner of my eye, I noticed a faint glow coming from the footwell of the right rear seat. Curious, I got out and opened the passenger door for a better look.

The floor mat showed a ghost outline of Mrs. DeLong's sneakers in what appeared to be luminescent green dust, the texture of which resembled fine-grained beach sand. Against the black background of carpet it resembled an emerald galaxy on a moonless night.

I knew just who I could ask about it.

Arriving home, I threw all my clothes, save my boxers, in the parking lot dumpster behind my apartment complex. A guiltless half-hour shower and two beers later and I was drooling on my pillow. Sometimes the single life is underappreciated.

Chapter 10

My first job today wasn't scheduled until 8 pm, so I had time to give the Lincoln a once-over. Drivers were expected to keep their assigned vehicle in top working condition in exchange for taking-it-home privileges. The local car wash was magically able to remove last night's stench from the undercarriage and I was soon on my way over to the coast.

Fee's farm was at the end of a long, graded, gravel driveway on a hillside above Half Moon Bay. The car's fresh layer of road dust was a small price to pay for a visit to the Polynesian Ponderosa.

Fee is short for "apostrophe" which is short for Ne'igalo-meatiga Fainu'u which means something along the lines of "unforgettable pain" in traditional Samoan. A widower and father to three grown triplet sons, Fee is a clean-living Methodist with the mischievous soul of a 320-pound brown leprechaun. His folks brought him to the Bay Area as an infant and he's been catching fish for a living since high school. We became inseparable at nine years-old while picketing a local Girl Scout troop intent on selling cookies in what had always been our spot to peddle tadpoles and turtles in front of Safeway. Now proud owner of two boats in Princeton Harbor, these days his main quarries are Dungeness crab and whatever species of finfish is running. His marriage to Teuila lasted for twenty happy years until she died unexpectedly five years ago from a brain aneurysm. Fee hasn't looked seriously at another woman since.

I can count the number of times I've seen Fee, at any time of year, and in any type of weather or situation, except in church, wearing anything other than shorts, flip-flops, and a t-shirt. He still irons his clothes the same way his wife did, and now looks like a middle-aged yurt on the first day of summer camp. His expression can be fierce but his nature is consistently sunny in the face of the violent Pacific storms that can wreak havoc in winter and the persistent blinding fog that can make summer navigation feel like playing Polo without Marco.

The forty acres of farm sat on a gentle grassy slope two miles from the ocean. A rambling wooden house painted rural white looked out toward the shore. Behind the residence was an updated old barn with an enormous glass roof. A small patch of pumpkins grew alongside an empty animal enclosure. Two pickup trucks were parked neatly nearby.

I pulled up and got out to watch Fee trying to teach his 600-pound sow to heel.

"Mornin', E-Z. Don't ask."

He'd coined the nickname to honor my devotion to IRS Form 1040EZ, for filers with modest incomes.

"Howya doin', Fee? Lookin' good, Trudy. You been working out?"

The hog actually turned toward me and snorted. Her truffle-training had been underway for a few weeks now. I was secretly dying to know how it was coming.

"You know how they say after a while people start to look like their pets?"

"Are you telling my pig makes me look fat?"

"Word to the wise? Keep her stripes in the closet this season. And don't be seen with her at all if she's in black."

My friend just smirked.

"OK. The suspense is killing me. Can she find fungi or not?"

"Rome wasn't built in a day. And there're still trust issues, I guess.."

Several months ago Trudy had been earmarked as the main dish at a traditional Samoan pig roast. Sensing trouble after weeks of double portions and the ominous arrival of banana leaves, she figured out how to unlatch the gate to her pen, and fled for her life. Fee had been out front picking up the morning newspaper in his underwear when he'd glimpsed his prize hog bolting toward the Coast Highway. Sprinting to the kitchen, he picked up a butcher knife, and thrashed after her through several thorny acres of artichokes growing on the neighboring farm. He had closed the distance by the time they reached the commuter-clogged artery down the hill. Chasing her in the median between north and southbound traffic had resulted in more than twenty 911 calls to the Sheriff's dispatcher. It wasn't every day you saw a blood-streaked Pacific Islander in his skivvies wielding a long blade in hot pursuit of livestock in the middle of a crowded thoroughfare. After a detailed explanation to the six responding deputies, no charges were filed, and Fee was shamed into commuting Trudy's sentence. She had not forgiven him.

"Have you two tried therapy?"

"I switched vets when he suggested I learn German.."

"Hmm.."

"..but the loofah does seem to help with the angst....and the boys have offered to cut back on the b-a-c-o-n..."

"We're capping-and-trading with some vegans online. Hey, Bill!"

The boys had appeared on the porch: Gilbert, Dean, and Brandon, identical triplets, 23 years-old, each an even six feet tall and 300 pounds, still a notch under their old man. All had shaved heads and Fu Manchu beards. I was godfather to the three of them.

"Morning guys. How goes it?" I asked.

Fee had returned his attention to Trudy, rubbing her flaps and folds with forced affection.

"Good girl. Such a good girl…"

"Get a room!", came the chorus from the porch.

My old friend turned toward me, but spoke to his boys.

"The three-headed menace is really startin' to piss off the old H-O-H."

"Hard-of-hearing?"

"Head-of-household."

"Hey, we're not the one re-purposing the pork here…"

Fee faced his sons and narrowed his eyes. I broke a slightly tense silence.

"Gentlemen. Gentlemen. Let's not…what's Samoan for *quibble*?"

"No such word." Fee replied firmly.

In perfect sync, the triplets looked down at their feet, grins growing across their faces. Their dad's hard expression broke into a quiet chuckle as he shook his head. He paused before continuing.

"Listen up. Your godfather had a rough ride last night. Any chance you boys could take a look at the Lincoln?"

♦♦♦

The tricked-out barn out back was loaded with natural light. You entered through tall sliding doors onto a rubber-topped concrete slab floor loaded with giant Olympic barbells, three stout bench press stations, and the same number of squat racks. There were no pulleys, cams, or exercise machines of any kind to be found in this unadorned shrine to gravity. From the rafters above the weight pile hung three football jerseys: number 54 from the Miami Dolphins, number 63 from the Minnesota Vikings, and number 68 from the San Diego Chargers, each bearing the Fainu'u name across the back. Emblazoned in the middle of the floor was the giant bearpaw logo of the University of California.

The triplets had each won an academic scholarship to study engineering at UC Berkeley. There, while graduating with Bachelor of Science degrees in three and a half years, they had comprised the entire starting defensive line of the Golden Bears, who changed their scheme to accommodate a nose tackle and flanking defensive ends. (In high school, the boys had played both ways and simply pivoted 180 degrees at change of possession to assume their offensive roles as center and both guard positions.) They were Academic and First-Team All Americans on a defense that allowed the least amount of rushing yards in the nation. Gilbert, Dean, and Brandon were each drafted into the NFL in the first round and went to different teams. Despite avoiding serious injury and gaining All-Pro recognition as rookies, they retired together after their second season. The press releases credited their true passion for pursuing technology. But anyone who knew them also knew that the three brothers (or *Uso*, as they sometimes called each other) couldn't stand to be apart for long. And pro football's not in the business of family reunions.

The Fainu'u Three took their signing bonuses and two years' worth of salaries, became savvy angel investors in a couple of promising tech startups in San Francisco and the Silicon Valley proper, and used the remainder of their nest eggs to refurbish their dad's barn. Today they hardly paid any attention to football at all.

Behind the spartan gym was a more Athenian workspace. After burning off energy heaving iron around in front, they'd typically repair to the back of the building to a state-of-the-art tinkerers lab containing an impressive array of electronic testing instruments from digital oscilloscopes and multimeters to function generators and logic analyzers. Across the room stood tall tanks of various compressed gases alongside a vented and hooded work pod and vacuum chamber. Nearby was a long wooden table underneath a wall's worth of mechanical tools, each hanging neatly from a pegboard within its own carefully described silhouette. Toward the rear of the space were three large computer workstations with monitors. A 3D printer sat off to the side. A freight elevator connected the lab with a further trove of devices and materials upstairs. Short of smashing atoms, there didn't seem to be a whole lot that couldn't be observed, tested, repaired, or fabricated in this old hay barn.

The triplets' initiative and ingenuity were lifelong and legendary. Years ago as Cub Scouts (and apparently strict constitutionalists) they devised their own community service project in Half Moon Bay. Like throughout much of the country, the scourge of drunk driving had led to the establishment of intermittent sobriety checkpoints in San Mateo County. After the times and locations of these controversial roadblocks were ascertained, the third-grade Fainu'u brothers would take up positions just up the road from the police gauntlet. As the lineup of stopped cars grew, three little boys in blue beanies would knock on each driver's window. Gilbert would offer single Tic Tac breath mints for five dollars, Dean would add two squeezes of Visine for another five-spot, and Brandon would recycle any incriminating open containers for a flat twenty-dollar fee. One evening, a tipsy car registered to the mayor but driven by an undocumented nail technician rolled over one of their skateboards and suffered a flat tire, leading to scandal, a successful mayoral recall, and the end of the Cub Scout roadside assistance program.

The Lincoln looked almost prehistoric parked inside the Fainu'us' next-gen garage off the weight room. But you'd have thought Gilbert, Dean, and Brandon were the pit crew for the Mars rover from the attention they were showing the car's passenger compartment.

"Is that a skip relay?"

"Looks like it."

"But where's it pulling current?"

"Look under the terminal. 12 volts going on 20."

"How many megahertz are you getting?"

"Like...300."

"So...all Wi-Fi repeaters create their own EMF's...and too many fields in proximity can cause interference...then these secondary components must be shielded."

"A faulty syllogism at best.."

"OK, Shakespeare. What's a *syllogism*?"

"Is that what happens when a clown gets too excited?"

The brothers erupted in giggles.

"Hey! Wanna hear my elevator pitch?"

"No, Uso! No!"

"No, Uso! No!"

One broke wind like a mournful tuba. Two more BRAPS made them a trio. The giggling grew louder.

These were the sounds of three adults hatched from a single egg. Each time they finished one another's sentences, an angel lost his wings.

♦♦♦

Feeling like dead wood amidst the technical talent in the garage, I stepped outside into fresh air to join Fee, who had just returned his jumbo hog to her enormous pen. He closed the gate and checked the new electronic latch twice.

"You should see the spotter drone they're buildin' me. They say it'll be able to send high-def video of schooling fish right back to my phone. It even works in the fog! Then they're gonna rig up a remote submersible with a sonar array to see where the crab are runnin' along the bottom. We'll make our limits before the other guys even get outta the harbor."

"Is Harley on board?"

I referred to an old mutual classmate who'd become the district's Fish & Wildlife warden.

"Knowin' what a stickler he is, I already ran it by him. Anchors aweigh. But the truffle project's still hush-hush. In the meantime, I gotta little treasure hunt planned as a shakedown for Trudy. Are you in?"

"You wouldn't be talking about the time capsule?"

Fee's grin could've been measured in candlepower. Before I could press him I noticed the deck-of-cards-sized apparatus peeking out from under the bottom of his t-shirt.

"Is that the new pump?"

He nodded. My friend was a lifelong, insulin-dependent, Type I diabetic who'd managed his health with grace and grit for as long as I'd known him.

"The boys set it up for ya?", I continued.

He lifted up his shirt, and gently patted the plastic pack attached to his belt.

"Pancreas in a pocket. They're even workin' on encrypting it against hackers."

Nearby, Trudy oinked and wallowed as coquettishly as her girth allowed. Fee looked her way.

"Do you think now that we didn't eat her I can claim her as a dependent?"

♦♦♦

"The reason you aren't getting any power to your onboard outlets is...this."

Gilbert motioned with one nitrile-gloved hand to a tabletop and what looked like a hockey puck with a nub antenna and several multi-pin connector ports visible around its circular edge.

"And the reason your customers aren't going to be happy with you is...this."

Brandon, similarly-gloved, produced another gadget, this one resembling a button-less, square-shaped TV remote control.

"Unless they like singing karaoke into...that."

Dean rolled the capture head of a very small microphone over next to exhibits one and two. His hands were also clad in blue synthetic rubber.

Fee and I had just re-joined the boys in the lab. It had taken them less than an hour to locate and identify the non-native devices that had quietly hitched a ride in the back seat of the Town Car. No one said a word for at least ten seconds as this unwelcome news began to sink in. My shirt started to cling to the fresh sweat at the small of my back. There may be a lot more to Lara Fratelli than fills the eye, I thought suddenly.

"So the Lincoln's electrical is fine but someone's actively eavesdropping on my passengers."

Dean nodded and wandered into the weeds.

"The reducer seems to interfere with pretty much all electronic devices for about a three-foot radius from the rear center armrest console."

"..leaving the front seat largely unaffected.."

"The charge indicator on a particular phone or tablet would show a steep drop-off in battery capacity. This false low-level reading would likely prompt your passenger to plug his or her device into a connection, where both sides of every phone conversation could then be heard live or recorded. And...it looks like this bad boy could also capture the content and contact data stored on SIM cards and flash drives and stream it all by 4G to the listener's lair."

"This set-up may or may not be designed to put a follow-bot on every phone. But it's theoretically possible. We'd need a few days to look at the code to get a better idea," Brandon added.

Gilbert took his cue.

"The mic looks like a third-layer redundancy, and probably picked up everything said inside the cabin. If it's any consolation, your sockets did continue to push current. Just not enough to get the AED to turn over when you needed it for Mrs. DeLong."

"Is this the kind of set-up the NSA might use?"

All three boys shook their heads. Dean elaborated.

"They use custom, purpose-built stuff. We're not saying this isn't pretty sophisticated. Just more off-the-shelf."

"Is there any way to locate like...an IP address or something...where the eavesdropper might be listening?," I asked.

"Anybody going to this length would for sure be using Tor or I2P behind a VPN," replied Gilbert.

"Uh-huh."

"They're anonymizing proxy networks that basically bounce the signal from relay to relay around the world. Next-to-impossible to track," Dean translated.

"Encryption by obfuscation," Gilbert further clarified. "Or a permissionless distributed database consensus if they used a blockchain protocol. Oh, and we didn't find any fingerprints or sebum on any of the components either. Clean as whistles."

There was another collective silence before I got even more nervous.

"Whoever's behind this...whoever's listening...are they likely to be concerned about the interruption *right now*?"

Again, three heads shook. Brandon responded.

"The transmitter works on-demand. They won't know they're off-line."

"But when you guys first started going over the car, could they have heard you talking about what you were doing?"

Dean weighed in.

"Nah. The first thing I did when I got in the back seat was remove the cap to the outlet under the rear armrest. The microphone came off in my hand. They musta set this thing up in a hurry."

"You know Bill, we can do a deep dive if you let us hold onto this little bug-set for a few days or so…"

I shook my head.

"I can't thank you guys enough. But could you please put it all back in working order right away?"

"Really?" Brandon looked puzzled.

I nodded. Fee got my drift.

"Coventry." He said, nodding knowingly.

"Coventry." I nodded back.

"Where witches gather wood?" Gilbert flailed. Fee grimaced.

"World War II? Anybody? A city in England? Without asking Siri?"

"Old school badass Winston Churchill let the Germans bomb it so they wouldn't know the Allies had broken their code, or so the story goes," Dean explained.

Fee nodded and patted him gently behind the neck.

"Kudos, grasshopper. Brandy and Gilly, 'Those who fail to learn from history are condemned to repeat it.'"

"Maybe if they'd just slipped a worm into the code the Nazis would've bombed themselves. War over."

I changed the subject.

"Do you guys have any ideas on the green substance on the floor mat?"

Dean spoke for the group.

"We're all over it. We'll ping you as soon as we get the spectroscopy results. "

"I owe you boys. Thanks."

"Any chance you could maybe swing by sometime with a ham?," Brandon whispered.

Chapter 11

On the drive back over the hill I pulled into the unpaved parking lot of a closed farm market, got out of the car, and called my swim buddy, Carl Frost. Without mentioning the Fainu'us at all, I told him I'd found what I suspected might be a listening device in the Town Car. He sounded surprised.

"That's definitely over the line. Have you had anyone look at it? Your boss? Someone at the dealer?"

"No. It's just my hunch. Should I start yanking out wires?"

There was a pause before Carl replied.

"That's probably not the way to go with something like this. The feds would want to keep it all up and running so they could trace the tap back upstream. Tip your hand and lose the advantage. What's your boss like?"

"No-nonsense. But fair. You don't....."

"You may not want him to know what you know just yet. For everyone's benefit."

"It *is* his car…"

"Has he ever shown an unhealthy interest in your clients... business-or-otherwise?"

"Nah, no way he's involved in something like this. One, he's too busy, and two, too honest. He once Yelped himself down to three stars - just to combat complacency. Plus he could've retired by now with all the lost diamond earrings and backseat baubles he's returned to people over the years."

"Be that as it may, I'd hold off on breaking the news to him until after you speak with Janet Farr. You still have her number?"

"Yup. I'll give her a call. Thanks Carl. I appreciate it."

"They're stretched pretty thin over there right now and she's about to go out on maternity leave. But she'll be in touch. Keep me posted, will ya? It keeps me young."

Chapter 12

I felt a little funny dropping by the hospital to see how Mrs. DeLong was doing. I didn't want it to seem like I was angling for an "attaboy" for my late-night roadside fumblings. But my involvement had required a level of intimacy I certainly hadn't expected and in some weird way I felt I should pay my respects, as it were.

She'd been transferred out of intensive care and onto a medical floor. I stopped by the nurses' station on her ward and was directed to her room by a friendly Filipina RN.

"She hasn't had any visitors since I started my shift. Let me make sure she's decent."

She poked her head in and out of the patient room and motioned me inside, whispering.

"You're her driver? You saved her life, you know."

I was pretty sure only her first sentence was true and I smiled feebly. She parted the patient curtain on its ceiling track and left me suddenly bedside.

Mrs. DeLong was propped up by two pillows but looked alert, hair and makeup in order, and wearing her usual red silk scarf under a beautiful purple robe. She immediately reminded me of one of those formidable grande dames from the golden age of Hollywood, a once-attractive, now sparrow-framed harridan who deployed her wide, dark eyes like talons to eviscerate the less-wary, which meant me and pretty much everyone I'd ever met. The idea that less than 24 hours ago this woman's brain had been without oxygen for a few minutes was incomprehensible. But if I was expecting to hear the smoke and rye rasp of a resurrected Bette Davis, I was to be disappointed. She nodded at me with a small, closed-mouth smile, took a Post-it pad and pen from the rolling tray cantilevered out over her bed, and started writing.

She couldn't speak. The scarf hid the tracheostomy scar which I'd noted only in passing while starting CPR. But it was now clear that she had no voice at all, and what I'd interpreted all along as an extreme reserve must have been the result of some earlier insult to her vocal cords. She pulled the first small square off the pad and handed it to me.

IS THE GRATUITY STILL INCLUDED ? was written in large letters.

I laughed out loud. She trembled gently and silently with mirth.

She began writing again. This note read simply: **THANK YOU.** I smiled and nodded.

Her next page said: **FOR THE 3 BROKEN RIBS.** We both laughed simultaneously in our own fashion at that one.

"How are you feeling?," I said finally.

She resumed writing.

A LOT BETTER SINCE THE NEW PACEMAKER.

I had a sudden sick feeling that the bugs in the back of the Town Car were somehow to blame.

YOU'VE GOT TO GET ME OUT OF HERE.

The last note seemed a little desperate. I lowered my voice a little and tried to smile conspiratorially.

"The cuisine a little lackluster?"

She narrowed her eyes and sighed through her nostrils before putting pen to paper once more.

CAN YOU BE HERE TOMORROW AT 11:15 ? P.M. ?

I knew that was after visiting hours. I was guessing it was right around the time the nurses were at their busiest, giving report or passing out meds.

BRING A CHANGE OF CLOTHES. DO YOU HAVE A CAR OF YOUR OWN?

I nodded slowly but must've looked skeptical.

I'LL PAY YOU DOUBLE

"You want to go on a charter in your present condition?"

WHAT YOU MAKE IN A YEAR.

She extended her right hand and I shook it against my better instincts.

Chapter 13

A properly-executed traffic merge is a triumph of timing, empathy, and luck. It should be graceful and seamless, like playing cards neatly shuffled before a winning hand; or egg whites lightly folded into angel food batter; or the tiny teeth of a zipper as they line up to turn a yard of dark fabric into a little black dress.

My distracted exit out of the hospital parking lot made the docking of the Hindenburg look elegant. A collision was averted only by the quick reflexes of the shuttle bus driver who flipped me the bird after taking evasive action. She had a chest that could keep a TV tray level and possibly a runny tattoo of upset bowling pins at the small of her back. I could've kissed her.

My boss was magnanimous about my late-notice request to take an unspecified number of days off for mysterious reasons starting tomorrow evening. I was at first grateful and then nervous about his ominous lack of interest or concern. Either bookings were down or I was padding some sort of pretext for him to fire me. Then I registered the name of my next passenger. I needn't have worried. I'd be doing him a favor.

Henri Van Kempt, a pallid, middle-aged transplant from the Netherlands, was a notoriously brilliant systems programmer with a nine-digit net worth and a rapidly blinking gaze that was said to indicate his brain's refresh rate. He usually wore a front-facing fanny pack which served as both lunch box and *Star Wars* reliquary, and a too-tight faded-beige hoodie that made him look like a stale eclair. Nobody but my boss, and by extension, me, would drive him anywhere anymore.

Pretty much everyone in the local livery trade consistently rated him as their most difficult passenger. Ride-shares had blacklisted him entirely. He wasn't big on rude remarks or prone to illegal behavior. He never stiffed a driver or ran into traffic. He just had a way about him that made you... uncomfortable.

He cried. A lot. Out and loud, and with real, wet, honest-to-goodness tears. In "if lemurs chopped onions" quantities. Everything and nothing seemed to set him off. And very few drivers could handle the drama. My boss had raised four kids on his own and could tune out Armageddon. I really needed the job.

With moist eyes, red nose, and earbuds in place, Henri got in the car with his usual unconscious flourish, already playing his laptop keyboard like a baby grand, his fingers pausing periodically to work a few strands of flossy gray ponytail between his teeth while awaiting further heuristic inspiration. Something about the thrum and motion experienced by riding in the back of an automobile at night calmed him enough to assemble some of the most sought-after software code anywhere. In a very real sense the car was his muse. He must have been on a roll, or a deadline, or both. We burned through a tank of gas and two boxes of tissues in several big lazy circles across six bridges and seven counties. I had plenty of time to think while he sobbed.

It was hard to imagine what anyone listening must have thought about the inconsolable Dutch genius. He hadn't plugged into any of the car's outlets during the trip so I could hope that no one had hijacked his intellectual property. After leaving him at a forlorn gentlemen's club that probably featured strippers on hospice, I headed home.

Before my meanderings with Henri, I'd put in a call to Special Agent Janet Farr at the FBI. She didn't pick up, so I left my contact information on her voicemail. Shortly after, Brandon Fainu'u walked me through the simple disabling of the wireless component that had likely interfered with Mrs. DeLong's pacemaker. I did as instructed. I couldn't live with another on-the-job near-miss. He assured me (via encrypted SMS) that with this hack the perps would be none the wiser and still missing very little of what was said or done inside the Town Car.

Then Dean Fainu'u left a message while I was in the shower. The early findings from the first round spectroscopy on the green dust from the rear floor mat suggested a compound consisting of at least one element with an "unstable nucleus".

Radioactive is such a highly-charged word.

Chapter 14

"You've got a sleepy little isotope of lithium that acts like tritium, dresses up like depleted uranium, but puts off less measurable radiation than glow-in-the-dark watch hands. By all standards, the level's so low as to be harmless. "

First, Dean sought to head off my panic. Then Gilbert.

"Put it this way, Bill. The granite countertops in your kitchen emit more alpha particles in a day than a truckload of this pixie dust will in a hundred lifetimes."

"He really means it's got a half-life of 5204 years, give-or-take, but you get the point." Brandon, ever the stickler.

"We were just rounding up, Bran Flake."

"Rounding up brought down Chernobyl."

"Does banal rhyme with anal?"

"Why the green tinge?", I asked, still amused that they thought the kitchen in my apartment could have granite anything.

"You'd usually suspect copper, but we detected only a trace in the test sample."

"We did see a curious strata of organic precipitate, though. Diatomaceous earth."

"Biogenic silica synthesized by diatoms - algae fossils - skeletons, really - for sure from the Cenozoic Era - probably the Pliocene Epoch. Found in both lake and marine deposits. Sometimes near the surface in deserts."

"It's used to filter swimming pools, isn't it?" I asked.

"Yup. And wine. It's got a host of other uses, too."

"...in agriculture, pest control, to stabilize dynamite.."

"...plus it's highly absorbent and it's a really good thermal insulator."

"The weird thing is that here it seems to be acting like an electrolyte in the composition."

"..while the metal's mimicking both anode *and* cathode."

"Sorry guys. My last chemistry class was in high school. I scraped by."

"The previously unknown substance looks like a compound that's been subjected to enormous heat and pressure."

"Enough to have changed the atomic structure of its original constituents. Maybe from a blast of ionizing radiation."

"My last physics class went even worse."

"Someone nuked your sample."

"What?"

"And now, apparently you've got a rare material that's both safe to handle *and* produces a slow and steady supply of electrical energy, all on its own."

"You mean like a battery?"

"A legacy trickle battery."

"One you could put in your smartphone or tablet and never have to charge or change."

"Ever."

"The Holy Grail of consumer electronics."

♦♦♦

My twitching chin must have ended the connection. I quickly re-dialed the Fainu'us' lab.

"Sorry. I must've....anyway...wouldn't exposing a naturally radioactive substance to even more radiation make it even more dangerous?"

The boys darted in and out of the conversation like bike racers drafting to stay fresh.

"Not necessarily."

"Under certain conditions there's a process called trans-mutation that can occur, by way of nuclear reaction or radio-active decay, where parent elements or isotopes combine and end up being converted into completely new versions of themselves."

"..and strange as it sounds, it can effectively neutralize their volatility."

"...and erase their outlaw past."

"Offering them a fresh start."

"Picture...Bonnie and Clyde...giving birth to an Eagle Scout."

"...who ties off his own cord for that last merit badge."

"For what it's worth, Bill, please tell Mrs. DeLong we'd love to invest at any stage."

Head buzzing and suddenly dry-mouthed, I thanked my godsons and hung up the phone. My fridge turned out to be pretty much empty, so I'd need to make an overdue grocery run if a cold beer was in the cards. When I went to grab my wallet, I noticed the thin stack of Post-it notes I'd collected from Mrs. DeLong during our "conversation" in her hospital room. They were all stuck together to the billfold's worn leather. As I peeled them off to throw them away, I stopped short. Each note was now completely blank. But it wasn't as if the ink had just smudged off; it was as if her words had simply vanished into thin air.

I pulled the squares apart gingerly and looked them over, one-by-one, front-to-back. I recalled Mrs. D using a soft-tip pen of some sort, and predictably, the Post-it's bore no discernible imprints of any kind. My subsequent pencil rubbing revealed no impressions of the writing which I'd seen occur before my own eyes.

I was on the verge of bothering the Fainu'us one more time, when I remembered that their dad and I had ordered away for "disappearing ink" from the back of a comic book when we were kids, and if memory served, the invisible could be made visible under the application of low heat from a clothes iron or conventional oven. Ever the early-adopter, I spread out the loose papers on a turntable plate, popped them into the microwave, and sat an anxious vigil, squinting through the glass of the oven door, hoping my little retro-experiment didn't go up in flames.

Sure enough, after less than 90 seconds - or about two Hot Pockets in bachelor time - letter-by-letter, Mrs. DeLong's words reappeared. And there was another, longer message, in the same script, but smaller, written on the back of one of the sheets which I'd not seen before:

MR. FEENEY,
IF I SHOULD DIE BEFORE I WAKE,
FIND GWENNIE:
ANOTHER OLD RED-NECKED BITCH.
SHE'LL LEAD YOU THERE.

AAA-UT-T34 162/262
PUSH COMES TO SHOVE
550 AM
DEUTERONOMY
YOU'VE GOT THE GREEN LIGHT.
I TRUST YOU'LL DO THE RIGHT THING.

♦♦♦

There's nothing like a morbid message with your name on it to usher in a good night's sleep. I stayed up way past any sensible bedtime trying to decipher Mrs. DeLong's homespun haiku. I wasn't sure about the commanding tone, but her earthy self-assessment made me grin.

Gwennie was going to stay a mystery for the time being. I couldn't think of anyone who went by that name. And where this *Gwennie* would presumably be leading me was anyone's guess. The alpha-numeric string vaguely rang a bell, but the biblical reference was a real head-scratcher. That part of the Old Testament didn't number chapters and verses that high. And was it **550 AM**, as in local time-of-day, or perhaps a radio station on the left side of the dial?

Maybe I'd just ask Mrs. D to clue me in in person tomorrow night.

Chapter 15

The morning arrived early and I headed down to the general aviation facility across the main runway from the commercial concourse at Norman Y. Mineta - San Jose International Airport (SJC) - a grandiose appellation for a facility so scarce with overseas connections. (Think IHOP confusing itself for the League of Nations.) Today was the Adam Smith Memorial, the annual, invitation-only fun-raiser celebrating the late Scotsman's talismanic "invisible hand", with hijinks and feats of derring-do, and all for a noble cause: the endowment of the Longevity and Life Extension Institute of the Silicon Valley - dedicated to "disrupting mortality and putting forever within reach". The actual reach-to-grasp demographics were rarely discussed during the festivities, where this year's raffle involved guessing how many technology Brahmins could squeeze into a shimmering Gulfstream G650ER parked under a soaring arch of tethered gold helium balloons. Unofficially, the slogan for the gala was "Only a douche checks a bag", though it appeared nowhere in the promotional media. Similar tin-eared bonhomie was pretty standard around these parts during a boom period. Millions of dollars were raised, drams of booze were swilled, and legions of limos returned the revelers home in time to heckle their gardeners or coach Little League. They're already taking suggestions for next year's sweepstakes. How many narcissists does it take to fog a mirror?

I made it home in time for a quick nap. An email notification from PayPal pinged me awake. Sixty-thousand dollars had just been credited to my account. "Half now - half later" showed up in the comments field on the transaction confirmation page. I'm a little embarrassed to admit that I wasn't as creeped out as I should've been, but I guess privacy takes a back seat to penury. How Mrs. DeLong knew my email address, that that was enough to go on to send funds to a recipient via PayPal, *and* my last year's adjusted gross income within a few hundred dollars, was beyond me. She seemed like the least-connected, most offline person I could think of. Next thing you know I'll find out she made her fortune mining Bitcoin.

I didn't know where we were headed or for how long, so I just threw a bunch of comfortable clothes in a pack, grabbed my shaving kit and sleeping bag, and headed toward the hospital in my ten year-old econobox. Hope she doesn't mind going casual.

Chapter 16

It was quiet in the hospital's main lobby. Both the piano and harp were draped and unattended by the calming musicians who were brought in during the day to help distract from the often grim business ahead. Somehow the harp seemed an odd fit for this venue; not necessarily the instrument most likely to give reassurances of successful outcomes and happy discharges. At least they'd thought better of posting an angel or hanging a scythe.

The elevator doors opened and out spilled a young dad holding a sleeping toddler, followed by a shapely female wearing blue surgical scrubs, shoe covers, cap, and mask, as if she'd just stepped out of the OR. Several blonde locks had escaped fetchingly from under her headcover. She slipped nimbly past the father and son, her eyes fixed on her phone. Someone with somewhere to be.

I checked my watch and rode up to the 3rd floor. It was a little after 11 pm. I walked through the visitors' lounge just outside the medical ward and then down the hall to the nurses' station, where I was glad to see the friendly RN who'd just yesterday cleared my patient visit. She was speaking into a desk phone when she looked up and caught my eye. Her face fell. After composing herself, she reluctantly held up one finger to keep me nearby. I turned to watch a subdued white-coated code team slowly push a crash cart from Mrs. DeLong's room.

"Sometimes the heart just gives out. There were no indications from the monitor until..."

Just outside the room the nurse stopped and touched my arm.

"I am so sorry."

I had no idea how to respond and just nodded self-consciously.

"You can see her before they...they have to bring her downstairs."

"Oh...I don't know.."

She opened the door. I hesitated, took a deep breath, and followed her inside.

Mrs. DeLong's sallow corpse sneered back at the living. Her mouth gaped open, blue lips crenelated like a clamshell, chin slammed down against her collarbone. Murky eyes, visible between lids fixed in a final grimace, stared sightless up at the pink-cheeked chef braising lamb shanks on the muted television. It appeared that Mrs. DeLong had not gone gently.

There was an unmistakably malevolent atmosphere in the room. It was so still, it was if she'd taken all the air with her wherever she'd gone. Coal mines and deep caves and grain silos and pharaohs' tombs came to mind; places where life looked over its shoulder. Places where you sent someone else's canary.

A large-gauge intravenous catheter was still stuck in her neck, and two of the leads from the now-silent bedside monitor could be seen under the top of her gown, which had been hastily arranged to salvage what little dignity a flatline afforded. Mercifully, but unexpectedly, there was no smell at all.

Her hands had been folded with care over her middle, the nail beds already a muted purple-grey. But their peaceful pose belied a violent end. A dead giveaway.

Her left pinkie finger had been snapped grotesquely, at a right angle, at the middle knuckle. And there was a curious amount of swelling for someone without circulation. I turned to question the nurse only to find myself alone in the room. As I shrank away from the bed, I noticed Mrs. DeLong's signature red scarf on the floor near an IV stand. I bent to pick it up and saw a single, blank Post-it note crumpled in the corner. I grabbed it as well, just as two orderlies appeared in the doorway with an empty gurney.

Once back out in the hallway I again stopped by the nurses' station.

"Her finger...the little finger on her left hand...when did that happen?"

"Oh...I know...it looks so bad. But sometimes the hands will fall into the hinge of the bed when they're attempting resuscitation. It's not so delicate, I'm afraid. But she'd already expired by the time they got there."

"But why would it swell if it happened after her heart stopped?"

I could see I'd put her in an uncomfortable position when her phone rang again. She hesitated and sighed.

"Excuse me. I'm sorry."

She broke eye contact and picked up the phone. The two orderlies rolled their new passenger away, her tight, white shroud creased like butcher paper.

Chapter 17

My car may as well have been autonomous for all the thought I put into the ride home. It's a miracle no one on the way was hurt.

I found myself staring at the glass turntable of my microwave again as it rotated another Post-it through the vegetable setting. The ding of the timer finally nudged me back into the present.

This go-round, the letters on the note were a little shaky, but apparently still in Mrs. DeLong's script.

ts'ídá háadi da

I plugged the strange strand of symbols into a search engine, which determined that the words were probably of Athabascan origin, a large family of indigenous languages of North America, spoken from Alaska to Arizona. A few more keystrokes revealed that the letters constituted a phrase used in Diné Bizaad, the idiom of the Navajo of the desert Southwest. In English, it simply meant:

never

Who was she "telling" this to, and what was the question being answered? Did the more jagged handwriting indicate something sinister about her interlocutor? Had it been written under duress? Who would've understood this? Mrs. DeLong could write in *Navajo*?!

Too many questions, but too late for answers tonight. I mumbled a little prayer for the deceased, climbed into bed, and closed my eyes. Mrs. DeLong's death mask appeared in ghastly detail right behind my lids and I sat up with a start. If that weren't enough, something I'd never noticed before would be keeping me awake for a while longer. The broken finger was appalling. But recent. The rest of the hand and the other one folded beneath it had looked rough and calloused, like they belonged to someone else. Someone used to getting them dirty.

Chapter 18

My phone began vibrating shortly after sunrise. The plummy voice on the other end seemed almost put out that I'd answered.

"Thomas Lippincott speaking. I represent the late E. J. DeLong."

"That was awfully quick."

There was no reply.

"What can I do for you Mr. Lippincott?"

"You can fulfill your obligation for which you've been handsomely remunerated."

"Sorry?"

"I presume you've had a look-see at your bank balance as of yesterday?"

"Oh, of course. Just tell me where to send a wire and I'll return the funds today."

He made a miffed, sniffing sound like I wasn't fully housebroken.

"That won't be necessary. But it is imperative that you complete your trip with Mrs. DeLong."

"Excuse me?"

"Her...remains. I'm told they will be ready for pickup tomorrow. You are to accompany them to Utah."

"I...uh...don't think that's part of..."

"A small urn is all, Mr. Feeney. Surely you have room?"

"By the way, whatever happened to *Mr.* DeLong?"

"I haven't the vaguest. And you are to receive the second half of your agreed-to remuneration upon....execution."

"You want me to scatter her ashes someplace?"

"The location to be forwarded to your email. On your honor, Mr. Feeney."

"Where would I pick them up?"

"Instructions also in your inbox."

"You know I'm not exactly sure what Mrs. DeLong had in mind in exchange for the *remuneration*, in the first place. I only know I was supposed to drive her to some undisclosed location."

"I'm afraid I can't help you there. I'm privy only to the compensatory terms of your arrangement."

"Will there be an autopsy?"

"Surely not. My understanding is that she suffered from a pre-existing heart condition and that her status had been frail for some time. Why do you ask?"

"How long have you represented Mrs. DeLong?"

"Twenty-nine years."

"Then you have my condolences."

That sounded snarky, but I hadn't meant it to be, and he didn't take it that way.

"In point of fact, I've not once laid eyes on the decedent in all that time. She was the soul of discretion. I daresay your association was out-of-the ordinary."

Chapter 19

I was able to get the charge nurse from the hospital on the phone. She confirmed that Mrs. DeLong had hosted no outside visitors, save me, from the time of her admittance to the time of her death. The patient services office then reported that there were no known speakers of Diné Bizaad on staff anywhere in the facility, nor did the telephone-based medical translation service offer interpretation in the Navajo language.

It's probably not all that hard to obtain a spare pair of scrubs in a quiet linen closet somewhere in a major medical center and gain unauthorized access to a patient room. But the degree of malice required to intentionally mutilate the finger of a vulnerable older woman recovering from a cardiac event was probably harder to come by. I couldn't prove it, but I had a strong suspicion Mrs. DeLong had been tortured for information of some sort. Probably about something green and glowy with enormous profit potential.

And her defiant, possibly final, one-word note read like she just might have died keeping her secret. *Never*.

I still had to decipher her Post-it instructions. Those included in lawyer Lippincott's follow-up email had only mirrored those revealed earlier in her own handwriting. I guess

Gwennie would still be filling in the blanks. Incongruously, a straightforward street address was spelled out as the location where I was to meet the funeral director and fetch the ashes: the Starbucks at Stanford Shopping Center. This was a little "left coast" even for me. I hope they get her name right on the urn.

Meanwhile:

AAA-UT-T34 162/262
PUSH COMES TO SHOVE
550 AM
DEUTERONOMY
YOU'VE GOT THE GREEN LIGHT.
I TRUST YOU'LL DO THE RIGHT THING.

Working a throwback hunch, I headed over to the local American Auto Association (**AAA**) office in Palo Alto. As a member in good standing, I was provided a complimentary old-school, folded paper road map of Nevada and Utah (**UT**). There, along the southeast margin of The Beehive State, smack dab in the middle of quadrant **T-34**, at the very edge of the Navajo Indian Reservation, was the hairline intersection of Highways **162** and **262**; chapter and verse, of a kind, from the motorist's bible, as it were. Utah has a Moab, and a Canaan, and a Jericho, and plenty of other places with names from the original Hebrew Scriptures, but I didn't see any mention of a **DEUTERONOMY** anywhere.

I spent the next few hours online reading the fifth book of the Old Testament from beginning to end. In short, the Israelites remain stiff-necked and don't always take direction well, but Moses, now 120 years of age, continues to lay down God's law, and then dies. There is milk and honey, and jealousy and wrath. There are blessings and curses, brimstone and burnt offerings. A lot of "Do's" but a lot of "Don'ts". Dietary restrictions. Marital proscriptions. Harsh judgment and terrible consequences.

I was no closer to figuring out the balance of Mrs. DeLong's riddle than before. And I had to wonder why on earth she'd chosen me.

Chapter 20

I used the drive up to Aquatic Park to mull over the events of the past few days and ended up with only a dull throbbing between the temples. The cold bay water has a way of focusing your attention on the here-and-now and I welcomed the distraction. After splashing around for 30 minutes or so, I stumbled back across the sand into the clubhouse. My head was still numb from the swim when I joined Finbar in the sauna.

"What's on the agenda, Fin?," I inquired as he yawned.

"Rum, sodomy, and the lash. Reminds me of the old parish picnic."

"Have you seen Carl around?," I asked after a respectable interval.

He shook his head before responding.

"He's usually come-and-gone by now."

We continued in silence, each of us savoring the superheated air.

On my way back down the Peninsula, traffic came to its customary standstill. I started to query my phone's GPS about routes to Utah, when I caught myself and powered off. I didn't want to make following me to whatever awaited in the desert any easier than it had to be.

Chapter 21

After giving me a ten-minute tutorial on SIM card swaps and burner phones in their garage, the Fainu'u triplets were hard at it inside my car sweeping for electronic remora. I'd brought them twenty pounds of applewood-smoked, nitrite-free bacon which I'd picked up at a gourmet butcher shop on my side of the hill. It had been vacuum-sealed in clear plastic and I'd carried it past Trudy's pen in an opaque Radio Shack bag on the off chance she could read. She hadn't even deigned to look in my direction.

"Bill, you ever hook up with a lesbian?"

"That could be hot. Just sayin'."

"Not that I know of. Why do you ask?"

"Oh, nothin'."

"That's kind of a strange question."

"It's just the only chick's gonna be impressed by a base model diesel crossover also probably digs sensible shoes. If you know what I mean."

"Thanks. Everybody needs reliable transportation."

"True dat."

There was a bit of a ruckus after someone's phone pinged.

"Did she just swallow that whole thing?"

"That's nasty!"

"You go girl!"

I leaned my head into the passenger compartment. Trudy showed up in a livestream video on Gilbert's mobile. She was chowing down on giant cobs of corn right outside.

"Is that the feed from one of your Dad's security cameras?"

"We're piggybacking it onto the new site we're hosting."

"She's trending in Yemen."

"..already viral in Denmark."

The brothers burst into laughter.

"Meeting unmet needs overseas."

"Farm-to-fork meet barnyard-to-boudoir!"

"We're going all in on SEO in the #taboo/fetish space. Should have the analytics back in a few hours."

"Are you guys gonna run ads or something?"

"Maybe subscriptions for premium content.."

"..if we can just get her into a thong before Ramadan.."

"..she should scale easily for Yom Kippur."

"Your Old Man know about this?"

"Which one?"

"Current or former?"

"Oscar Schindler or Mayer?"

The synchronized siblings wrapped up and hopped out of the car, closing their three doors as one. It was a little like watching Cirque du Soleil do auto repair.

"You're clean, Bill."

"Nobody but you on board this trip."

"Well...nobody but you and..."

"Sorry about Mrs. DeLong."

"Safe travels to Utah."

Chapter 22

I met the undertaker at the Starbucks in the Stanford mall at a few minutes after six in the morning. She was dressed to-the-nines, wore a fair share of jewelry, and had the most erect, confident posture I'd seen in quite a while. With an unlabeled shopping bag in one hand, she walked right up to me like she'd known me forever.

"Bill, hi, I'm Michelle Li. Mr. Lippincott described you to a 'T'. Please accept my sympathies."

I'd never encountered the man face-to-face, but I didn't want to seem impolite.

"Hi, Michelle. Thank you. We really weren't all that close.."

Michelle bee-lined over to a small table with two chairs by the window where we sat opposite one another. She set the bag down on the floor beside her and looked at me with a quick apologetic smile as she tapped the Bluetooth earpiece affixed to one ear. It appeared to be encrusted with either large diamonds or small rhinestones. She looked away and spoke into the mobile.

"Hey, Callie. Can you let the stagers in in 45 minutes? Great. Thanks. Yeah. The broker tour starts at 10, so they'll have to hustle. Right. Bye."

She turned my way again.

"Pardon me for that."

"You're also in real estate?"

She nodded and handed me her card in one movement.

"Going on five years now. I've learned to compartmentalize."

She leaned forward and dropped her voice to a whisper.

"I once held a wake next door to an open house that I ended up selling to the widow for 50K over list."

She smiled impishly before leaning back and putting on her funeral face. She picked the bag up off the floor, removed a container shaped like a large Chinese takeout carton, and set it between us. It looked to be made of some kind of tasteful, high-end cardboard and was itself wrapped inside another, clear plastic bag.

"Mr. Lippincott suggested you would be scattering the cremains. I don't mean to presume anything, Bill, but I always advise more of a gentle, pouring motion. And keep your eye on the weather. A stiff breeze can bring back the dead."

"Thanks for the hint."

I slid the curious urn over toward my side of the table, fighting off the urge to flinch. It was warm to the touch. Not potholder hot, but at least body temperature. And while it wasn't exactly inelegant in design, you could still be forgiven for mourning the moo shu pork.

"Do you do many old-school funerals still these days? You know...embalming...the whole deal?"

She shook her head.

"Keep it simple. That's my motto. Frankly I find many of the old-school practices to be predatory. Upselling grief, *casketeering*, whatever you want to call it. Profit's one thing. Taking advantage is another."

I nodded appreciatively. We stood up and shook hands.

"Again, Bill, my condolences."

I had to ask.

"That's some Bluetooth you've got there. Those're.."

"Real. My ex thought I'd never know the difference. Word to the wise: cubic zirconium's just another name for conflict diamond."

Chapter 23

I like a good mystery as much as the next guy, but something about this one had me a little outside my comfort zone. I placed Mrs. DeLong securely behind the passenger seat and headed southeast.

Leaving the Bay Area, and after traveling the length of the San Joaquin Valley on I-5, my route took a dogleg left on CA 58 into the Mojave Desert at Barstow, where I steered clear of the wheeled stampede from Southern California to Sin City. The suspiciously well-behaved return traffic from Vegas back to L.A. plods by comparison. God knows what happens when you stay.

On Interstate 40 I passed through Needles into Arizona, crossing the Colorado River, here only a slack ribbon of water lamenting its own dissipated course, like a child bride dragging her heels on her wedding night. By now pretty much all the West's rain and snow is spoken for before it ever hits the ground.

Just outside Flagstaff, now high in the pure mountain air, I pulled into the mostly-full lot of a roadside diner. The Tyrolean-themed restaurant was tidy and well-lit, with an evenly-stacked woodpile to one side of the stone chimney, and the Health Inspector's seal of approval in a neat frame to the right of the entrance. There was the sound of music coming from inside.

I was escorted across a mostly-filled dining room to a small table by a severe blonde woman who handed me a leather-bound menu as I took my seat near the stage. I'd stumbled into a dinner theater production of the actual *Sound of Music* performed by a large family of towheaded singers. Despite the familiar tunes of the innocent childhood classic, the place felt unwelcoming, and I feared this reimagination was headed in an ominous direction: a plucky Jewish governess had been accidentally hired to look after the Minister of Propaganda's children following an incomplete background check. I showed myself back out to my car as Frau Goebbels led into *How Do You Solve a Problem Like Shoshana?*

I ended up thirty minutes further east on legendary Route 66 at a Dairy Queen where the quesadillas bear scorch marks some say resemble the Virgin of Guadalupe. The line was long but moved quickly. Several patrons eating soft serve cones also appeared to be praying the rosary.

Flyover country is seriously underrated.

Chapter 24

After a forgettable night on a motel mattress in Tuba City, well inside the vast tribal lands of the Navajo, I was back in the car aiming northeast in the general direction of Monument Valley and the Four Corners region. There are flatter parts of the West, and possibly some with vistas as grand, but it's hard to imagine another place that offers the same level of giddy horizontal vertigo to those passing through by automobile. Once you settle into the wide open, the directional arrow on the GPS begins to look more like the emblem of the ancient hunter-gatherer than the signal of the modern satellite-guide.

My cell pinged me right back to earth with geo-tagged half-off offers for trail mix and turquoise. At a windswept truck stop I quietly slipped my phone between the diesel tank and cab step of an idling 18-wheeler pointed in the opposite direction. I hoped this would let me go dark for a while.

♦♦♦

The junction of Highways 162 and 262 forms a right angle in the middle of Montezuma Creek, population 335. The town fronts the pretty San Juan River and is surrounded by an exposed geology worthy of the Flintstones. There is an elementary school and a high school and a lot of open space.

Now what?

I drove up and down the handful of numbered surface streets that crisscross the city limits. Most of Montezuma Creek lies within the Navajo Nation, with a small section wedged into the State of Utah. The city limits, like much of the border lands around it, were laid out in a bit of a patchwork, with territorial boundaries starting and ending seemingly around every corner. After wandering aimlessly for more than an hour, not really knowing what to look for, I found myself on the northern outskirts of town, slowly trolling the Utah sector. Like some sort of prank monument to a language arts class, a battered makeshift street sign at a lonely intersection read: EMPUJAR in one direction and EMPUJÓN in the other. Where **PUSH** COMES TO **SHOVE** in Spanish.

Only one corner had any improvements: an abandoned auto tire store with cracked paint but intact windows. I pulled into the empty parking lot and up to the bent newspaper rack by the front door and got out. I almost tripped over the empty water bowl under the rusty faucet protruding from the side of the building. **GWENNIE** was spelled out in bold hand-written letters on the dented stainless steel.

Puzzled, I leaned down and vacantly turned the valve handle to the screech of tired metal threads. Water spurted onto my pants leg and into the bowl below. I quickly spun off the spigot and looked up into the fixed glare of a blue-eyed coyote wearing a crimson kerchief.

ANOTHER OLD RED-NECKED BITCH. Mrs. DeLong remains full of surprises.

"No bark but b-i-i-i-g bite."

The voice of an older man came from behind me. I might usually have whirled around from the start, but instead found myself unable to move.

"What's with the scarf?," I asked.

"She's a coy-dog mix. Got her daddy's teeth and disposition. The neckerchief keeps the ranchers from shootin' her on sight."

"Are they common?"

"Quite rare actually. Most breeders quit tryin' altogether. Had high hopes of sellin' 'em up in the suburbs as *Lobodoodles* or some such. Real smart. Not so great around kids. Or strangers."

The compound canine displayed her fangs and snarled on cue as I turned a few degrees to glance at an elderly white man wearing a starched shirt and bolo tie.

"So...this is Gwennie?"

"With an 'i-e'. Just like on the bowl."

"Is she...with you?"

He just snickered and pulled a fresh newspaper out of the broken machine. He put a quarter in the slot after the fact.

"Honor system."

"So who feeds Gwennie here?" She dialed down the growl.

"Feeds herself. Betty waters her when she's in town."

"Mrs. DeLong."

"If you say so. I only know her by Betty."

"Are you from these parts?"

"Originally from Salt Lake. Moved down a few years ago."

"How well...do you know Betty?"

"Not very. Can't recall even once sharin' words with the woman. Keeps to herself mostly. And the only one I've ever seen use the airstrip."

He pointed with his chin past the single railroad track and across a large expanse of weedy tabletop rock to a limp windsock alongside a dirt runway. A lone pickup truck was parked at one end.

"How do ya like your Subie?"

He nodded at my faithful steed.

"Love it. It's a real workhorse."

"My daughter had one kinda like yours. She used to pitch softball up and down the state. Ended up runnin' away with her catcher. Her mother blames the all-wheel drive."

He ambled away alone with his paper, leaving Gwennie to wonder how I might pair with tap water.

Chapter 25

With ears back and tail tucked ominously under her lowered body, the coy-dog stalked me step-for-step, tango-style, as I edged slowly toward my car. My childhood paper route had taught me to avoid direct eye contact with unfamiliar canines so I made sure to keep Gwennie well within my field of view without meeting her stare head on.

I was feeling around blindly behind me for the driver's side door handle when she launched herself past my shoulder through the open window into the back seat. After corralling my bowels, I watched her focus her nose on my backpack. As she sniffed intently around one of the outside zippered pockets, the raised hackles on her back toppled like furry dominoes. She turned to look at me.

I reached carefully around her head, unzipped the pocket, and pulled out Mrs. DeLong's scarf. Gwennie's sniffs turned to sighs as she buried her nose in the folds of red silk.

Fortunately she showed little interest in the cardboard urn which rested only about a foot away. I wasn't looking forward to breaking that news.

After thoroughly luxuriating in the scarf's signature scent, she looked up almost sheepishly; the open irony lost on neither of us. Then without so much as a running start, she flung herself back out the window, landed gracefully, glanced back over her shoulder, and trotted off in the direction of the airstrip.

I followed her in my car across gravel, over the railroad track, and through patches of dead grass to the end of the runway where she'd stopped alongside the pickup. The doors to the dusty 4x4 were unlocked, and Gwennie quickly took up a spot in the front passenger seat, shaking her head vigorously from side to side.

The vehicle's interior was unremarkable, but clean. The glove box was empty. There was nothing hidden behind the sun visors or under either of the floor mats.

Gwennie continued her conspicuous demonstration of head-wagging. She didn't seem wet. Maybe a burr in her ear? Or some sort of infection? I finally noticed a slight metallic glint coming from under her kerchief: a collar ring. And the key to the truck. Carefully dampered with a rubber coat to resist jingling. Her prey still wouldn't hear her coming.

I put the ashes and my pack behind the front seat. The engine turned over and the gas gauge read full. The single band radio dial was set to - wouldn't you know - **550 AM**. With the volume up, the frequency emitted only a fax-like warble through the dashboard speakers. Blue LED letters at the bottom of the rearview mirror scrambled back and forth between all eight compass points. With the radio off, the compass recovered its bearings and held fast. No hidden tracking device within a stone's throw stood a chance. I turned the dial back to the on position and left the volume on a bearably low setting.

I popped the clutch and ground a few gears before getting back in the groove with the manual shift, a practice gone the way of exploratory surgery and the rotary dial. Mrs. DeLong might have left the key in the ignition without worry.

Chapter 26

Taking direction from a huffy four-legged navigator is something I'll say never happened if asked. That she seemed to know where we were going somehow made it even worse.

Snout turned left, I turned left. Snout right, I followed suit. Muzzle pointed up equaled straight; down meant slow or stop. It was rudimentary but effective communication; only once removed from passing Post-its with another taciturn female.

We left the airstrip, bounced over spotty asphalt for about three miles, and then veered off onto a graded dirt road, which quickly turned into a one-lane washboard, and finally a glorified game trail demanding the truck's high ground clearance. Throughout the bumpy ride Gwennie remained on high alert to any chance of her driver taking one of many possible wrong turns off the business end of this nameless mesa. For my part, the concentration required to keep from hanging an axle up on rock or bogging one down in sand was total. It wasn't like there was anyone around to come to our rescue; we hadn't seen another soul since leaving Montezuma Creek more than an hour ago.

The temperature was only in the low 80's outside but by the time we pulled up in front of a single-wide trailer above an oxbow bend in a dry wash I was drenched in sweat. As far as the odometer was concerned, we hadn't moved a muscle or a mile since we'd left the airstrip. Mrs. DeLong thought of everything.

Gwennie squeezed out the passenger window and ran up to the front and only door. A large camouflage net, secured by knotted ropes to flexible poles staked into the hard earth, was suspended over the structure. Also concealed from overhead view was a small array of south-facing solar panels carefully angled under a jut of rock further upslope from the seasonal creek. A sturdy water pipe, painted a background blend, followed a short, steep gully from a well-hidden pump house to the deep gravel in the middle of the dry channel - and presumably the aquifer underneath.

There were heavy bars on all the windows and the reinforced portal looked like the entrance to a bank vault. My companion only had to wag her head once this time. There was another key under the kerchief around her neck, this one the color of graphite, which I hadn't noticed earlier. It was lightweight, had a matte finish, and looked like carbon fiber. It opened the door lock on the first try.

♦♦♦

Gwennie sat patiently on the outside landing just beside the door. There was a dog bowl under a water faucet next to the front steps which I filled for her. She lapped thirstily as I stepped into the trailer.

Lights and air conditioning went on automatically. A single pair of well-worn women's hiking boots was lined up neatly on the industrial-grade carpet just inside the entrance. Out of respect I popped off my own boots, setting them down next to Mrs. DeLong's.

For a place so buttoned-up the interior was actually quite cheery. One-way windows looked out through metal bars to the dramatic canyon wall across the wash below. There were all the usual kitchen appliances, a bright sitting area with a neat desk, and a comfortable, if austere bedroom. But I didn't see a computer, telephone, television, radio, or any other electromagnetic link to the outside world anywhere.

The closets held only two small pairs of beige coveralls, a wide-brimmed hiking hat, a miner's helmet and headlamp, and an empty backpack. Two surveyor transits, still fixed atop their folded tripods, leaned into opposite corners. Binoculars hung from the handle of an unlocked gun cabinet; inside stood a high-powered, high-capacity semi-automatic rifle and a pump-action shotgun. Boxes of ammunition lined the shelf above.

The bathroom was spotless. The medicine cabinet held only a single toothbrush, a newly-opened tube of toothpaste, sunscreen, lip balm, and a bottle of tiny white nitroglycerin pills.

From the back window, I could see what looked like a compact composting septic system around the corner of an outcropping. Much closer were six large solar storage batteries bolted to the aluminum siding under the canopy outside the kitchen. Inside, rubber-handled flashlights were tactically distributed on most flat surfaces throughout.

Grid, schmid. I can already see Michelle Li's breathless listing for this *prepper's pied-a-terre.*

♦ ♦ ♦

Gwennie was pacing in half-circles on the gravel. When I got outside she sprinted away, then raced back, took my hand gently in her jaws, and pulled me back up the steps into the trailer like a dyslexic Lassie returning a shut-in to a house fire. She let go of my fingers, grabbed the nearest flashlight in her teeth, and bounded back outdoors and through the open passenger window into the pickup.

We crossed the dry creek and climbed faint switchbacks to the top of the facing escarpment in 4-Low gear, the sure-footed truck showing no signs of slippage through the impossibly-tight turns. After a steep descent into a slot canyon, the primitive road ended abruptly at what looked like the edge of a debris field. It was as if one side of the mountain had simply collapsed under its own weight and blocked any hope of forward progress. Without hesitation, Gwennie pointed her nose right, and for the next thirty minutes we scrambled off-road at funhouse angles up and down the sides of two mirror-image arroyos, dodging deep cracks and crawling over wide caps of slick rock. Suddenly, she nodded us to a stop in front of a large, rust-colored boulder plugging a recess in a sedimentary wall, the length of which looked like it had been seared by an enormous blowtorch.

Once out of the truck the coy-dog eyed me and then pawed at the chockstone. I rapped on the rough surface with my knuckles. Hollow. I ran my fingers over its nooks and ledges and studied its contours up close. Just out of sight under a knee-high overhang, I felt a fist-sized knurl, like a handhold in a climbing gym. I pushed with one sweaty hand. Nothing happened. I tried pulling. The six-foot-high false boulder swung open slowly on a swivel track. Made of some sort of lightweight gunite material sprayed over an aluminum frame, its color and texture blended seamlessly into the surrounding sandstone landscape. The prop rock even hosted an honest-to-goodness piñon tree in one of its cracks.

Gwennie wasted no time brushing past me into the void.

Chapter 27

My first few steps inside the earth were made easier by the daylight spilling in from outside. At the first bend I turned on the flashlight. What lay ahead was a tapered tunnel bored into the rock, a downward sloping mineshaft about eight feet in diameter, with a flat floor and rounded walls. Gwennie trotted ahead of the flashlight beam. I stopped and looked back toward the entrance behind us. Already the sun barely registered. One hand-lamp, one bulb, a few batteries of unknown vintage. I had to be out of my mind.

The coy-dog's footfalls grew fainter as I tried to keep up. I was walking faster than I would've liked but I didn't want to lose her, or truthfully, her me. As we got deeper the temperature hadn't dropped as much as I'd have thought, and I remained covered in perspiration. I turned around several times to shine the light back in the direction of fresh air. The slight downward pitch seemed to have leveled off and I had to be careful to remember which way was out.

Suddenly my knees bumped into Gwennie, I stumbled, the flashlight flew from my hand and....darkness. Like you have to not see to believe. Then…quiet. All I could hear was my own heartbeat. And that little noise a coy-dog makes when rolling her eyes.

I leaned over and felt around frantically for the light, located it near my feet on the ground, and tried to turn it back on to no avail. OK. OK. Just find and follow one wall back out to sunshine. One mindfully deep breath and a muttered prayer later...and my jaw dropped open and I let go of the flashlight again as my vision adjusted to a 360 degree viridescent spectacle. I could now clearly make out Gwennie's profile and the shape of my own hand against the jade-green glow. We were standing in a horizontal cylinder whose ceiling, walls, and floor resembled the interior dome of a planetarium - only with the densely-arranged planets, stars, and galaxies surrounding us completely, even underfoot, and glittering like tiny emeralds in deep space. Pixie dust. The mother lode of what Mrs. DeLong brought back to California on the soles of her shoes.

I ran my fingers over the warm, glazed surface of the shimmering rock, hard and smooth as kiln-fired glass. It was impossible to focus on any one spot and I just gaped for what seemed like an eternity. Or a second. It was hard to tell. Finally, shifting my gaze, I caught Gwennie staring at me. It was too dim to see her expression exactly, but the tilt of her head made her seem...Curious, maybe? No. More like concerned. Fretful. As in "Where's Miss Betty?"

At once my own inner voice registered a different concern and quickly cued the panic. Exactly how many chest X-rays had I undergone in the last three minutes?

I bolted toward the entrance, hands in my pockets, trying to limit further contact with the walls. Gwennie beat me outside.

◆◆◆

We four-wheeled back to the trailer in about half the time it took to make the outbound trip. I found a water hose coiled up on a reel under the foundation apron and screwed it onto the tap out front, thinking I'd at least give Gwennie a cursory rinse-off. She was having none of it, and effortlessly kept out of range of the spray. I stripped off my clothes and doused myself frantically.

I doubled down by heading inside for a long shower in Mrs. DeLong's bathroom. With no internet to check for decontamination hacks after radiation exposure, I was flying blind. For all I knew, the application of H2O might just be fanning the flames. I closed my eyes and let the cool water run over my head, picturing my gonads glowing like Fat Men and Little Boy.

After drying off and throwing on the only change of clothes I'd brought to Utah, I slumped down on the couch in the living room. Somehow I hadn't noticed the boxy apparatus sitting on the floor behind Mrs. DeLong's desk. It didn't look like any office machine I'd ever seen. It had a slot tray reader for something called a radiation dosimetry badge, as it said in fine print just under the plastic cover.

The power cord to the device was unplugged and wound up in a tidy pigtail knot on the carpet. I plugged it into the wall outlet and pushed the ON button. From the small LED screen I chose PRINT HISTORY. A few seconds later a three-foot strip of thermal paper curled down to the floor.

Month-to-month figures starting in 2003 and ending last year showed a slow but steady decline in the count of *millisieverts*, which I guessed were a measure of the radiation absorbed by the person who'd worn the badge. I was also supposing that the lower the number, the better. At least the trend looked headed in the right direction.

There were however, a few short spikes along the downslope of data points. Were these the result of mysteriously-brief radioactive releases, or just signals that the badge-wearer, presumably Mrs. DeLong, had spent a bit more time at ground zero during those months? Also, it appeared she'd either stopped visiting the tunnel entirely last year, which seemed doubtful, or just stopped wearing a badge for some reason. Maybe, like my godsons had insisted about the test sample, Mrs. D had concluded that the health risk had become negligible.

Regardless, I decided to put off a return to the green grotto for the time being. *The walls were warm*, for God's sake.

I rubbed my eyes and looked over at the bookshelf across the room. Plainly juxtaposed against a lineup of hard-cover mysteries in glossy dust jackets was the cracked leather spine of the Holy Bible. What had I missed the first time?

♦♦♦

As I pored over **DEUTERONOMY** in print I wondered how much each different Bible version mattered to the message. Mrs. D's copy was the American Standard which lacked some of the formal flourishes of the King James that I'd waded through earlier online. This time she went easy on me.

My eyes whiplashed to a stop in the middle of Chapter 14; verses 9-10 had been highlighted in bright yellow felt pen.

These ye may eat of all that are in the waters: whatsoever hath fins and scales may ye eat; and whatsoever hath not fins and scales ye shall not eat; it is unclean unto you.

I flipped ahead impatiently through the next twenty chapters all the way to the end looking for more yellow accents. Zip.

OK. So Moses put the kibosh on eating shellfish. Maybe a hygiene thing? Probably tough to keep crustaceans from killing you in the desert without some way of keeping them cold.

I looked up and out the window. Desert. And then across the room at the refrigerator.

The cool side of the appliance held only a few plastic water bottles, a carton of eggs, a vacuum bag of ground coffee, and an unopened stick of butter. Behind the freezer door, under a full tray of ice cubes, was a bread loaf-sized package covered in white fish wrap. I took it out and placed it on the counter next to the sink. Printed on the paper tape holding everything together was a trademark showing a green duck with orange feet and a grinning yellow bill holding a rod and reel: the very same logo which branded the sterns of *Lucky Duck* and *Lucky Duck II*, Fee Fainu'u's fishing fleet berthed back in Half Moon Bay.

♦♦♦

Mrs. DeLong had my full attention. I directed it toward unpacking what turned out to be a whole, cooked Dungeness crab inside a clear plastic bag under the paper fish wrap. Using cutlery from a drawer by the sink, I painstakingly cracked the red shell and picked through the delicate meat like an ancient Etruscan priest reading entrails. Neither a proud nor a Eureka! moment.

Replaying an old standard, I gently folded the white wrapping paper to fit it inside the wall-mounted microwave, set it on the turntable, pressed one minute, peered through the window glass, and crossed my fingers.

Like deep bruises surfacing on skin, blue writing appeared on both sides of the paper.

I carefully removed it from the microwave and spread it out on the kitchen counter.

On one side was a detailed schematic of what looked like the green grotto. There were several views of the space: overhead, sectional, and rotated diagonal, each with dimensions, angles, and elevations carefully described. Then there were draft drawings of core samples showing cross sections taken at various sites in the tunnel. Around the edges were tables and graphs stuffed with chemical formulas and equations.

The flip side was covered with meticulously hand-rendered figures depicting a round wafer and an oblong capsule. An asterisk noted that they were enlarged for illustration. Below was a multi-flow chart labeled with symbols for ohms and amps, watts and volts.

No one had to tell me I was in over my head here.

YOU'VE GOT THE GREEN LIGHT remained a riddle. To do what exactly? And **I TRUST YOU'LL DO THE RIGHT THING** seemed more of a taunt than anything at the moment. Frustrated, I couldn't think of a reason to stick around without much deeper technical context. In any event,

I thought I'd give the trailer a once-over before heading back home for some enlightenment.

Predictably, there was little to suggest anything further at all about Mrs. DeLong anywhere. None of the mystery novels seemed to carry any embedded messages, most of the drawers, cabinets, and storage places held only batteries or ammunition, and any personal touches other than the work clothes, toiletries, and what was left in the refrigerator, were glaringly absent. Then, on my final sweep through her bedroom, I saw something I'd missed earlier right there on her nightstand. Blocked from casual view by a reading lamp but directly visible from the vantage point of someone in bed, was a rectangular photograph in a thin silver frame.

It was a class picture of eight kindergarteners and their teacher huddled around a flagpole in front of a single-story stucco building. The inscription read: **Chimney Flat School** and the year **1974**. It showed a happy group of kids, all smiling or laughing, and all Native American by appearance, with straight black hair, dark eyes, and brown skin. Five girls and three boys and one round-faced female teacher who looked like a grown-up version of her students. The littlest girl, on the far left, had noticeably sharper features than her classmates.

Chapter 28

Gwennie sat next to me again in the co-pilot seat as the truck slid and twisted toward Montezuma Creek. But this time I couldn't even look in her direction. For one, she might not always be available for guide duty and I needed to learn the route on my own if I had any hope of making it back this way again. Plus, I was about to break her heart.

Just outside the narrows of the first canyon, I made a hard turn uphill and followed a steep ridgeline to an overlook I'd spotted earlier. We made it to a point which faced almost directly west and offered an unobstructed view of raw creation all the way to the horizon. I stopped the pickup, reached behind the front seat, removed the urn from the plastic bag, and stepped out of the cab. Gwennie followed tentatively.

The air was warm and still. I rested the cardboard urn on the table rock, struck a match, and lit the corners of the container.

As the thick paper burned, I finally looked down at the coy-dog, who stood transfixed, staring at the low flame. It didn't take long for the fresh embers to spiral and float away and leave the denser gray remains behind.

For her, there were no stages. No denial. No bargaining. No acceptance. No chance to "process" the lifeless ore at her feet. Her grief was without preamble.

Her hind legs wobbled and briefly gave way before she recovered stoically to a sitting position. With ribs heaving and throat quivering, she pointed her muzzle straight up toward the sky, squeezed her eyes shut, and opened her mouth. But there was no piercing howl or high, lonesome sound. There was no sound at all. She finally lowered her head and curled up next to the short mound of ash and trembled in silence. It was the saddest sight of my life.

As I hunched down to pat her head I saw a small metallic glint coming from the pile of cinders. Locating a scrubby branch of creosote, I gently fished out a button-sized silver disc, likely a neglected pacemaker battery that had resisted cremation. It had time to cool as Gwennie grieved.

♦♦♦

Gwennie continued to stare vacantly out the open passenger window as we exited the lost labyrinth. The first signs of civilization, barbed wire, now bordered the dirt road.

My feeble attempts to console her had failed and each time I'd tried to stroke her fur her shivering had only grown worse. She eventually pulled her head back inside the cabin and started to flail her paws up around her neck in what looked like an attempt to rip off her collar.

I stopped the truck and unfastened the collar ring. She began thrashing and tearing at the kerchief with her fangs and

I couldn't help her for fear she'd shred my fingers. Suddenly she fell quiet and looked over at me beseechingly.

I carefully unknotted the red fabric and pulled it from around her neck. She nuzzled my hand and vaulted out the window.

I sat still in the truck and watched her spring over the wire fence and lope across a broad fan of prairie sage, her shoulders back and head held high, until she disappeared over a gentle rise. It couldn't have been more than a few minutes before the rifle cracked and I knew she was home.

♦♦♦

My car almost seemed too civilized after the long day in the truck, which I'd gassed up and left back at the end of the runway in Montezuma Creek. But there was still plenty of daylight left and I wanted to pay a visit to Chimney Flat.

I was already missing my companion, least of all for her pathfinding prowess. Gwennie, though half-dog as I reminded myself, was unrecognizable as either Hollywood's hapless cartoon cut-up or the shape-shifting trickster of traditional tribal lore. She'd somehow managed to toggle gracefully between species and shown ours a loyalty larger than life.

I wasn't proud to have abetted her death, but I was there and I owed her. I'm sure Mrs. DeLong wouldn't have wanted to be the cause of her suffering, as it's been said that to be worthy of devotion is to not occasion its display. Whoever rushed Mrs. D toward the abyss back in California has a lot to answer for.

Chapter 29

Chimney Flat sits in a gap between two parallel rock ridges that incite air of different pressures to back-alley battle. It's remarkable for its formidable gusts, and for its curious lack of sustained winds. I got out of the car in perfect atmospheric stillness and hadn't gone two steps before being pasted by a haymaker of red dust. Like wind shear that can threaten aircraft close to the ground, it calmed as quick as it came and left me believing in phantoms.

The little school from Mrs. DeLong's bedside photo wasn't hard to find. It was right off the two-lane blacktop and looked virtually unchanged from the forty-odd year-old image I now held in my hand. The tan flag of the Navajo Nation flew high from the pole out front. In stark contrast, across the street, the Stars and Stripes hung inexplicably at half-staff in front of the U.S. Post Office. These days it seems like every letter carrier with GERD plunges America into a period of national mourning.

Between recurring bursts of wind I heard the steady whine of an approaching electric cart. A lean man wearing ironed jeans, a blue cowboy shirt, sunglasses, and a ball cap bearing the eagle, globe, and fouled anchor insignia of the USMC appeared from around the back of the building.

"Can I help you?"

His tone was matter-of-fact. Very *Semper Fi.* Your best friend or your worst enemy. Pick one.

"I'm trying to identify someone in this picture."

He climbed out of the cart and approached. I handed him the class photo.

"Miss Begay's kindergarten class. I had her too. A coupla years after these kids. She died young. Diabetes, I think."

"Do you recognize any of her students?"

"Let's see...that one looks like....Clifford...Clifford something...Could be something Clifford. Ahh. What was that kid's name? Those two don't ring any bells. But that's Susan Doubletree there. With the dimples. Heard she became an actress. Off-Broadway. Maybe *On* by now. Who knows? Where'd you get this?"

"A friend of mine had it on her nightstand. Elizabeth... Betty DeLong?"

"Had?"

"She passed away very recently."

He removed his hat with unconscious respect.

"You knew her?", I asked.

"Everybody around here knew her. Not many white women lived on the Rez. She was Susan Doubletree's mom."

"Did Betty have a husband at the time?"

He shook his head.

"She fell for the local war hero. Ray Doubletree. Got her pregnant and then got himself killed. Over in Germany. Multiple combat tours in Vietnam and he gets rolled by an M60 in Europe. Never made any sense to me. Green Berets in main battle tanks? Maybe that's just the Army."

"Do you know how Betty lost her voice?"

"Think it was cancer of the...thyroid, maybe? Does that sound right? The story goes her dad's mining outfit won a bid to extract uranium on Diné land back in the 50's and 60's. Pre-EPA. Hardly any regulations to speak of. Prospectors and wildcatters everywhere. The *Glow Rush*, some called it. A lot of our people got lung cancer from the radon. The tailings are still screwin' up our water. It ended up killing most of her family outright, I think. They said she got sick just from laundering her dad's coveralls. You from San Francisco?"

"The suburbs, yeah."

"The climate was supposed to be good for her health. I remember when she moved out there. After Susan went east to college and never looked back. Broke her heart that her kid had no time for native ways."

Something about his conspicuous use of third-person personal pronouns when discussing Betty DeLong reminded me of a custom of some Diné I'd read about who forever refrain from uttering a person's name after his or her death. The latent anthropologist in me had to ask.

"Is that a taboo of sorts...to speak the name of the departed out loud?"

He paused and I made out a squint behind his sunglasses.

"You could say that."

"No offense. Just curious."

"None taken. Twenty years a Marine. I'm used to your ways."

He grinned and continued.

"In boot camp one of the DI's used to get in my face about the whole Navajo superstition thing. The 'goner gag rule' he called it. I reminded him about the native code talkers of WWII. He eventually came to appreciate our culture and even swore he'd at least never speak *ill* of the dead again. If anyone asked, he'd just say, 'No comment on the deceased. But boy what an asshole when he was alive.'"

We both laughed.

"How is it you know so little about your friend?"

He'd been sizing me up all along.

"The truth is, *friend* may be a stretch. I've known...I knew her for four years and never felt it my place to ask."

I proceeded to tell him the rest of the truth, save the bit about the untold fortune holed up in a mineshaft only a few ridges over. It took me less than a minute.

"Any of you Silicon Valley limo guys drive electric these days?"

"There's still the range issue for practical commercial use. But you've gotta stay relevant with the young money, so my boss has been mulling it over. Whaddya got under your hood there?"

I nodded at his cart as we both leaned into another blast of wind. If he answered, I didn't hear him. He just motioned for me to follow.

♦♦♦

Lee Thomas, USMC (Ret.) gave me a front seat guided tour of the enormous mothballed ordnance plant which sat directly behind the Chimney Flat schoolhouse. We carted over the single railroad track and around the perimeter of the one-story, 300,000-plus square foot, steel-sided, concrete-floored facility.

The little classrooms had been converted from the plant's original front office, circa 1968, or about 15 years after the factory had been built in anticipation of the needs of the U.S. Department of Defense after the Korean War. It was designed to produce ammunition for rifles, pistols, and light machine guns. Electricity from the huge coal-fired generator upwind of town provided reliable power. Fresh water was plentiful in the shallow aquifer nearby. But not a single bullet from the plant had ever been fired in anger. Or ever produced in any numbers. The crimping mechanisms, primer lathes, and shell casing molds had only been powered up periodically to keep the lines lubricated in the event of a declared call to arms. A victim of excess capacity, the plant remained on inactive duty all though the Vietnam conflict. The DoD held the factory in ready reserve and provided funds for ongoing maintenance, a continuance of the right-of-way for the rail spur, and the upkeep of the two-lane road which split the town in two. Finally, in 1974, the Diné people assumed complete interest in the site after the passage of the controversial Navajo-Hopi Settlement Act. Lee Thomas augmented his military pension with a small stipend from the tribe to watch over the facility; a one-man rampart retained to keep entropy at bay.

While some of the original manufacturing lines and tools had been sold for scrap, the bones of the old ammo plant were solid. Lee followed a strict schedule of preservation triage and had been remarkably successful in beating back the elements in this dusty environment. At one time, livestock feed had been warehoused under the massive roof, and for years the site hosted youth recreation and after-school programs. But today all was quiet.

Chimney Flat itself suffered only collateral damage from the litany of social ills exacerbated by the gambling casinos on other parts of the reservation. Gaming was now a proven profit center for the Diné. But to Lee it was an affront. Just another subsistence economy, without the fresh air. An awful lot of desperation touched too many lives around here to begin with without loading the dice with lady luck. The once-and-always Marine hadn't yet been able to convince the Tribal Council of the abandoned bullet factory's transformative potential. He'd already proposed its value as a fulfillment center and anchor to a tax-friendly enterprise zone. There had to be better jobs than dealing cards and pouring firewater.

Chapter 30

When your mind is two states behind, you don't always see what's right in front of you. The swaying trailer of an 18-wheeler outside Los Banos finally scared me straight to a rest stop where I put the seat back and dreamed I'd only dreamt the past twenty-four hours. I woke to the rising California sun and headed northwest on the final stretch toward home in early commuter traffic.

After buying a new smartphone (porting my old number) at a Verizon store right off the freeway in San Jose, I steered toward Mrs. DeLong's old place. It was more-or-less on the way and I thought maybe I should see if there were any newspapers stacking up in her driveway. I'd check her mailbox and deliver whatever was in it to lawyer Lippincott's office.

I turned down her street and slowed to a crawl. Every week for the last four years I'd picked her up and dropped her off right across from the incongruous white-columned Georgian with the twin palms out front. Right here, where three days ago stood a stone-turreted estate.

The huge house had been scraped to the dirt. A temporary chain-link fence surrounded a now-homeless acre: three heritage oak trees and a large pile of rubble. A hulking Komatsu bulldozer sat quiet in what used to be the driveway.

It struck me suddenly as very Navajo. Dare not speak her name. Destroy her hogan so her spirit won't dwell. I guessed right that there'd be no obituary.

♦♦♦

I found Thomas Lippincott's number and gave him a call from the car. He was out of the office taking a deposition.

I then sent Fee a text to let him know I was on the way over to Half Moon Bay. I took the "chunder road" route via CA 84, which winds up and over the Coast Range in a series of stomach-sloshing turns under a dense canopy of Sequoia sempervirens, some of the tallest trees on earth. Dim ravines and steep drop-offs edge both sides of the asphalt. The passage was constructed in the 19th century to haul timber from remote groves to San Francisco Bay and finally up to the City itself where home builders shingled rooftops with old growth redwood; a practice more precious than practical: like gargling with champagne or flossing with a Stradivarius.

A low-slung bullet bike shot past me and disappeared around the shaded bend ahead. With my windows up I saw him before I heard him. The last two things I remember were an acrid odor and the tumble-dryer view out the windshield.

♦♦♦

Dangling from my shoulder belt, I came to with a raging headache. There didn't seem to be any bleeding, and a quick once-over revealed nothing obviously broken. The car had ended up passenger-side down and seemed to be jammed between a large tree trunk and the steep uphill slope. A deflated white airbag hung limply from the steering column like a ghost that had given up. The windshield was intact, but both front windows - driver and passenger - were gone, one apparently shattered on impact, the other impaled by a low branch. Cool air vented through the cabin. There was still a residual metallic smell - similar to an empty pot burning on a stove - but I didn't see smoke, nor could I locate the source of the scent.

My cell phone, still snug in its holder on the dash, showed a black screen and I couldn't get it to power on. I was starting to think I'd been out long enough for the device's battery to drain when I looked over and saw the car's sturdy digital clock. I'd been off-road for less than five minutes. I pulled myself out the window and scrambled fifty feet up the steep, duff-covered gully to the highway. A peleton of speeding Spandexed pedal pushers, all thigh and mighty, swore at me, one after another, for blocking their route, as they swerved past and out of sight. My Good Samaritan arrived shortly thereafter in the form of a recumbent bicyclist, a mostly-solitary sub-species of enthusiast shunned for their low, poky profiles and lapsed-Amish vibe. He had a whip antenna on the tail of his rig and was able to patch me through to the auto club by CB.

♦♦♦

From the front seat of a CHP cruiser I watched the tow truck right my car and winch it back up to the road. After passing the field sobriety test I'd talked the trooper out of calling me an ambulance. Neither the cop nor the tow driver was surprised that the engine started up without a hitch. They helped me change the one flattened tire and suggested a front end alignment. I was cited for distracted driving, a charge I didn't protest, and was told I was free to go.

The headache only got worse and I drove myself to the ER in the satellite clinic at the coast. A CT scan revealed nothing worrisome and they discharged me with a few packets of acetaminophen. I called Fee from a landline to let him know what happened and that he could expect me shortly.

The four Fainu'us greeted me on foot in front of their house.

"You sure you're OK?"

"Mild concussion. Tops. Normal pupils. No signs of head trauma. I feel like a drama queen."

"But you got knocked unconscious.."

"It's funny. I think I actually mighta blacked out *before* the crash. I dunno…"

"Weird."

"How's the headache?"

"Maybe a little better. Hard to say. Probably lack of sleep. My phone fared worse than I did...Sorry I'm so late."

Dean took the phone from my hand and looked it over. He turned and headed toward the lab.

"What do you guys make of this?"

I dug in my pack and handed over the fish wrap schematic.

"Oh...almost forgot. And this?"

I tossed them the silver disc recovered from Mrs. D's urn.

Chapter 31

I woke up in Fee's Barcalounger to find all four Fainu'us present and hovering. My updated three scariest words in the English language? Samoan male nurse.

"How long've I been down?"

"An hour."

"Fifty-seven minutes, twenty-two…twenty-three seconds."

Dean and Gilbert glared at their brother.

"Do you log your own rectal temperature?"

"..in like…Kelvin?"

Fee quietly browbeat his sons.

"We thought maybe we should wake you.."

"But that's the protocol only if you're actually concussed.."

"Which, as the boys now figure, you probably aren't. C'mon, E-Z. We're takin' you to Stanford."

Fee and Dean drove me in my car with Brandon and Gilbert following in their pickup. While I was sleeping, the triplets had looked at my car, broken open my dead smartphone, and determined that:

1) The phone battery had released almost all its energy in a single, rapid surge.

2) Said surge had been directed toward a specific component cluster located between two micro-capacitors and the main processor chip, causing them to overheat and release acutely poisonous fumes, which dissipated when the car windows shattered (and probably saved my life).
3) This hardware hack likely used location data from my phone to trigger the attack while I was driving on a particularly treacherous stretch of highway.
4) All the above indicated a high level of technical sophistication and unquestionably malicious intent.

Meanwhile, the silver disc didn't turn out to be a pacemaker battery, or a forgotten medical or dental implant, or an overlooked piece of the deceased's jewelry, but a high-end geo-tracking device likely planted in the urn post-cremation. While it appeared the pickup truck's jamming device had scrambled its circuitry, that still meant I'd been cyber shadowed at least all the way to the airstrip at Montezuma Creek.

My headaches were just getting started.

Chapter 32

I tried Thomas Lippincott's office again, this time using Fee's mobile. He took my call sounding unenthused at my existence.

"Everything was discharged per her expressed wishes. May I presume you completed the disposition of the remains?"

"You may. Did her daughter have any say...about the house?"

"Mrs. DeLong was quite clear about her intentions. I'm not at liberty to discuss the details. The balance of your remuneration will be released to your account later today. Additionally there is a bank safety deposit box key bequeathed to you from the estate here at my office. The contents of the box - undescribed in the will - are now your property. Please present yourself at your earliest convenience for its conveyance."

"I'll try to get by your office later today."

"Is there anything else?"

"Do you know anything about Mrs. DeLong's educational background? What she studied?"

He sighed a little longer than necessary. I wondered if he irked as easily with clients on the clock.

"She held a doctorate from the Colorado School of Mines. In exactly which discipline, I don't know. Surely one can put two and two together?"

One thanked the counselor through gritted teeth and hung up the phone.

♦♦♦

Chelation therapy is fairly undramatic by emergency room standards. The outpatient is given successive intravenous solutions, in my case, a shot of EDTA with a chaser of penicillamine, drugs designed to bind with toxic heavy metals in the bloodstream and flush them out of the body by way of urination. Ultimately, they also infuse you with a few life-sustaining minerals to replace those the treatment strips away as a side-effect.

The Fainu'u brothers had persuaded the skeptical medical staff at Stanford Hospital to run an expensive, comprehensive screening of my blood. Sure enough, my system contained highly unusual, sub-lethal levels of three rare earth elements: erbium, neodymium, and ytterbium, and the arsenic-like metalloid, antimony.

After keeping me several hours on a drip and scheduling a return appointment to re-check my blood levels, the doctors gave me clearance to drive myself home. Before leaving to head back toward the coast, Fee & Sons handed me a burner phone and made me promise I'd call once I got back to my place. Getting in my car, I thought better of stopping by Lippincott's office in my feeble condition.

But it was sort of on the way, and what doesn't kill you just makes you a fool.

♦♦♦

Lippincott was the middle name etched in grey stone on the pyramidal sign in front of the law firm on Page Mill Road. Inside the lobby, the walls were paneled in narrow strips of deep cherry wood, giving the space a hip gravitas reinforced by the single adorning statement: a three-story chandelier of hand-blown colored glass hanging in front of the reception desk. I gawked, reflexively clutching my wallet.

A very pretty Asian-American woman smiled at me as I approached the counter.

"May I help you?"

"Yes, thank you. I'm here to see Thomas Lippincott. My name's Bill Feeney."

"Certainly, Mr. Feeney. One moment please."

She picked up her house phone and murmured into the receiver. I couldn't hear the reply.

"Mr. Lippincott is with a client at the moment, but his assistant has asked me to give you this."

She produced a sealed envelope showing the outline of a key inside and set it down gracefully, just out of my reach. Again she leaned under the desk, this time returning with a three-ring notary logbook and a small inkless thumbprint pad.

"We ask for a driver's license...or other photo ID.."

I passed mine over for her inspection. She took it and wrote the number down in the log before returning it.

"...and your signature here please.."

I signed on the appointed line.

"..and...if you wouldn't mind..."

I held up my right thumb and she smiled and nodded. I rolled it over the pad and pressed it against the paper inside the square next to my name.

"Thank you Mr. Feeney."

She smiled and slid the envelope across the counter.

"Thank you."

"Have a good day."

"You too."

On the way to the car I opened the envelope, found the address to a bank written inside, and removed the key. The branch was scheduled to close in a few minutes but was only a block away. As I started the ignition, my mobile chimed, telling me my PayPal account was another 60K richer.

Somehow my signature passed muster at the bank and the assistant manager left me alone in the vault with her key dangling out of one of the two lock cylinders in the door to a large safety deposit box. My key turned the bolt and I removed the deep drawer and set it on the table in the middle of the room. Inside was a Pelican protective case the size of a small ice chest with a single sturdy key lock on one side. A thin manila envelope sat on top. I opened it carefully.

Inside was a warranty deed, dated almost 18 months ago, and recorded in San Juan County, Utah, showing ABC, a Limited Liability Company registered in the State of Nevada, transferring title of real property, to another Nevada LLC, listed as XYZ. The attached plat description from 1963 showed an enormous parcel of undeveloped land, located wholly within the State of Utah but bordering the Navajo Nation, and likely encompassing the area of the green grotto. A third sheet of paper, the Articles of Organization for Limited-Liability Company, embossed with the seal of the Secretary of State of Nevada, showed my typewritten name and a passable facsimile of my signature under the words: Principal - XYZ, LLC. Fourth and fifth sheets of paper outlined an ongoing mechanism by which an impound account, controlled by ABC, LLC, would pay any and all property taxes to the appropriate state and federal authorities - in perpetuity.

Without my knowing it, I'd been sole owner of 31,000 acres of desert wilderness, "all mineral rights thereunder and all improvements thereupon", for a year and a half. I suspected this type of title transfer - by using anonymous shell companies - was a way to shield the details of ownership. I also suspected that ABC was an alias for Mrs. DeLong. Leave it to the great state of Nevada to live up to its pledge of complete translucency in government.

After I let everything sink in for a minute, working another hunch, I dug the carbon fiber key to Mrs. DeLong's Utah hideout from the deep recesses of my front pocket and gave it a try. Bingo.

In what I hoped was only an abundance of caution, the heavy case appeared to be lined with a thin sheet of lead. Set firmly upright in the protective egg-crate foam inside were twelve chrome-colored capped cylinders the size of large test tubes. Each was labeled meticulously with date and description: the core samples from the grotto. To my relief, none felt hotter than room temperature. I pulled the case from the drawer, returned the drawer to its slot, reset the lock, and thanked the banker on my way back out to my car.

The tingling in my right hand - thumb to be exact - started shortly after I'd turned back onto El Camino Real. My shoulder got involved as I pulled into the parking space under my studio apartment. It felt like a pigeon was fluttering inside my chest by the time I made it up the two flights of stairs and slumped down against the outside of my door. I didn't offer much resistance as the pretty law office receptionist pried the Pelican case from my hands.

Chapter 33

My neck was killing me and I woke up grouchy. (Apparently, as I would learn, a couple of jolts from the defibrillator had caused my back to arch and my head to bridge up off the floor outside my apartment.) The first thing I saw through a gauzy daze was Gilbert Fainu'u eating what looked suspiciously like applesauce intended for me from the tray beside my hospital bed.

"Welcome back, godfather. Brandon ate your Jell-O."

"Hey Bill."

"Hey Bill."

"How ya feelin' E-Z?"

"Who do I have to thank…"

"You'd have done the same for us." Fee, ever-magnanimous.

"You guys...again?!"

"Forget about it."

"The slate is clean."

"If we kept one."

Brandon was swiping one finger side-to-side across his phone screen.

"Speaking of clean…do you want the hottest or just the lowest bidder? For your sponge bath?"

"It's like TaskRabbit for tramps."

"Tinder for gimps."

"Uber for the loose."

"eBay with benefits."

"There's even a large-font dropdown for MILF's.."

"Talkin' dirty after thirty. My idea."

"MILF's? At his age? Are they gonna be talkin' dirty in like...Latin?"

"I can see lots and lots of endings. Few happy."

"You three! Outside! Now!"

"Just sayin'..."

"And scrub your souls in the fountain out front while you're at it."

Fee glared them out of my single room.

"Sorry."

"Don't be. I've never felt so alive."

You could hear the triplets laughing all the way down the hall. Fee approached the end of my bed.

"They wanna keep you here under observation for a couple of days."

"What happened?"

"You collapsed outside your apartment. When we got there we couldn't find a pulse..."

My friend swallowed hard and took a few seconds to compose himself. This made me feel even worse.

"Ever since your last ride with Mrs. DeLong the boys have made sure to carry a fully-charged AED in both trucks. You didn't call us like you were supposed to so we went over to your place."

The lump in the throat thing was getting contagious and I felt my eyes start to well up. Fee broke the moment by proffering one giant fist which he bumped into one of mine.

"By the way, this had fallen between you and your front door."

He handed me the manila envelope from the bank safety deposit box.

"Did you happen to take a look?", I asked.

He nodded.

"Don't know whether to feel happy or even more scared for you now."

Then he stepped aside as a gaggle of white coats materialized around me: one attending physician and her flock of downy residents.

"How are you feeling Mr. Feeney?"

The captain of the medical scrum was a young woman of South Asian descent with an accent I'd place somewhere in the Big Ten Conference. Maybe Minnesota.

"Bill. Fine thanks. I guess. My neck's a little sore."

She turned to address her minions at a slightly lower volume before returning to me.

"Probably from the defib in the field. You are a very lucky man. Your friends saved your life."

"I know."

She looked over at Fee who looked out the window in silence. She then pulled her stethoscope up to her ears and listened to my chest.

"It appears your heart suffered no permanent damage from the interruption to its normal rhythm. We don't believe the toxicity from the heavy metals was the proximate cause. Do you remember how you felt in advance of your collapse?"

"Like I'd swallowed a dying bird. My right arm tingled first. It started in my thumb…"

"Do you have a garden?" Her pretty brows formed symmetrical question marks.

I shook my head.

"I live in an apartment. Surrounded by asphalt. Why?"

"Your blood contained a small amount of aconite alkaloids. They're found in certain plants. Have you heard of wolfsbane?"

"From Greek mythology?"

"And Shakespeare, Keats, Joyce...it's even referenced in *Dracula* I think. It can be deadly on contact with the skin. I've been here eight years. And I've asked around. No one can remember ever treating anyone for either rare earth or aconitum poisoning. Against the odds you've survived two nearly-fatal encounters with different exotic toxins within 24 hours. In Russia, this would make you their senior journalist. I think you should first buy a lottery ticket and then have a word with local law enforcement."

Chapter 34

Special Agent Janet Farr wasn't anything like what I expected. Still, there was something vaguely familiar about her that I couldn't quite put my finger on.

"I'm just coming from my last ultrasound. Two buildings down as a matter of fact. I'll be happy to be eating for one again soon. Mind if I..."

She looked like she needed to sit.

"Please. Thanks for stopping by."

She landed with an airy thud in the thick-cushioned chair under the TV and quickly elevated her feet by way of the lever under the armrest. When she exhaled through partly pursed lips, her lank ginger tresses blew up and down over her forehead like the nodding pneumatic mascots in the better corners of used car lots. Despite everything - including the comically-distended midsection over an otherwise thin frame - she was not unattractive. She seemed quite comfortable in her own skin - even coated as it was in a thick, powdery layer of makeup.

"Carl got me up to speed on the deep background. But tell me more about your last coupla days. They sound pretty ridiculous. Did you talk to anyone in the Palo Alto P.D. or follow up with CHP?"

I shook my head. She reached down into her handbag and took out a small notepad.

I told her everything. Mostly.

"Utah's a pretty big place."

I nodded.

"Keepin' the exact location close to the vest. Smart. Are you sure you could find it again? Without.."

She flipped back to refer to her notes.

"....Gwennie?"

"Yeah. I believe I could."

"The test sample your godsons analyzed...is it still in their custody?"

"My understanding is that they had to - in their words - 'waste' all the material to complete the assay."

Agent Farr's poker face dipped slightly as she clicked her ballpoint closed.

"From the sound of it you have at least two parties who were willing to 'waste' you. In the first case to silence you outright, possibly to keep the existence of the material hidden, and in the second to get their hands on the substance, maybe to reverse-engineer it to their benefit. You being collateral damage. Does that seem about right?"

"That would be my take too."

"Have you got somewhere safe to stay for a while once they let you out of here? Preferably with lots of large, loud people around at all hours?"

"I'll figure something out."

She looked at me like she was mulling something over and then heaved herself up out of the chair.

"Call me if anything...I mean anything...comes up. I'm gonna have a word with the lab here in the hospital about your two tox screens and see about getting you a guardian angel from security. Then we'll have to hear what Mr. Lippincott has to say for himself."

"Don't sweat the muscle. Believe me, I'm covered."

She grinned when I looked toward the hall and the noisy approach of the Fainu'us.

"Thank you...for taking this all seriously."

"Carl's an old friend and you've got either a heck of an imagination or a hell of a story. My money's on the story."

With one hand supporting the small of her back, she headed belly-first for the door.

"Well, I really appreciate it. By the way, when's your baby due?"

She grimaced but kept moving.

"Last week. If she hurries maybe she can still make her prom."

Chapter 35

"Now that someone's stolen the core samples, it's definitely not a trade secret."

My godsons were wheeling me out of the hospital having commandeered a chair from a grateful, overextended orderly. Fee was in front of me, point man of my protective phalanx.

"But it is in the queue for disposition at the PTO. Searchable by the application number on the schematic you found in Mrs. D's freezer."

"He means Patent and Trademark Office."

Gilbert spelled it out for me.

"So it's part of a patent application?"

"Probably for a utility patent to protect the process of formulating and exploiting the chemical compound."

"The illustrated casings for the battery would be *prior art* and those designs not covered."

"Is there some way to know for sure?"

"She submitted a non-publication request. It veils the nuts and bolts of the application until protection is granted and all the details are made public. Which usually takes about 18 months."

"Is it likely to be granted?"

Three heads nodded.

"Do you have any idea when?"

"18 months from initial filing makes it.."

"Next Tuesday."

"Give-or-take."

I noticed the three brothers exchanging glances as we got into the elevator. No one said anything as we descended to the ground floor. They pushed me out into the hall off the rear lobby and stopped directly under an AED set in a clear plastic sconce on the wall.

"You know I think the walk'll do me good.."

Six large hands gently pressed me back into the wheelchair. Fee rubbed his chin and then looked me head on.

"Mrs. DeLong filed the patent in your name."

"Huh?"

"We'll go get the truck."

Gilbert, Dean, and Brandon hustled toward the parking lot.

♦♦♦

"You can do that? File in someone else's name? Unbeknownst to...whomever?"

"That would be you. Unbeknownst to you. And yes, it seems you can. And, according to the boys, it seems she did."

Even though I wasn't quick enough to be able to game out all the implications of this piece of news, I knew they could be staggering and was honestly glad to be sitting down. Fee continued to push me in the wheelchair toward the exit. We were almost at the walk-in door to the ER when I saw a familiar face out of the corner of my eye.

"Mr. Singh?"

Fee stopped. Sanjay Singh, Sand Hill savant and long-time paying passenger, was seated in a chair by himself in the overflow waiting area, a magazine opened spine-side up in his lap. He looked like he'd rather I'd not spotted him.

"Bill. From the limo company?"

"Bill! I didn't recognize you in civilian clothes."

He noted the wheelchair.

"What happened?"

"No worse for wear. Their lawyers make you ride in this crazy thing until they can get you safely off the property. By the way, this is my buddy Fee.."

"Sanjay. Nice to meet you Fee."

"You too."

Mr. Singh shook hands without leaving his seat.

"How 'bout you? I hope everything's OK."

Sanjay Singh gave a tortured look, leaned forward, and lowered his voice.

"You know how they say if you have an adverse reaction to those little blue pills to see your doctor immediately?"

He nodded at his lap.

"Going on five hours now."

Fee gasped and started to tremble with suppressed laughter. I couldn't think of any appropriate words of solace.

"Wow. I'm...sorry."

He responded at his usual warp speed, words slightly out of sync with lagging lips.

"Do you think they apply leeches or something? I'm too afraid to search it. I've been trying all afternoon to bring down the swelling on my own. I don't think I've touched myself this much since *Gandhi* won the Oscar."

"Yikes."

My oldest friend pretended to be tying a shoelace and buried his face in my back.

"Has anyone seen you yet?"

"I called ahead but I can't exactly walk in there to check-in in front of all those people."

The dog-eared issue of *Southern Living* tented nicely over his privates but probably served as a bulwark against graceful ambulation.

"Do you want us to ask for.."

"No. No. No. I'll call again in a few minutes. Thanks."

We sat three feet from each other avoiding eye contact, but Sanjay Singh had a thing about unfilled silences.

"It was my wife's idea to get the prescription. 'To put the tikka back in the chicken.' Her words. But all I really want to do at sexy time is ogle my big screen. Old war movies, mainly. Mrs. Singh has tried everything: *Patton*'s speech in an olive drab sari; not Facebooking for *Thirty Seconds Over Tokyo*; last weekend she begged me to *Sink the Bismarck!* Repeatedly! The kids didn't seem to notice but Alexa kept recommending plumbers in North Dakota."

Fee slumped over like a circus bear, holding his sides. A no-nonsense male nurse approached Mr. Singh, took his arm, helped him to his feet, and led him quietly through a side door.

Chapter 36

A few days of R&R at the Fainu'us' was pretty much just what the doctor ordered. They fed me like a potentate, gave me my own room, and even on tiptoes kept about as quiet as a buffalo charge. I found it oddly soothing and slept like the dead. At mealtime I learned that Trudy, through firewalls and fatwas, was still racking up "Likes" like nobody's business. Fee didn't ruffle easily, but I couldn't ever remember him squeezing his eyes shut so tightly when he said grace.

"Hey Bill, we've been able to run a few more tests on your green dust.."

"..mostly confirming what we knew.."

"..but fleshing out the timeline a little more."

"I thought you guys had to *waste* all of it in your first go-round."

"We always save a little for contingencies."

"Plus, you brought home a fresh batch between the treads of your shoes."

"We took the liberty."

"How do you know where things stand in the whole patent process? Is that public information?"

Fee looked up from his plate and frowned with suspicion. Brandon finally broke the silence.

"Patent examiners usually start at about GS-7 or 8."

"..i.e., they don't make a whole lot."

"Still you gotta be pretty smart to get the job."

"Add in student loan debt.."

"..predictable envy of former classmates in the private sector and..."

"We bribed an old fraternity brother."

"Blackmailed, technically."

"But he still has a great story we can never tell his grandkids."

"So they'll lift the veil for a price?"

"How do you think patent trolls usually get first dibs?"

I was already out of my depth.

"What does a patent troll do exactly?"

"They obtain the rights to new or existing patents and make money by licensing the intellectual property.."

"..or by suing companies that may have infringed on the IP."

"They don't actually produce anything of value themselves."

"The polite term is *NPE*."

"*Non-practicing entity*."

"Like a surgeon with hiccups."

"..or a Catholic without guilt."

"A quarterback with a sore arm."

"Two flutists with gingivitis."

"Three pianists with dysentery."

"Four limbo dancers with hard-ons..and a restraining order!"

"Fi...."

Without looking up from his plate Fee slammed one open palm down on the table. All our water glasses jumped, and like re-set needles on a skipping record, the boys changed their groove without missing a beat.

"The trolls have their defenders but most people around here say they stifle innovation."

"It's a safe bet they have their own sources inside the Patent Office too."

Fee turned my way.

"Did the FBI ever get back to you?"

"Just got a text from Agent Farr before we sat down. The receptionist in Lippincott's office was a temp filling in for the full-timer who suddenly took ill herself right before I showed up. Totally false identity. Even the employment agency was bogus."

"Jesus."

The boys were jolted. Never before had they heard their dad take the Lord's name in vain.

Chapter 37

"Didn't you say she was Asian?"

All five of us had repaired to the living room. I nodded in reply to Brandon.

"And quite attractive. Right up until I realized she didn't have my best interests in mind."

"That's weird. We pulled a hair sample off your fleece before the paramedics got there. Long. Dark. Female. Definitely not yours."

"But definitely not East or South Asian either. Possibly Caucasian. But only part."

"She sure looked Asian. Chinese, I'd have guessed."

"So you can only rule in or out a few broadly geographic roots?", Fee asked his sons.

Gilbert nodded as Dean explained.

"Right now the bottleneck is at the bisulfite conversion stage of the sequencing protocol. Genetic origin testing is at the very limits of today's forensic science. And we'd still need blood or teeth to tell her age."

"Could she have been wearing a disguise?"

"Heavy theatrical makeup?"

"Maybe colored contacts and blepharal prosthetics?"

"We also found statistically significant levels of lithium in that one strand."

"Indicating?"

"She's been taking prescription meds for manic depression.."

"..bipolar disorder.."

"..for years."

Fee stood in thought, slowly spinning the vintage globe in front of a wide-eyed trophy sailfish, mounted to look like it died doing what it loved most - frolicking over the fireplace.

"Did the FBI agent ask to see your old phone? Or the tracker you found in the urn?"

"No. Come to think of it. She didn't."

"Anyone else find that strange?"

We all decided that we did, but also didn't know quite what to make of it. Fee turned to his sons.

"So what more did you learn today about the green dust?"

The triplets answered their dad by facing me.

"So we took a sample over to the grown-ups' bench at Lawrence Berkeley Lab."

"The director owed us a favor."

"No disclosures were made and he gave us free run of the apparatus."

"We were able to drill down deep on the rate of decay."

"And we came up with a start-date. Or year, anyway."

"A high-energy, catalyzing event gave rise, or birth, if you will, to the new material in 1971."

"Everything points to a single genesis explosion. Probably Uranium 233."

"Utah musta been rockin'."

♦♦♦

Fee and I trailed the triplets outside to the barn.

"You sure you can't remember ever.."

"..selling crab to Mrs. DeLong? Who I never even met before?"

I nodded. He shrugged.

"We had a pretty good season, so a lot of people dropped by the harbor. But that's definitely my brand on the fish wrap."

"I still can't figure out how she knew we were friends."

"Well, she sure knew how to set the hook. Kinda weird with all the riddles, though."

Once inside the lab we were treated to a demo the boys had scratched together before dinner. Gilbert dropped a chrome-colored capsule the size of a grain of rice into my open palm.

"More or less from Mrs. D's specs."

"Yours now, Bill."

"Filled with an unadulterated sample of green dust recovered from the bottom of your shoes."

Dean placed a similar shiny prototype into a tiny metal cradle attached to a voltmeter. The needle jumped. Brandon explained.

"Enough amperage to operate any known mobile device. Effectively forever. And not even harmful if swallowed."

"Running the numbers from the tunnel schematic, we figure you'd need approximately 131 cubic meters of substance to supply all 8 billion humans with at least one legacy battery. Even if the potency degrades with the delta from ground zero inside the cave, there should be more than enough raw material for everybody.."

"..to have ten kids and still throw away their chargers."

"The energy density's so impressive, there might even be enough surplus for homes and offices. Maybe throw in a vehicle or two."

"All of which will make you a very, very rich man."

"If you make it 'til next Tuesday when the Patent Office opens."

Chapter 38

There was an immediate consensus among the Fainu'us that my next idea was ill-advised. But I wasn't about to let a solid hunch go to waste and would need to make a date with Lara Fratelli, rookie chauffeur and chief bug-planting suspect. Who may or may not have also tried to kill me.

I had none of her contact information but she'd said she worked for Victory Coach, and I took a gamble that their livery enterprise might be insured by the same company as ours. I called their office, got the dispatcher, imitated a compliance officer, and politely demanded that Ms. Fratelli report for a random drug and alcohol screening at the nearest testing facility within the next two hours. Most drivers who wanted to keep their jobs had submitted to this minor indignity more than once.

Against the odds my ruse worked.

About 90 minutes after my phony summons, an annoyed-looking Lara Fratelli pulled into the testing station parking lot going too fast, barely missing a fire hydrant with her Lincoln's front bumper. She stepped out of the car in full driver attire, as lithe and comely as before, bounding on the balls of her feet like a ballet dancer whose curves had derailed a budding career. She steamed up the steps to the door of the facility. After several minutes had passed, I followed her inside.

Vanguard Testing was a one-woman band operated by a middle-aged eyeshadow enthusiast from Azerbaijan who'd previously practiced cardiology in the old country. The wall in the waiting area was covered with certificates and citations permitting the collection or extraction of a panoply of fluids and other human tissue specimens under the authority vested by the State of California. Several official portraits of U.S. Presidents from both parties looked down at the lone couch. Fashion magazines were fanned out neatly on a low glass table. The reception counter was unstaffed. All surfaces were spotless but smelled of cinnamon and sweat.

Just as I sat down, the single interior door opened and Lara Fratelli emerged, fluffing up her hair with one hand. Thickly accented English followed from behind her.

"We send to lab today. Results to boss in 48 hours."

"OK. Thanks."

Lara replied over her shoulder, and then muttered, "I guess."

I caught her eye just as she turned the handle to the door to the parking lot. She looked startled, but gave little away.

"Oh. Hi."

"You too, huh?"

I hoped I sounded more nonchalant than I felt.

"Yeah. They told me these tests would be random. I just wasn't expecting them so often."

"I've gone more than a year between visits before but I know another driver who got called in two days in a row. No telling, I guess. So...how.."

The lady from the Caucasus tilted her head out flirtatiously from the small reception window.

"You bring paperwork, yes? No shy bladder today? I close 5 pm sharp, OK?"

Sensing my embarrassment, Lara turned back toward the exit but then, as if reconsidering, faced me again, and whispered.

"You wanna get a cup of coffee? After you're finished?"

She beamed and I nodded enthusiastically. Troy would've sacked itself for that smile.

"The Philz...around the corner?"

I gave her a thumbs-up and watched her slip out the front. I then handed my own doctored paperwork to the tester who led me three steps to the open toilet stall and handed me a plastic cup.

"Up to line. Please."

She tapped at the mark on the side of the cup.

"Will be just outside. If slowpoke again, you want soothing sounds of nature or Cosmo magazine?"

"No more soothing sounds. For the love of God. Please."

She left briefly but long enough for me to open the labeled dry test tube in the rack on the exam counter and remove several dark strands of Lara Fratelli's hair.

I was soon peeing fitfully as the one-time heart doctor coaxed me along from just outside with tips on *De-Cluttering Your Boyfriend: Best Vacays for The Vajayjay.*

Chapter 39

Anyone with half a brain and our checkered history would've skipped out on the date at Philz Coffee with Lara Fratelli. With her hair samples now secure in a sealed envelope in my pocket, I'd already gotten what I'd come for.

At a busy strip mall I pulled into a spot alongside an autonomous test vehicle bristling with antennae, cameras, and LIDAR. Behind the dashboard sat two millennial "safety drivers", eyes cast down at their open laptop screens, free hands gripping steaming cups, hoping to fend off the damp of the mid-morning marine layer - what everyone now out Instagramming their suspicious moles used to call "fog".

Inside the cafe Lara was seated at a table for two with her back to the wall and an unobstructed view out the front window. The Fainu'us had insisted I take a prophylactic oral dose of activated charcoal to reduce the absorption rate of any poison(s) she or anyone else might try to ply me with - and had warned against mixing it with anything containing milk - so I went with a small bottle of orange juice, headed over, and sat down just as she finished dabbing away a latte foam moustache from her upper lip.

"OJ? I couldn't do this job without coffee."

"A little java goes a long way in my system. But probably too much information," I explained.

"I don't know what she's talking about. You don't seem all that shy to me.."

Her laugh at my expense had just the right pitch and timbre. Throaty and genuine. Rousing. The rest of her was even more attractive than I remembered. Drop-dead beautiful.

Oh, boy. I can't let my guard down for a second.

"Sorry. I couldn't resist. That lady is really a kick," she added.

"That's one way of putting it."

She grinned, brandishing her whole arsenal of dimples, then unaffectedly tossed her hair. I checked her pupils. Slightly dilated.

Everything pointed to this being an unlikely infatuation. In a region where six-figure incomes are dismissed as minimum wage and the culture embraces the wisdom of newborns, a forty-something with breath hinting of government cheese doesn't exactly qualify as a *catch*. But a little voice inside kept telling me that females this desirable are often written off as unattainable, and while undoubtedly on the receiving end of much attention, can often lack for genuine affection.

That didn't take long. I was now about ready to blame Obama for bugging the limo.

♦♦♦

Unfortunately I'd played way out of my league before. And there really is such a thing as too good to be true. For me, long ago, there was Irene.

She was bright, fun, and there's-a-God gorgeous. She was also traditionally Catholic, and we'd never slept together, which probably should've raised a few red flags. But the truth was, she had a body worth waiting for. Flawless. (Although looking back, she did seem to yawn more than was healthy.)

The night of our engagement she lay splayed out on the bed like some golden goddess, wearing nothing but the new diamond ring and a...CPAP mask. An early, almost-artisanal effort. Picture orthodontic headgear strapped to a fireplace bellows, like a Victorian era contraption devised to cure hysteria and shunt men's passions toward map-making.

I told her I thought I was gay. It was just easier that way. Those were simpler times.

"Do you ever wonder why Betty DeLong chose you to keep her little secret?"

Lara's query jolted me right back to the present.

"Ex..cuse me?"

"I think you heard me."

Her beguiling face wore a twisted vixen grin; frightening and erotic at the same time. I took a good long while to collect my thoughts.

"Who *are* you?"

Over by the register a bearded and top-knotted barista bellowed out a customer name for beverage pickup.

"E-Z!"

"E-Z! Your order's ready."

It took me a second to realize he was talking to me. Puzzled as I hadn't ordered anything, I got up from our table.

"I'll...uh...be right back."

"I expect you will."

I faced the counter and saw a tall, plastic-lidded cup with my nickname initials penned on the side. The busy wait staff didn't have time to even return my gaze, so I figured probing for information was futile.

The piercing shriek of shredding rubber stopped all conversation in the cafe. Tires smoking, the self-driving car slammed through the front window, splintering glass and wood, and crushing Lara Fratelli against the tastefully exposed brick behind her.

Chapter 40

It seems as though every time there's a non-terrorist-related runaway car incident, it involves a senior citizen mistaking gas pedal for brake, or some similar story of driver befuddlement. At first glance, this case looked an awful lot like a high-tech version of the same, as the two ornamental motorists in the autonomous vehicle insisted their software had, to their utter bewilderment, lost control of both navigation and acceleration and that their frantic attempts to intervene manually had been ignored. Three representatives of the NTSB had joined the Palo Alto P.D. and the CHP in questioning the distraught young engineers, who'd probably be reliving the nightmare of their wild ride for years.

All employees and patrons of Philz Coffee were sent home after their debriefs with the Police Department. Having been seated directly across from the single casualty, I came in for particular scrutiny, but added little, and withheld mention of the mysterious nature of the beverage order that had clearly saved my life. There would be no going back on that omission, as any delayed "recollection" of such a crucial detail would cast me in a very dark light with the authorities. I was counting on the predictable rush to blame the haste of the tech industry to promote driverless transportation to frustrate any further lines of serious inquiry.

The crowds cordoned off across the street dwindled quickly after the medical examiner removed Lara Fratelli's broken body from the shattered entrance to the coffee shop. As the ante had been raised with extreme prejudice, I thought it best to put Special Agent Janet Farr deeper in the loop of this developing horror show.

Scrolling through the short list of contacts on my burner mobile, I pressed her number. From the plastic bag of personal effects hanging from the handle of the coroner's gurney came the ringing of the dead woman's phone.

Chapter 41

"So you're saying the hot limo driver *was* the FBI agent?"

"*Phony* FBI agent...and maybe the Asian receptionist too, if the boys are able to match the hair. But that's not the kicker."

Fee stared at me over a stack of crab pots on the deck of the *Lucky Duck* in Princeton Harbor.

"I'm pretty sure the cops'll find out her real name was Susan Doubletree. Unrecognized actress. And Mrs. DeLong's estranged daughter."

"No way!"

"Way."

"And Mrs. DeLong wasn't a Mrs. anybody. We all just took her for a widow and she never disabused anyone of the assumption. DeLong was the name she was born with."

"You piece this all together from your trip to Utah?"

"This Navajo guy...long story."

"What about your swim buddy? The ex-FBI guy? Didn't he hook you up with Miss Doubletrouble there to begin with?"

"Carl Frost. Yeah, he's gotta be right in the thick of this somehow. Remind me to ask the boys how to decontaminate the Lincoln for good."

"So who do you think ordered the coffee...using your nickname?"

I shrugged.

"Does anyone else know you by it?"

I shook my head and speculated.

"Someone's probably been tapping my phone for months. If not longer. Likely yours too."

Fee closed his weary eyes and rubbed one hand over his face. I felt guilty about troubling my friend.

"I am genuinely sorry you got sucked into all this."

"How sorry? One-to-ten."

"I'm serious. I'd give anything.."

"Really?"

"What?"

"Trudy. She's brought shame on the family. And make it look like an accident."

"Or an honor killing."

Fee fished his ringing phone from his pocket and put it on speaker.

"Bill's here. Whaddya got?"

Brandon's voice came in loud and clear.

"The hair from Bill's fleece matches the ones from the testing station."

As everyone let that percolate, all I could think about was the fast-moving blonde in the surgical mask brushing past me outside the elevator on my very last visit to see Mrs. D at Stanford Hospital.

Susan Doubletree had also murdered her own mother.

Chapter 42

I needed some serious counsel in a hurry if there was any chance of getting out in front of what the Fainu'us assured me was about to happen once the Patent Office revealed my name as the exclusive holder of possibly the most valuable piece of intellectual property on the planet. No one with my utter lack of experience in these matters had the slightest chance of making too many coherent decisions once that bell tolled.

I called my boss and told him I was available to work, knowing that Sanjay Singh had a long-standing return reservation with us from SJC back to his home in Saratoga after his monthly day-trip to Los Angeles. My godsons drove me over the hill and helped me remove and destroy the remaining listening devices in the Town Car. Two hours later the VC was in the back seat as the sun was setting.

"Welcome back, Mr. Singh."

"Sorry to keep you waiting. Some lady in coach went full paleo and tried to eat the captain's comfort dog. It was heartwarming to see so many fellow passengers step up with their seat belt extenders to help restrain her. God I love flying commercial."

"Wow."

"Before takeoff, the allergy queen on the aisle tried to bump me from the window because he'd *seen a peanut* in his seat back pocket. I told him I was pretty sure the *depiction* of a peanut in the gift basket ad in the back of the in-flight magazine wouldn't trigger anything except maybe his neighbor to stab him in the eardrum with his million-mile pretzel."

"When did you start being such a people person?"

Sanjay Singh paused and I figured my days in livery were numbered. Then he snorted a single laugh.

"Well played, Bill. And please, it's Sanjay. Good to see you back in the saddle, as it were."

"Thanks. Hope they were able to quiet everything down with you, as well. Without too much...discomfort."

"I found the homeliest nurse in the ER and had her whisper 'supply chain management' over and over in my ear, hoping against hope we might be able to avoid the needle. No such luck. Enough said."

"Ouch. How are things in Silicon Beach?"

"Innovation may know no zip code, my friend. But how many truly great ideas ever get started in a carport?"

I was warming up my own proper elevator pitch when his phone rang.

"Hi, Emmett. I got the new deck and the P&L. "

Sanjay opened his laptop and turned on his mobile's speakerphone.

"Look...you've got product-market fit, you're building for scale, your team is deeply technical...blahblahblah...So what? You're still missing the point. Your code is elegant but your

UX is execrable. Your puppy's peeing the paper but shitting the sofa."

A self-assured disembodied voice filled the cabin in reply.

"All our c-levels are pivoting toward more horizontal, deeply transparent leadership, enabling our customer-facing team to pull focus on increasing engagement and enhancing contrast with others in the channel."

"You sound like you're troubleshooting my television. Close your kimono and listen up. More users successfully faked their own deaths last quarter than logged onto the site a second time. The Board wants to go in a new direction. Up. Sorry."

"You're firing me?"

"According to your recent blog post, your 'true North' oriented you toward.."

"..innovation and giving back. Exactly! Exactly!"

"But according to your recent expense reports, your *magnetic* North pointed you toward Ukrainian lessons and a nanny for your au pair. Today only, we're offering you a soft landing in our office as an entrepreneur-in-residence. It's a 12-month deal and then you and whatever your shares are still worth are on your own. If you bring your dog to work I will walk it up to 280 and throw a lamb chop in the fast lane."

Click.

Sanjay closed his laptop just as we arrived at his neighborhood of large homes on large lots. The architecture was uniformly Tuscan-inspired, and from the beautiful setting in the rolling California hills you might think you'd moved to Italy if you could overlook the Golden State Warriors flags flying from every other terra cotta roof. I stopped at the end of his gated driveway and turned around to face him and tell my story. But he had slunk down low in his seat and was peeking out at his house like a panicked toddler. I followed his gaze through the leaded glass of his kitchen window, which typically framed a bright, busy family tableau. Tonight there was only candlelight.

♦♦♦

"Drive! Drive! Before she sees us!"

"Where to?"

"Who cares!? Thursday...the kids are at friends'...I forgot movie night.."

I sped away from the house while Sanjay voiced a text message.

"Flight delayed. Don't wait up."

We backtracked out of his quiet bedroom community into the strip mall sprawl of the South Bay. After re-posturing himself as a grown-up in the back seat, he motioned to a Peet's Coffee outlet between a chiropractic office and a picture frame store.

"Here! Do you drink chai?"

"Sure."

I pulled into the lot and parked in an open spot.

"When's your next pickup, Bill?"

"You're my last one, actually."

"Can we make this a charter?"

"No sweat."

"I owe you."

He bought us both an Indian tea and we took them back to the car at his request and to my relief. The carnage at Philz Coffee was still fresh in my mind.

"Here. Join me in the back. You'll get a crick in your neck turning around like that. Please."

The legroom and cabin space in the back of the Lincoln were impressive. Even side-by-side we were separated by several feet. It was really a lot more comfortable than sitting on wooden chairs in a coffee shop.

Sanjay had a few things to get off his chest and I would have to wait for my opening.

"My daughter's had her license for all of six months and she's already been cited for three moving violations. We insisted she deal with the consequences herself. So she sets up a webcam in her room, re-names herself after our Dachshund and her first car, and *strips* her way through *traffic school. Sparky Corolla* only got outed after they seized her guidance counselor's computer and...Don't even get me started on the *Internet of Things*. With all my investment diligence in that space I still failed to anticipate her boyfriend's penis showing up on our thermostat."

"Pretty hard to see around that corner." I tried to be sympathetic.

"Sorry Bill. Your turn. Tell me your tales of woe."

He was uncharacteristically silent through the whole telling. I withheld no detail. When I was through, he sat unmoving, eyes forward, fingertips steepled over the bridge of his nose.

He eventually blinked, took in and released three deep breaths, and turned to face me.

"You are so screwed."

Not the words I was hoping for.

"You should've asked me to sign a non-disclosure agreement. I'd have said 'No' - all VC's do - and now I wouldn't be trying so hard to unhear what you just told me. If all this is even remotely true...essentially that alchemy is real... then the financial upside to you personally...and the collateral windfall...well you're talking just *staggering* numbers here. That kind of reach across markets is genuinely disruptive, but remember, lots and lots of people, especially in the energy sector, *hate* being disrupted. My first question to you is, who nuked the mineshaft in Utah? 'Cuz if it was Uncle Sam - and who else could it have been - you're about to have a bit of a falling-out."

Chapter 43

Sanjay read me the boilerplate rendition of the riot act I'd heard him hone on naive wunderkinder over the years, but it felt a little watered down, probably owing to my age and the fluky roots of "my" breakthrough - and perhaps even his dormant appetite for genuine risk. He cut quickly to the chase.

"As I see it, if you can stay out of Guantanamo, you've got three options: sell your patent outright, license the IP, or go into the battery business. There may be variations, but those are the general themes. Can you give me a quick demo of the prototype the Fainu'us put together?"

We made it over to the coast in just under an hour. Brandon, Dean, and Gilbert totally nailed it - even fashioning a custom battery housing adapter for immediate use in most smartphones. Sanjay Singh, notoriously stingy with praise, positively gushed over the boys' mastery. They were, in turn, flattered by his attention; Singh was an old lion by Silicon Valley standards, but a lion just the same. He'd made his name inventing an optical inventory scanner while working for Argon Industries, and his fortune from successfully circumventing the non-compete clause in his separation agreement and selling a knock-off of his own invention to all franchisees of the convenience store chain where his parents had worked after immigrating with him from India. Venture capital was really just a very lucrative way to get him out of the house these days.

"You know what Bill...let me reach out to Tom Moore. I know for a fact he's sweating his keynote next Monday in Cupertino after the preview he gave at the last Board meeting. OS updates do not headlines make."

The boys nodded, clearly impressed with Singh's high-level access.

I was a little skeptical.

"You want to read him in on all this?"

"It's entirely your call."

Chapter 44

Tom Moore, dean of Silicon Valley CEO's, was exactly the way he was portrayed in the tech press. Lean, bespectacled, genteel, ascetic, he combined the expressionless manner of a small town funeral director with the tactical genius of Erwin Rommel.

Moore, Singh, and I faced each other in a triangular layout on treadmills in the chief executive's home gym. Sanjay and I dogged it on slow and low while Moore strode quickly and evenly on the steepest incline setting. He spoke without even breathing hard.

"We can offer you 250,000 non-statutory options tomorrow morning as a good-faith retainer.."

Sanjay countered.

"A quarter-million restricted stock units. And the use expires at the conclusion of your keynote."

Moore looked up high as if counting ceiling tiles.

"One million NSO's. You'll provide us with two prototypes - one for the demo and one for R&D."

"Both to be returned to Mr. Feeney at close-of-business Monday."

Sanjay Singh arched one eyebrow and aimed his cellphone camera at the big boss. Moore continued.

"Cameo, Inc. lays no claim to the exclusive intellectual property of.."

I helped him out.

"William J. Feeney."

"William J. Feeney..here to my immediate right.."

♦♦♦

Sanjay Singh had seemingly just shaken down the CEO of the world's most valuable technology company. But Tom Moore was the anti-pushover and I started to wonder what he knew that we didn't. Sanjay read my thoughts.

"Cameo's last earnings call was a big disappointment. Their stock price is going to skyrocket after the keynote. All because of your battery. Believe it or not, Moore got you on the cheap. And it may cost me my Board seat, but he'll pay through the nose when the time comes. And he'll be OK with it."

How a million Cameo stock options was "on the cheap" was the exact kind of talk that made Silicon Valley the object of so much open loathing in the outside world. But Singh would have none of it.

"Look...I've got more money than I know what to do with. But the truth is, Bill, I haven't seen the end zone in years. This is like first and goal on Super Bowl Sunday. If you want my advice, I'll do it just for the shits and giggles."

Chapter 45

Sanjay eventually let me drop him off at his home well after midnight. It was almost 2 am by the time I made it back over the hill again into the Fainu'us' protective custody. I woke up early to make breakfast for everyone. It was the least that I could do.

Around 8:30, I received an email from the law office of Thomas Lippincott. Attached was a document requesting my signature, stating that I agreed to distribute 1% of the annual profits from any commercial application of my pending battery patent or $250,000 per year - whichever amount was smaller - to an Alice Devine Croft residing at an address in Coral Gables, Florida. The document was not a legal demand, but more of an appeal by the Estate of Elizabeth DeLong, as represented by Thomas Lippincott. Payments would cease upon Ms. Croft's death.

Lippincott actually answered his phone but could or would share nothing about the backstory of the strange petition other than to say that he had been sending $250K every year on Mrs. D's behalf to the same person at the same address for as long as his firm had been retained.

There were only three Alice Devine Crofts that came up in my internet search, and only one with an address in

Florida. Born in 1965. With a listed phone number - likely an old landline.

A drowsy female voice answered.

"Hello?"

"May I please speak with Alice Croft?"

She yawned before responding in a gentle drawl.

"Speaking. Who is this?"

"My name's Bill Feeney. I'm calling from Palo Alto, California. I believe we both have had dealings with an attorney named Thomas Lippincott."

There was a long pause.

"You may have had *dealings* with Mr. Lippincott. I wouldn't call what I've had with him exactly that. Two phone conversations in almost thirty years is more like it. But he's been a faithful correspondent, yes."

I decided to show my hand.

"I just wanted to let you know that the annuity payment from Elizabeth DeLong's estate will continue without interruption. Did you know she'd passed?"

"I've never even heard the name, sir. What is your business with Thomas Lippincott? Exactly?"

"Lippincott was the late Elizabeth DeLong's lawyer. She was your benefactor. I've become a conduit of sorts."

She said nothing.

"Pardon...but did you ever wonder who sent you the money all this time? Or why?"

"My mother received a check for as long as I can remember. Mr. Lippincott continued to send the checks to me after she died. It was just me and Mom. My father died when I was three. I've always assumed it was the Army's way of keeping us quiet. Who's Elizabeth.."

"DeLong."

"Her name's never been on any of the checks. Thomas Lippincott always signs 'em."

"Is Croft your.."

"My ex-husband. He's been out of the picture for twenty years."

"If you don't mind me asking...what was it that you think the Army wanted to keep quiet?"

She sighed.

"My father was an Army medical officer. A psychiatrist. What were the chances of him getting crushed by a tank?"

Chapter 46

I called my boss and explained that I'd need some more time off to attend to a health issue, which, as it turned out, would be the most prophetic lie I'd ever told. He sounded puzzled but understanding, and told me to come back to work when I was ready.

I signed the document from Lippincott and walked it in its return envelope down the Fainu'us' long driveway to their mailbox for pickup. Fee gave me a stern look upon my return to the house: I was to go nowhere without an escort.

During my short absence Alice Croft sent me a link to her father's obituary in *Stars and Stripes* newspaper:

06-June-1968
Major Kirk Jackson Devine, USA, M.D., age 29, of Wilmington, NC died in a training accident in West Germany. He received his medical degree from Johns Hopkins University in 1964 and completed his residency in Psychiatry at George Washington University Hospital. He leaves a wife and a three year-old daughter.

Stars and Stripes required a subscription fee to access additional archived obituaries. It turned out to be a small price to pay.

06-June-1968
Staff Sergeant Raymond H. Doubletree, USA, 10th SFG, age 27, of Montezuma Creek, UT died in a training accident in West Germany. His awards and decorations include a Silver Star, two Bronze Stars, two Purple Hearts, the Vietnam Service Medal, and the Joint Service Commendation with 'V' device.

Coincidence plus suspicious circumstance equals doubt squared. Alice Croft told me that her multiple inquiries over the years into her father's death had been met with polite condescension from the Army and dismissed outright by her mother, who was content with the original official explanation. Her parents' marriage had not been a happy one, and the Department of Defense and the Veterans Administration had gone to some length to continue the benefits accrued to her late husband.

Mrs. D had clearly had a steady source of income for a long time. Whether she'd inherited it from her wildcatter father or made it herself was unclear. But anonymously paying someone three time zones away a quarter of a million dollars a year for quite possibly fifty years seemed like an extraordinarily generous or *guilty* gesture.

Chapter 47

"Have you thought more about the business plan? T.M.'s making noises about your intentions."

Sanjay texted me to a burner phone the boys had secured. Tom Moore's people must have been up most of the night testing the battery prototype.

I was inclined against selling the patent outright. To put a dollar value on it seemed like dealing in complete fantasy. And no matter the size of the offer, it would feel like an abdication of my role as steward to the weird legacy of Mrs. DeLong. A winning lottery ticket and a pass-through. Like I'd be letting her down. A *disappointment.* But I was willing to have my mind changed.

Licensing the IP seemed a little more appropriate, and the option Sanjay favored. There could be a reasonable level of control over the proliferation of the product and the steep challenges of manufacture would be fobbed off on enterprises that had decades of expertise over the Swiss watch intricacies of the modern supply chain. But the Fainu'u brothers had already demonstrated that assembly of the revolutionary battery was surprisingly simple. And enforcement of IP rights could be a real headache in huge markets like China, with its dodgy commitment to such quaint Western notions.

The truth was, I was leaning toward reinventing the wheel right here in the US of A. Or, more accurately, at Chimney Flat in the Navajo Nation.

I texted Sanjay back.

"Do you think it's wiser to release the batteries slowly and build demand at a premium price point or focus on the long tail?"

Price point? Long tail?? Who was I kidding? I'm out of my depth at Coinstar.

"Right now you've got the best mousetrap. Leverage scarcity while you can, because you only get one shot to monopolize a commodity. Your patent app is vague about the catalyzing event. State actors will likely be breathing down your neck soon. Do you have any idea at all how Mrs. D could've initiated the reaction in the first place without alerting the authorities?"

I didn't reply.

Chapter 48

Several civilian nuclear watchdog groups have maps available online showing the locations and yields of all the verified atomic munitions tests conducted by the U.S. since the Manhattan Project. There are dates and detailed official - and unofficial - descriptions of the more than one thousand atmospheric, underwater, and even space tests occurring between 1945 and 1992. I was only interested in underground detonations near Montezuma Creek, Utah in 1971 - assuming the triplets had their date right.

There were thirty-four contained blasts catalogued by the Department of Energy that year (and similar numbers during the shoulder years) - one in the Aleutian Islands and the rest at the Nevada Test Site outside Las Vegas - four hundred miles from Mrs. DeLong's property. Yet the green grotto had clearly been ground zero for something.

Brandon suggested a different government agency might be able to help triangulate the actual day and date we were looking for. He and his brothers calculated that an underground explosion as small as a single kiloton could result in a localized earthquake as large as 5.5 on the Richter Scale.

More involved digging, this time into the digital archives of the United States Geological Survey, revealed that a remote networked seismograph operated by the University of Utah on behalf of the USGS registered an earthquake measuring 5.3 on the Richter Scale on March 18, 1971 - with an epicenter located 11 miles northeast of Montezuma Creek. The event date bore an asterisk in the margin and was annotated "calibration error - temblor unconfirmed".

The historical facts seemed clear: a measurable nuclear fission reaction had occurred in a mineshaft on Mrs. DeLong's land - probably in 1971 - possibly on March 18. It earned scant official notice at the time. The father of Mrs. DeLong's only known child died mysteriously in West Germany while on active duty with the U.S. Army on June 6, 1968. An Army psychiatrist died on the same date in the same area under similar strange circumstances. Mrs. DeLong, through her proxy Thomas Lippincott, had been paying the doctor's widow, and subsequently her surviving child, $250,000 per year since her husband's death. The beneficiaries claimed no knowledge of Mrs. DeLong.

The triplets and I spit balled possible scenarios.

"Her baby daddy offed his shrink."

"Intentionally - or like the Army said - by accident?"

"Why her guilt trip if it was an accident?"

"Why would the Army cover it up?"

"And what do they have to do with the bomb in the mineshaft?"

"Does anybody know if Trudy's fixed?"

"Huh?"

"Dad probably does."

"And we're going off topic here because?"

"We're gonna lose views if she gets knocked up. That's why they hid Elvis's wife. Ruins the fantasy."

"We may be too late."

"How? There's not a boar for miles."

"I dunno. But I thought I saw a piglet while mucking her pen."

"Probably just a fuzzy steamer."

"Scoop or swaddle? Tough call sometimes."

Fee walked within range of the discussion.

"Shouldn't you guys be double-checking the demo battery or something before the big reveal? And maybe making sure the backup works too?"

"We're good."

"Well then you three can help me pull the pots off *Lucky Duck II* bright and early. We've got a charter tomorrow. Sightsee around the Farallones. The reservation just came in."

Chapter 49

The boys removed the crab pots from the deck of the boat in the manner of an old-time firefighters' bucket brigade, passing the circular steel traps effortlessly from brother-to-brother from ship-to-shore. The floating berth in Princeton Harbor was now stacked head-high with the traps, their trailing lines wound around float buoys and cleat-hitched in a practiced blur.

As I helped Fee hose down the vessel with water from a shared utility tap on the dock I received an urgent text from Sanjay. Tom Moore was asking if the Fainu'u brothers could meet with some of his engineers in Cupertino ASAP to help fine-tune the battery interface in advance of his keynote. The triplets were delighted to be consulted and hustled off in the direction of their truck parked in the small lot just across from the Harbormaster's office.

"You OK with this? I mean...I can't leave you behind alone, so I guess..."

"It's just you and me. And the party of two. It'll be fun. Fair seas, right?"

I'd been out with Fee too many times to count, but the round-trip passage to the Farallones could get Poseidon to hork.

"Fairly fair. Swells from the northwest - 8 at 18."

That forecast for 8-foot swells at 18-second intervals was typical for this time of year and manageable for most landlubbers with over-the-counter seasickness preventatives or those lucky few blessed with natural sea legs. Treatment of mal de mer once underway is almost always pointless. I knew my limits and that patches and pills required pre-medication. So I gobbled down some candied ginger and slipped on one of the acupressure wristbands Fee kept handy onboard. The skipper himself was immune - he had the balance of a steeplejack in heaving seas and could eat sardines from a can with green waves breaking over the wheelhouse. Something about a self-leveling inner ear. Maybe inherited from his seafaring Polynesian forebears.

♦♦♦

Two middle-aged men, backlit by the morning sun and wearing ball caps, dark glasses, and windbreakers approached the *Lucky Duck II*. Both wore daypacks and each carried a pair of binoculars on a strap around his neck. The white one had a formidably bushy beard, the black one was clean-shaven.

"Bernie and Dale? I'm Fee. This is Bill, my first mate."

"Dale. Nice to meet you."

The guy with the facial hair had a familiar-sounding voice that I couldn't immediately place.

"And I'm Bernie."

Both passengers smiled broadly at us while bumping fists. Bernie looked a little unsteady on his feet as he stepped aboard and soon tumbled straight into Fee's arms - his hands briefly clutching the skipper's waist - before righting himself and tisking a bashful laugh.

"Never been on a boat this small. But don't you worry - I've got the patch."

He pointed at the beige circle behind his ear. Fee nodded.

"You're welcome to stow your gear below if you want. It's up to you. There are refreshments in the galley fridge - hot coffee or chocolate in the maker. Please help yourselves. Oh, and housekeeping hint: the head's a double-flush."

Fee then gave his safety talk: pointing out life vests, rings, and the raft, and the locations of fire extinguishers and signal flares. The *Lucky Duck II* was three bells beyond ship-shape; for a working vessel she was nothing short of immaculate. You could even breathe in the salt air untainted by fishy smells or fuel fumes. A custom ventilation system saw to that.

Fee turned over the twin engines, I cast off the dock, stern, and spring lines, and we were beyond the breakwater in less than five minutes.

The headwind coupled with the diesel growl to make conversation on deck difficult as we skipped over slow rollers out in open water. Dale and Bernie sat amidships across from each other like two intrepid school boys on their very first nautical field trip, hands clinging to the gunwales, knapsacks packed with reassuring notes from mom. Not the booze cruise types from the looks of it. More animal cracker than Captain Morgan. Thank God.

"How long will it take us this morning?"

"Two and a half, maybe three hours," I shouted back over the din.

Bernie knew more than he let on. Travel times to the Farallon Islands can vary dramatically depending upon a myriad of seasonal, atmospheric, and oceanographic conditions. These rocky redoubts - five or six loosely-defined islands and an assortment of islets and sea stacks covering a total of about 200 acres of dry land mass strung out over five miles of open Pacific - host an embarrassment of natural riches - from squadrons of seabirds onshore to colonies of marine mammals in their near waters.

Between Pillar Point Harbor and the Farallones stretches a marine sanctuary protecting species in air and sea from human influence for hundreds of square miles. Fishing is highly regulated and commercial trade traffic between Asia and the busy port of Oakland sails in carefully circumscribed channels strictly enforced by the U.S. Coast Guard. But the narrow inlets between the islands give cold comfort to all who dare ply those waters, for beneath the churning surface swims the stuff of nightmares: one of the densest known populations of great white sharks on earth.

♦♦♦

Less than ten minutes after leaving the dock, Fee, who was at the helm, dug his vibrating cell phone from his pants pocket. I was just off the bridge, between the skipper and the two sightseers, and out of earshot of the ensuing conversation. But I watched him pull up his t-shirt and fiddle with his insulin pump before ending the call.

"Everything OK?"

"Yeah. Yeah. That was Dean. They got some kind of alert that my new pump wasn't working. I musta hit the power button on something when we were casting off. Anyway, no worries. I got it turned back on."

He returned his focus to the gray-green expanse of water in front of us. You wouldn't know it from all the ribbing between them, but the Fainu'us were fiercely vigilant over their dad. I guessed that we had to be nearing the limits of 4G range and that they would've reached out over satellite phone or one of the available marine bands had we crossed that threshold. But it was a very good thing they called. I'd learned from my buddy that diabetes can go from controlled to crisis in a hurry.

"You have some idea what's on the agenda today?"

Neither man had demonstrated any interest in sport fishing. And while they'd brought binoculars, and there were always a few advance pods of humpbacks around, we were still a week or two away from prime whale watching season.

"Birds. They don't have landing status so they wanna get as close to Southeast Farallon as allowed."

They were certainly headed to the right place. The Farallones were either permanent or temporary home to vast populations of gannets, gulls, cormorants, petrels, murres, and even, in recent years, blue-footed boobies, one of the curious species credited by Charles Darwin for inspiring his theory of evolution. How these birds had adapted to the brisk climate of the North Pacific after generations in the Galapagos mystified even the parade of animal biologists granted limited stays of study on Southeast Farallon by the U.S. Fish & Wildlife Service.

Fee paused before continuing.

"Feel free to get some shut-eye before we get out there. This could be a long day."

I gave him a thumbs up and headed out of the wheelhouse. On my way down to the galley I noticed the two ornithologists were now sitting next to one another, their packs open in their laps. One was screwing a long lens on a camera, the other adjusted the settings on something like a combination spotting scope/rangefinder. They looked up and caught my eye, then smiled and nodded. I continued below, lay down on the padded bench behind the hatched lower fish hold, and dozed to the even roll of the morning swell.

Chapter 50

I woke to the *Lucky Duck II* yawing in broken seas. Fee must've throttled down the engines, which were now putting off only a low rumble. Glancing out the closest porthole I could see the sharp profile of Seal Rock, the small crag due south and only about 100 yards off Southeast Farallon. Large numbers of pinnipeds: seals, sea lions, and elephant seals, staged here year-after-year, almost unwittingly, like a whiskered prix fixe for the great whites that gathered to feast.

I climbed up to the wheelhouse. Bernie was steering the boat.

"Where's the skipper?", I demanded.

"A little under the weather."

He motioned to the corner under the instrument panel. Fee sat slumped on the deck with his back against the bulkhead, eyes at half-mast, a lazy smile on his face. He was humming a tune I didn't know.

"Fee!"

I squatted down at his level.

"I'm gonna take a look at your pump."

He offered no resistance, but his mass and torpor made it hard to find the device under his sweat-soaked shirt. I turned to Bernie.

"How long's he been like this? Where's...uh.."

"Dale?"

The second passenger had materialized behind me. I addressed him without turning around.

"Here...give me a hand. He's an insulin-dependent diabetic. Can you grab some orange juice from the galley?"

"That's so sweet of you to cover for your lush of a friend."

It took a second to understand what he'd just said. But the voice was starting to come back to me.

"What?"

"Yo-ho-ho and a bottle...and all that.."

Furious, I whirled around to see the now-beardless cheeks of "Dale" - and to stare into the unforgettably asymmetrical face of Glenn Fletcher, the man who knew everyone had a price.

He smiled and pressed the crackling blue arc of a stun gun against my neck.

♦♦♦

I never lost consciousness but dropped like a puppet off his strings. After the seizing and groaning stopped I rolled and looked over at Fee. Thankfully he too was still awake, but looking paler by the minute.

"Something's wrong with his pump. He needs some juice or he's going to die."

I lowered my voice so my friend couldn't hear my plea. If he was hypoglycemic, as I was convinced he was, he might get agitated, which wouldn't help matters at the moment. In the few times I'd seen him go low over the years, he'd only presented agitation once. They'd have to really hurt him then to get him under control. So I hoped desperately for his usual, slightly goofy compliance.

"His pump's doing exactly what we've asked it to."

Dale, AKA Fletcher, did smug like a frat boy Bond villain.

"What do you want?"

"I would really love your forgiveness for all this but... maybe too soon?"

Fee broke into a slurred, off-key version of Elton John's *Sorry Seems to be the Hardest Word* as Fletcher grabbed me by my shirt collar and dragged me up to a sitting position. He then placed a pen in my hand and dropped a sheet of paper into my lap.

"What's this?"

I started to read what looked like an affidavit of some kind.

"You're assigning your pending patent to another party."

I read on.

"Who the hell is Catalog, Inc.?"

"They're an aggregator of sorts."

"You mean a patent troll?"

"I prefer NPE. For what they pay me I'm happy to make that distinction. Your John Hancock and the skipper gets his juice. Don't make me give you another time-out."

I looked over at Fee, whose head was barely resisting the force of gravity, and signed my name.

"Once more for the notary."

Bernie relinquished the wheel to Fletcher, and removed a logbook and an inkpad from his pack. I signed, he countersigned and stamped, and then motioned officiously for my thumbprint.

"The last time someone asked me for that, she was trying to kill me."

"A little over-enthusiastic, that one," Fletcher noted.

"So you ran her over."

"Too much autonomy can be a dangerous thing."

"And you kept me around for my penmanship."

"And the location of the abandoned mineshaft. Or this is going to hurt you a lot more than it is me."

"Give my friend some juice and I'll tell you everything."

"No. No. After you."

"It's in Utah. The Four Corners region. Near the Navajo lands."

"Keep going."

"Montezuma Creek's the nearest town."

"How far?"

"I don't know exactly. I turned off all electronics. I don't have the exact coordinates."

"How did you get there?"

This wouldn't go over well.

"Some...one...took me there. An old friend of Mrs. DeLong."

"OK. Where's this.."

"The friend died soon after."

Fletcher, the main inquisitor, stopped talking and turned toward Bernie, who produced a rubber-handled tool that looked like a cross between a cheese grater and an abalone iron. A foodie's kitchen implement. A *zester*, I remembered an old girlfriend calling it. He tossed it to his boss.

Then, showing gameday form, Bernie kicked me squarely in the groin like he was attempting a long-distance field goal.

The force of his follow-through briefly lifted me off the deck, and that weird pain I hadn't felt in many years shot way up into my abdomen. The radiating ache was visceral. Almost *pulpy.* And reminiscent of having my gullible junk slammed in a sock drawer during a clumsy coupling with the hot-flashing spinster-succubus who had hired me, the boy-next-door, one day after school, to "help her with a heavy box". I still move furniture with the lights on.

As I doubled over, Fletcher grabbed my hair and yanked my head back like he was about to peel my scalp. Instead he ran the corrugated stainless steel across my forehead. Thin shreds of skin flapped down in front of my eyes like bloody hash browns.

Bernie returned to the helm just as Fee's sat phone rang. His insulin pump must've alerted the boys again. Fletcher yanked the phone from the listless skipper's drybag and hurled it overboard into the chop.

◆◆◆

"What's your plan?", I sputtered through the rivulets of blood now running down my face.

As I tried to stand, Fletcher executed a perfect leg sweep, sending me nose-first back to the steel deck. The impact sounded like cracking crab through bubble wrap and I soon began sloshing in a crimson puddle.

"You're becoming a bit of a biohazard here, Bill. And I'm losing interest in your wellness."

I blinked the tears out of my eyes long enough to see Fee still breathing steadily but barely conscious. Bernie had his eyes directed forward out the windshield, and I now noticed that both he and Fletcher were wearing thin rubber gloves.

"I'm thorry to bore you." I'd begun to lisp a bit through broken teeth.

"Can you give me solid directions to the source, or not?"

"I can take you there mythelf. I'll thow you the way. Justh get Fee some juth and head back to the harbor."

"I'm calling B.S. And Fee's pump's probably already put out an S.O.S. to his bouncing baby behemoths. Last chance. Details."

Buttons flew as he tore open my shirt and zested one of the nipples off my chest. I heard myself scream, rolled over onto my side, and curled into the fetal position facing the bulkhead. About even with my hands - now down around my waist protecting my abdomen - a rescue kit sat in its wall mount. As Fletcher raked over my ribs I yelled again to cover the sound of me unlatching a single flare, the top half of which I wedged under my pants leg into the arch side of my shoe.

Blood now poured freely from fresh wounds to the shallow veins just under my armpit, and Fletcher, panting from his exertions, had finally had enough. The flaying stopped as quickly as it had started. His voice echoed his disgust.

"I think we're done here."

Bernie helped his boss haul me up to my knees. They dragged me off the bridge and out toward the stern rail.

"Fair winds and following seas, old chum."

"I hope you attholes never thee another bird."

A sharp hammerfist to one of my ears knocked me dizzy and four hands tossed me headfirst over the side.

Chapter 51

A shallow breath, the flinch of impact, and I plunged deep under the surface. Somehow, maybe from years of swimming in the Bay, I avoided gasping upon sudden immersion in the 50 degree brine. And like blanching a vegetable in a gourmet kitchen, the cold water shock stopped the burning sting on my skin, and made the thudding aches in my mouth, nose, neck, and groin at least manageable. Definite pluses.

Now the bad. Blood, sharks, and dead ahead a rollicking 100-yard sprint to jagged rocks lashed with ocean surges from three different directions - sometimes all at once. Such pile-ups can triple the height of the surrounding waves just in time for a sudden shoal break to send foam and flotsam high onto the cliffs.

I popped my head up to see Southeast Farallon at 12 o'clock. *Lucky Duck II* loomed right behind me, its engines gurgling just above idle, blue diesel smoke settling at the waterline. I remained less than two body-lengths from the twin propellers which still spun fast enough to finish the fricassee Fletcher had started onboard. Both bad guys scanned the water, not thinking to look directly down. I filled my lungs, dove back under, and breast-stroked in the direction of the island, hoping my gray hair would be lost in the whitecaps.

To my left, Seal Rock was moving. Chubby undulations made it look like a pile of wriggling maggots. The seals knew something was up this morning. They weren't out sunbathing.

Two large dorsal fins stirred the surface to my right.

I reached down to my feet. I hadn't kicked off my deck shoes because I knew I'd need them if I made it to the island. These were floating loafers I'd found on the internet and so far seemed to be working as advertised.

I pulled the signal flare from under my pants leg and ducked under the waves again. With all the turbulence, visibility was poor, and I couldn't see the shapes or shadows of the patrolling sharks. We've all been schooled that we're not their preferred prey, but I was unlikely to survive even a test-bite from one of these giants. And you never know. Tastes change.

I twisted the starter cap off the flare, hunched over, and struck it across the primer. I couldn't work up much wrist speed underwater, but the scratching of the flint sure made a lot of noise. I really really hoped it wouldn't draw the wrong kind of attention.

Finally the magnesium stick ignited. I pivoted and waved it around like a frogman's lightsaber, trying to appear bigger, or more dangerous, or less appetizing than anything a shark had ever considered. But I knew one way or another I needed to stop the flow of blood - the catnip of the deep. The bleeding from my torso now mushroomed around me like a neon bait ball.

Holding my breath, I held the underwater flame to my chest and underarm, searing my flesh and cauterizing the open wounds. It hurt like crazy, but somehow not as badly as I would've thought. I'd probably just killed off the nerve endings. I couldn't bring myself to torch my face.

Now further behind me, the *Lucky Duck II* bobbed in a slow circle, safely beyond the surf zone.

Over the lapping of the water against my ears, I heard a distinctly electric whir. A drone carrying what looked like a small plastic package approached Fee's boat at a steep angle. It circled about fifty feet above sea level and then hovered behind the stern. Bernie appeared from inside the wheelhouse holding a large pistol. Using a two-hand combat grip, he calmly aimed and fired at least ten loud shots at the drone, which wheeled over sideways and splashed into the water.

It had to have been the triplets who'd launched the mini-copter. At least they now had a clearer picture of the dire situation on board the *Lucky Duck II.* God willing they were headed at full steam in our direction.

Bernie returned to the bridge and stood alongside Fletcher. They were no longer searching for signs of a floater. There were now bigger fish to fry. I was good as dead.

♦♦♦

The rest of the way across the channel involved a steady sidestroke interrupted by broad swings of the flare in an arc around my waist. The fins had submerged and I figured they were now circling in the murky space beneath me. The seafloor was only about twenty feet deep here and adding the mass of even one apex predator left an uncomfortably thin cushion of water between us. Some ichthyologists have suggested measuring these great whites by *displacement* for crying out loud.

Suddenly, the flare began to spit parks, and just like that, went dark. I dropped it from my hand and windmilled in a breathless freestyle toward the hard edge of Southeast Farallon.

The island offers no beach approach, protected cove, or even any real landing to speak of. A lone crane arm winches small craft by block-and-tackle up from the breakers directly to a dry rock shelf forty or so feet above the mean water line. Sometimes high tides and big combers crash over the top of the creaky, salt-streaked apparatus. Most visitors take a good look, turn around, and sail home.

I'm usually not fast enough in the water to time, catch, and safely body surf most waves. The rogue swell behind me stacked up like a pyramid and sucked me under its curl until I was looking straight down at a trough of dry rock. I skidded *up* the face to the crest and was deposited almost gently onto a bench of barnacles halfway up the cliff. The wave receded and I scrambled for slippery holds in the granite before the next wall of water slammed into me, dragging me down into the maelstrom below, and then flinging me into the air and up onto high ground.

I'd made landfall in one piece. Birds began pecking at my head.

Chapter 52

If the seas around the Farallones forgive your trespass, the Islands themselves welcome you with open talons. Thirty miles outside the Golden Gate but technically within the city limits of San Francisco, everything here with feathers acts like it's auditioning for Alfred Hitchcock. The biologists who rotate through on field assignments, surveying and observing in fog and gales, wear hard hats to fend off the beaks and bills of the very animals they're trying to protect. They also need to watch their step. It's hard to know where the land ends and the guano begins. And then there are the rats - voracious consumers of bird eggs - bequeathed years ago by cargo vessels, they've reproduced so prolifically that the U.S. Fish & Wildlife service has proposed carpet-bombing them with Zyklon gas - a variant of the chemical weapon used by the Nazis to murder millions of people in WWII. The optics of the campaign were so bad, the plan was called off and the rodents have continued to multiply unchecked. I don't know if there are any spiders or snakes or clowns around to speak of, but the naked hostility of the place fosters a lot of everyday phobias.

I swatted at several dive-bombing birds, resolved to eat more fowl, staggered to my feet, and headed toward the old Victorian that once housed the lighthouse tender. Offshore,

Lucky Duck II was still puttering in a small circle about where I'd left her deck. I prayed that Fee was still breathing.

The door to the circa 1870 building was unlocked and I stumbled inside. It was apparent that no one else was on Southeast Farallon at the moment. Probably a few-day lull between vetted researchers. The radio was a jerry-rigged contraption, powered like everything else in the dank building by a diesel generator just outside. I went back outdoors, found the ignition switch, and was able to fire the rusty old motor up.

Back inside I consulted the laminated wall poster, found the Coast Guard frequency, and put in a distress call. The connection was rough, and I was unable to answer back without lots of static, but I was pretty sure the young-sounding Coast Guardsman heard my plea on the other end.

I stripped off my wet clothes, found a ratty blanket and a portable electric heater, and warmed up just enough to stave off hypothermia.

The kitchen nook held a hot plate, microwave, drip coffee maker, and refrigerator. Small cabinets on the wall were mostly empty, save salt, pepper, ketchup, and several small stacks of chipped plates and cups. The drawers by the sink were strewn with mismatched cutlery. The fridge was empty, except for an open bottle of flat diet soda, which I guzzled through aching teeth. In the interest of time I warmed up a tall cup of water in the microwave and drank as much as I could stomach while scouring the cabinets again.

Bingo.

Toppled over behind the ketchup was a half-empty bear-shaped squeeze bottle of honey. I threw on a pair of old coveralls left hanging on a wall hanger, slipped back into my deck shoes, and located a thread-bare roll of duct tape. I used it to fasten the honey bottle to the waist of the jumpsuit and headed back outside, flipping off the switch to the generator. Large barrels of fuel were arranged on pallets nearby. A plastic gas can with a spout hung from a nail on the side of the low wooden fence around the small power plant.

I grabbed the can, found a tap on the bottom of one of the diesel barrels, and filled it to the top.

Taking and holding a deep breath, I squeezed my eyes shut and poured the slick, smelly fuel over my shoulders until I was thoroughly soaked.

♦♦♦

The fumes kept the birds at bay on my way back to the edge of the island. I prayed they would have the same effect on the sharks.

Timing the shore entry into the channel was a hit-or-miss prospect. I missed.

Mid-blink, a breaker came out of nowhere and knocked me sideways off the cliff top. A second wave from the other direction clapped me like a wet hand but saved me from face-planting onto a shallow shoal cloaked in giant kelp. Somehow, I squirted out into the channel.

The *Lucky Duck II* continued chugging in a tight gyre. Trying to read the swirling current, I aimed east of the boat in hopes the tidal flow would carry me near. A second vessel - an open-cockpit, outboard Panga favored by drug runners - approached as if out of nowhere, closing quickly. Then again I heard the telltale electric whir.

This time this drone circled higher, well out of pistol range. The Panga came right up alongside Fee's craft, their gunwales almost touching. One after the other, Dale and Bernie cleared the heaving gap between the two decks and abandoned my friend to his fate. I swam a little harder.

Only a single dorsal fin broke the surface this crossing and gave me a comfortingly wide berth. Though queasy, I was grateful for the diesel force field.

Between strokes I looked up at the Panga trying to escape to open water. It sped forward for less than ten seconds before spluttering to a stall. Overhead the drone hovered before dropping a salami-shaped object into the water. Bubbles trailed the tiny torpedo as it silently circled the stricken launch. I dunked my head back under the swell and continued toward the *Lucky Duck II*.

The haunting echo of a whale calf in distress reverberated from the direction of the Panga. I popped my head up into the silence above the waves. In the distance the skipper of the getaway craft fussed with the motor at the stern. The silhouettes of Dale and Bernie gestured angrily at one another. Plaintive whale song accompanied me under water all the way to the hull of Fee's boat, which floated too high for a swimmer to board unassisted.

Alert to the danger of the twin screws still spinning slowly beneath me, I wedged a hand into one of the bilge outlets and tried to bring my foot up to a narrow crease on the hull. Unable to gain a purchase, I let go and splashed back into the sea, narrowly escaping the propwash.

Then, directly above, the drone reappeared, the boat's bow line in its mechanical grasp. A loop dropped neatly in front of me, floating on the skin of the sea, and I pulled myself hand-over-hand toward the port side. I touched the steel plate and held fast.

To my right, less than a football field away, a female humpback breached the surface of the ocean, twirled on its vertebral axis and smashed its bulk across the exposed top of the Panga, which splintered and disappeared as if it were never there.

The wake from the whale helped boost me up the line to the deck of Fee's boat. Still not believing what I'd just seen, I scrambled to the wheelhouse. Fee was now sprawled on his back, unconscious, but breathing. I tore the plastic bottle from my makeshift tape belt and squeezed as much honey under his tongue as I could without choking him. He shook his head slowly and coughed.

The only sounds as sweet were the horn from the approaching *Lucky Duck* and the rotor slap of the Coast Guard rescue helicopter now overhead.

Chapter 53

Fee and I were being treated in adjacent beds at the Stanford ER and both our conditions had stabilized. We'd shared a ride in the chopper, my friend showing rapid signs of recovery after the triplets dosed him with Glucagon, even before the rescue swimmer had hoisted him up into the aircraft. Brandon, Dean, and Gilbert now hovered nearby, dodging medical staff and keeping the curtain open between us. Thankfully, Stanford was having a slow day.

"You guys made good time," said Fee, impressed.

"You may need to overhaul a few engines."

"All the intakes were smoking by the time we got back to the harbor."

"Thanks for lookin' out for us old guys."

"The pump setup worked pretty good. We got real-time blood sugars right off the satellite link."

"Sorry your care package got shot down."

"Hate it when that happens."

"The crab out there are gonna taste extra sweet next season."

"So that's what that wath," I added, also impressed, and still lisping.

They'd set my nose but my teeth would need to see the dentist.

"Just so you know, Dad, Bill's honey saved the day."

Fee's eyes filled up when he looked my way.

"Helluva swim, *Uso*. Helluva swim."

We bumped fists as the boys looked down at their shoes.

"My plan had a few holesth. Thankth you guysth for dropping me the lifeline."

"Wish we could've gotten there sooner. Those scumbags roughed you up bad."

"Are the docs planning on doing some skin grafting?"

"Thoundsth like it, yeah."

"Trudy wants to donate a nipple.."

"Celebrities with their causes.."

"Thank her for the offer. I think they can justh tattoo a new one on. By the way, did you guysth dithsable the getaway boat?"

"We jammed the throttle cable. Lucky that Panga was fly-by-wire."

"And the whale thoundsth?"

"YouTube. Uploaded to the aqua drone on the cruise over."

"In direct violation of copyright."

"Btw, we didn't share all of this with the Coast Guard."

"Did they find any survivors?" Fee wondered.

"Two boat cushions and a ball cap."

"Nature can be fickle."

"But nurture bats last."

Chapter 54

Fee was discharged into the care of the triplets. They were escorted in a second vehicle by three FBI agents who would be taking his statement in the comfortable setting of his own home over in Half Moon Bay and examining the floating crime scene now secured at her berth in Princeton Harbor.

It looked like I was going to be an inpatient again, for a longer stretch this time. I definitely needed a skin graft on my shredded forehead and probably another one or two on my burned torso. The doctors were mostly concerned about the risk of infection and were discussing whether to proceed immediately or to wait-and-see if the burns might heal without intervention. Everything hurt, but the broken teeth caused the most pain, and the trauma team took the unusual step of calling in a dentist to do a temporary fix right in the ER. They even did an ultrasound of my swollen testicles, and gave them a clean bill of health, but cautioned against engaging in vigorous sexual activity for the time being. No worries there. My bachelor shut-ins were content to cuddle.

The attending physician from one of my previous visits appeared at the foot of my bed. I recognized her playful dark eyes immediately.

"I saw your name on the intake screen. You've really *got* to work on your inter-personals."

I laughed and she frowned with a look of open concern few medical professionals could muster.

"No doctor should ever ask...but are you OK?"

Before I could answer she twisted her wrist and looked at an incoming message on her smartwatch.

"I'm sorry. I'm being paged to the ICU. I'll...uh...see you later?"

"Thanks for stopping by."

She patted my hand and was gone. Her colleagues decided to go ahead with the skin graft surgery and began the pre-op prep. I signed the release as they were wheeling me to the OR and nodded off into the ether before the ink was dry.

I looked up into the undertaker's eyes.

"Whoa! Whoa!"

I raised myself off my back onto my elbows. My forehead felt on fire and my ribs and side throbbed. Body and soul still seemed under the same roof.

"Where are the other two core samples, Mr. Feeney?"

Mrs. DeLong's mortician, stared at me intently. She was wearing a tailored pants suit and stood as ramrod straight as I remembered from our earlier encounter.

"Huh? Michelle Li? Right? Am I.."

"You're in the recovery room of the Stanford Medical Center. Did you hear me? We need to know what you've done with the missing core samples."

"Wait…Shouldn't you be hosting an open house or a funeral pyre or something?"

She produced a badge and a photo ID in a wallet.

"C'mon! *You're* FBI? *Too*?"

"We believe you to be in possession of unlawfully sourced materials critical to national security."

Two scrubbed-up recovery room specialists moved into my field of view, challenging my surprise visitor.

"I'm sorry. You can't be in here right now."

"Are you family?"

Michelle flashed her badge. The nurses were unimpressed.

"You're going to have to wait outside like everyone else. His doctor will come out when he's recovered."

"His doctor had no business putting him under before we could interview him."

"You can take it up with his doctor. Please. Now."

Special Agent Li clenched her teeth and pivoted gracefully, her long, straight hair sweeping across her shoulders like windshield wipers, as she clicked away on high heels.

Chapter 55

"Asked and answered. Stop badgering my client."

My attorney was a bulldog. He was actually Sanjay Singh's on-call counsel, who got to the hospital almost before I'd finished my text to his number one customer. Lawyering up seems so ridiculously entitled when you see it portrayed on TV - like you're too rich and guilty to answer your own questions - and I have to admit having Jay Montague at my bedside made me feel like a supper club Don with quicklime on his lapels.

"Do you believe the wiretaps planted in your work vehicle were intended to interfere with Elizabeth DeLong's pacemaker, and perhaps hasten her death?"

I was stunned by the question. Not only had I not seriously considered the possibility, I still couldn't believe Michelle Li's otherworldly time management skills.

"I assumed that the interference was coincidental. And unintentional. But I really don't know."

But what I did now know, according to Li, was that the FBI had recovered ten of the core samples that the late Susan Doubletree had snatched from my grasp. That left two unaccounted for from the original dozen in the Pelican case.

"Are we done here, Agent Li?"

Jay liked to move things along. Michelle was having none of it.

"Does your client understand that, while strictly speaking, he's not under oath, making false statements to a federal investigator is a felony?"

I shifted uncomfortably in the bed in my new hospital room.

"I haven't lied about anything. And while we're on the subject, how's the funeral business? The real estate market? Did the Bureau draw the line at dog grooming and wedding deejay?"

"A Special Agent is given reasonable latitude with respect to creating and maintaining operational cover during the conduct of an investigation. FYI, Mrs. DeLong's remains were treated in accordance with professional standards."

"The GPS in the urn being part of the premium package? I'm curious, do you really moonlight selling houses?"

"I keep a current broker's license. This is an expensive place to live. There. Your turn. Is there more than one device?"

Jay butted in.

"You don't have to answer. I advise against it."

"Device? I don't know what you're talking about."

"Trust me, you do *not* want a NEST showing up unannounced."

Michelle Li's voice dripped with menace.

"A what?"

"Nuclear Emergency Support Team. Deadly serious, those people."

Jay interrupted.

"This has gone on long enough. We've been above-and-beyond cooperative here and you're now openly threatening my client. Look around, Agent Li. This is not the time and place. Bill, if you want to keep me around, you will not say another word."

I motioned for Jay to come closer. He leaned in and I whispered into his ear. He then forwarded the question to my inquisitor.

"Do you know a Carl Frost? FBI retired?"

Without replying, Li turned and walked out of my room again.

♦♦♦

Sanjay Singh had joined Jay Montague at the foot of my bed and shared his lament.

"Regrettable but inevitable, I'm afraid. Washington casts a long shadow."

The lawyer elaborated.

"The Feds could claim that your patent is invalid and unenforceable due to the circumstances that gave rise to your discovery."

I corrected him.

"Elizabeth DeLong's discovery."

He nodded and continued.

"As the IP was assigned exclusively to you, in terms of culpability it matters little whether your role in the provenance was creative or custodial. This is only conjecture on my part at this point, but I can imagine the government making one of two contentions: first, that the process that produced the substance required a reaction that could only have been caused naturally, in which case the patent application should have been denied, under the provision that excludes naturally-occurring processes from protection, or, second, and more likely, that the catalytic event that created the substance could only have been initiated by employing stolen government property."

"The *device* she was asking about."

Jay nodded to Sanjay's deduction.

"Not the kind of thing that's supposed to be easy to get your hands on. In practice, it looks like one slipped through the cracks somehow. Of course no oversight committee in Congress with a top-level security clearance would ever make this public."

"Congress?!"

I couldn't hide my panicked falsetto. Jay continued.

"Losing a nuke back in the 60's - if it even happened - is not something that the Pentagon or any of its sister bureaucracies would want to own, even today. Losing a nuke and not knowing it, or making minimal effort to retrieve it, would effectively gag the leadership from disclosure. Beyond embarrassing. Possibly still indictable. A legacy security risk. At the very least a blow to near-term defense spending."

Sanjay tied it all up with a bow.

"So even if they wanted to tug on your short and curlies, they're between a rock and hard place."

Jay preferred the noose.

"Which makes them many, many times more dangerous."

Chapter 56

Two days of hospital bed rest did wonders for my condition. They'd removed the packing from my nostrils, my skin grafts had started to heal, and all swelling - everywhere - had gone down. Plus my doctor smelled nice.

Jackie Banerjee, M.D., was a hospitalist born in St. Paul, Minnesota who'd assumed her supervisory position at Stanford after four years as an attending physician at Northwestern Memorial in Chicago. She spoke with the earnest flat accent still common in the Midwest, had smooth sepia skin, eyelashes a giraffe would envy, and matte-black hair that made her white lab coat look like it was lit from within. Two small swooshes of gold adorned her earlobes like raindrops curling in a summer breeze. I didn't see a wedding ring.

She'd just replaced the dressing on my forehead.

"The graft's taking nicely. You may not even notice it once it heals. The ones over the ribs and armpit will take longer. How are you tolerating the pain?"

"I'll chew on a towel before taking Oxy."

"I'll prescribe some extras from housekeeping."

She winked and patted my hand again. There was a long silence as she bit her bottom lip with even white teeth.

"You can tell your doctor anything, you know."

And I did. Pretty much everything. She stood at the foot of my bed, arms folded circumspectly across her chest, a frown on her face as I gave my abbreviated version of recent events. After I'd stopped talking, she nodded her head up and down.

"I'll drop by again at the end of my rounds. You seem to live a very interesting life. I should've looked harder at the Humanities."

And just like that she was gone.

♦♦♦

Fee appeared shortly thereafter, laptop in hand.

"The keynote's about to begin."

He opened the screen and logged into the Livestream from Cupertino.

Employees, fanboys, and press filled the auditorium in Cameo's colossal circular headquarters. Massive glass columns supported transparent walls that reached several stories into South Bay skies - leaving all to gape and wonder why Scientologists had remodeled the Vatican. The imperial spaceship aesthetic messaged without subtlety that the future was here. Right under the golden calf.

Most Cupertini were predictably eyes-down, tapping away. When the house lights dimmed, the crowd hushed, until the High Priest strode out in person onto the stage. The ovation was polite but unsustained. Clapping was a long time to be away from your phone.

Keeping with tradition, Tom Moore's larger-than-life image was projected onto a floor-to-ceiling screen behind him, dwarfing the flesh-and-blood version in front by comparison, and leaving much of the audience with an unfortunate case of picture-in-picture vertigo. The pocket-sized CEO, known as *Tom Thumbnail* in Parsec circles, held the latest model mobile in hand. He swiped to open, and his home screen replaced his jumbo likeness.

"Welcome to Cameo World 2019. Today it's not about what's new - but about what's missing. Notice anything on the dashboard here? Or rather, *not* here?"

All the widgets familiar from last year appeared in outsized glory. But now conspicuously absent from the upper right corner was the battery status icon.

It took only a moment before the crowd gasped in unison.

"Forget your charger? Forgot to charge? Forget about it! Welcome to the Bambino 24-7: the best Bambino, the best smartphone, the most *unstoppable* device *EVER*!"

The applause thundered - the crowd now on its feet.

"Let me show you the one truly groundbreaking feature it has - or should we say - *lacks*..."

His smug smile drew raucous, approving laughter as he touched the settings icon.

With a loud bang, shards of metal and glass exploded back into Tom Moore's face.

♦♦♦

After an uncomfortably long interval, a security guard arrived to render aid to the stricken executive, while six hundred people posted video of the appalling scene online.

"What...just...happened?"

Fee's voice suddenly sounded like that of a much smaller man. I had no words.

The Livestream continued without context or commentary. Dean, Gilbert, and Brandon vaulted onto the stage to help tend to Tom Moore, who was now sitting on the floor, face blackened like a chimney sweep, holding a hand over either his forehead or one of his eyes - it was hard to tell exactly. The security guard had vanished from the scene entirely. Finally the Livestream went dark.

"He doesn't look too good."

"At least he's still alive."

"Did you notice that security guy bail right before the boys got there?"

"Yeah. Wonder what that's about."

My phone received a text alert. It was from Sanjay: *Sabotage. No feds w/out Jay present. No press. Memes already viral.*

The message contained a GIF embedded at the bottom. It showed an edited loop of a self-satisfied Tom Moore holding up his latest prototype followed by a closer shot of him sitting stunned on the stage, face and hair singed, covering one eye with his hand. The caption read: *Patch needed for new Bambino*

Chapter 57

The broad selloff of CMEO stock on the NASDAQ was immediate - the share price plummeting 60% in the first three minutes of trading after the smoke cleared in Cupertino.

Tom Moore was airlifted to, yes, Stanford University Medical Center, where a temporary news blackout had been imposed regarding his condition.

Sanjay Singh had joined Fee in my room.

"'He's in surgery' is all they're saying. The Board's meeting in emergency session in about 90 minutes and I don't know what to tell them."

He turned toward Fee.

"I spoke with your boys right on scene. They were unable to locate the demo phone. Just tiny fragments so far. But they did retrieve the other prototype from R&D."

Fee looked quite concerned.

"Sounds like Tom Moore's lucky to be alive."

Sanjay hemmed and hawed uncharacteristically.

"Is Gilbert the quieter...slightly more...serious...brother?"

"That's Dean. The sensible one. Who dates gingers because they're hypoallergenic."

Fee shrugged. Sanjay briefly raised one eyebrow and then moved on.

"So...uh...Dean believes the better part of the phone survived. He saw the security guard take something out of Tom's hand right after the blast. Nobody's seen the guy since."

"Tough to do forensics on evidence that's not there. Do you think it'll be the FBI or ATF who conducts the investigation?"

I wasn't very clear on the division of duties within federal law enforcement. Neither was Fee, who opened his hands, palms toward the ceiling, in a gesture of surrender. Sanjay knew who to ask.

"Jay'll know. But I'll bet, mission and jurisdiction notwithstanding, it's whoever gets there first. Does it matter?"

"Maybe not. But we're already on a first-name basis with the FBI. And I think they handle industrial espionage."

Fee squinted his displeasure.

"The patent trolls?"

"Could be. Or some other party."

"Any ideas?", asked Sanjay.

"I have an inkling."

"Should we call the nurse?"

Sanjay ignored my old friend and continued to probe.

"Your inkling?"

I really didn't want to appear paranoid or presumptuous.

"I'm...I don't know. Obviously. I shouldn't say anything until we know more."

"To the contrary, Bill. Speak up. Shout it from your window, because as it stands right now, the authorities are going to be looking first and foremost at Fee's boys. Innocence can get lost in the rush to means and opportunity."

Fee looked down and shook his head without saying anything.

"That's crazy. This is my responsibility. Can Jay represent the triplets?"

I thought it was the least I could ask for them under the circumstances. Sanjay was resolute.

"I'll make sure of it."

"Why wouldn't I be the prime suspect?"

"Your option deal with Tom Moore. Where's the motive? You only make money if the share price goes up. I was hoping you'd reap the bump after the groundbreaking keynote. You'd have been better off selling plasma."

Chapter 58

My godsons were interviewed separately - each with Jay Montague present - in the FBI field office in Palo Alto for more than six hours between them. While not exactly exonerated by the dozens of audience cellphone videos of the red-blazered security guard snatching the smoldering remains of the demo device from Tom Moore's blackened hand after the explosion, along with the affidavits of six Cameo engineers who had closely shadowed them during the dry run of the prototype the night before the keynote, the Fainu'u brothers were thanked for their cooperation, and consented to make themselves available for future *discussions*. To my astonishment, I hadn't heard anything from the authorities.

Sanjay, without divulging any privileged information, reported back from the emergency Board meeting that a decision had been made to delay the appointment of an interim or successor CEO pending the outcome of Tom Moore's surgery. A message to the public, tailored to reassure all stakeholders - shareowners or not - contained remarkably little PR spin, but served its purpose in calming the markets and staunching the selloff. Some late-day profit-taking signaled at least a pause in the race to the bottom. Confidence in the continuity of Cameo's stewardship was not in question.

The written statement made no mention of the cause of the explosion, but naming the FBI as the lead agency overseeing the investigation implied intentional rather than accidental origins.

Within hours, overseas exchanges opened their floors, rattled at the prospect of commercial terrorism. Cameo stock plunged another 10% in early trading. The contagion spread across the tech sector worldwide as the bears turned to gold.

♦♦♦

Sanjay left the hospital to attend to whatever it was he needed to attend to. Fee stuck around and had been joined in my room by Jackie Banerjee, having recently finished her shift. As we covered the pleasantries, I could tell Fee was impressed by the recast of my latest visitor, who was now without her lab coat, wearing designer jeans and a pale beige turtleneck, complemented by a thin gold bracelet around her left wrist. I caught Fee peeking at her bare ring finger and then nodding approvingly in my direction. If she saw, she didn't let on, as she expressed her admiration for the durability of our friendship.

"Sounds like you two have had each other's backs for a long time."

She then put her head down, one hand shielding her eyes, flashing the universal sign for embarrassment.

"Wait...that really didn't come out right, did it?"

She looked up and smiled as Fee and I laughed.

"That's all right. We've agreed to see other people."

Fee winked at me. She recovered gracefully.

"I envy you guys. I've lost touch with almost all my childhood friends. I miss that."

"It's pretty overrated, actually."

She looked at both of us and laughed softly while shaking her head. Fee turned for the door.

"I'm starvin'. Anybody want anything from the cafeteria?"

"No thanks."

"Thanks for asking."

"See you in a bit."

He headed out toward the elevators.

"So...how does a Doctor of Medicine know so much about literary allusions to wolfsbane, anyway?"

She looked a bit surprised at first.

"You mean, harkening back to your bout with aconitum.."

"How did you ever find the time?"

She smiled again, this time a little more Cheshire Cat.

"I crammed a lit course or two in between calc and organic. To keep the current flowing between left and right."

She tapped her forehead twice with her forefinger and I responded.

"Great minds! My roots are also in the hard sciences. I used to drive by the Livermore Lab all the time."

She laughed.

"Do you miss the Midwest?", I asked.

She nodded from side-to-side suggesting ambivalence.

"The people sometimes. My family's all there. But not the climate."

"Did you grow up in The Twin Cities?"

She shook her head.

"On a farm about three hours northwest."

"So you're a farmer's daughter?"

She nodded.

"My grandfather worked for the Indian Ministry of Agriculture and was posted to the U.S. as part of a commercial exchange working group in the fifties. Both my parents were born here."

My face must have registered surprise.

"..and I can still barely spell Minneapolis.."

♦♦♦

We went back and forth like this for a while. As genuinely delightful as she was, I had a nagging suspicion about why such an alluring, accomplished woman would be spending even a minute of her hard-earned free time with someone sporting more bandages than King Tut. In a vulnerable moment, I'd willingly given her information I'd intentionally withheld from the FBI. I'd spared most of the details, but painted a pretty complete picture of the revolutionary potential of the coveted green dust. I could now only hope to count on her silence. She could definitely do the math. That was a lot to hope for.

I did my best to keep my doubts from showing. The flirtation was fun - a welcome distraction from the persistent pain of my knitting skin and the tumult surrounding the terrible attack on Tom Moore. And our rapport seemed genuinely unforced. Chemistry, our old science teacher once taught Fee and me, is all about reaction, and is almost impossible to fake. Maybe she just really liked comforting the afflicted.

Fee returned from the cafeteria accompanied by Sanjay Singh. The VC hadn't been gone all that long, and I was surprised to see him again so soon. Jackie looked over. I reflexively made the dopey assumption that because both she and Sanjay were Indian, they must be acquainted. Statistically, this may be the dumbest form of racial profiling. There are more than a quarter-million people of Indian origin living in the Bay Area alone. As I pondered the long odds in quiet shame, Jackie slid past Fee into Sanjay's open arms.

"Yes, Bill. We all *do* know each other."

"Hi, Uncle. What are you doing here?"

The embrace was warm but indeed avuncular.

"Bill used to drive *me* around like *I* was a big shot. But in a few short hours...when the Patent Office opens.."

He checked his wristwatch as we all talked over one another.

"..for the record, a privilege I haven't earned.."

"..*he* will join the ranks of Tesla and Edison as the rightful heirs to Newton."

"Really pissing off Fig and Wayne," I demurred.

"My humble friend here is going to need to make himself scarce for a few days. Is there any chance of an early discharge?"

Sanjay looked at Jackie. She furrowed her brow.

"That's not yet medically supportable."

Singh didn't argue but dug in his heels with his posture. She turned toward me and continued.

"It's true that your risk of infection is greater in here than if you were in a more isolated setting at home...As long as you agreed to stay put...You'd need help with dressing changes.."

Fee rolled his eyes and nodded grudgingly. Sanjay made the arrangements.

"Jackie, do you still have your place in Pacifica?"

"Yup."

"Fee's in Half Moon Bay. Would you be amenable to a house call or two? As needed?"

Jackie smiled.

"I'm down."

Chapter 59

Jackie and Sanjay trundled me out the rear entrance of the hospital near the ambulance bays where Fee was waiting in his truck. According to Sanjay, who'd just heard from a fellow member of the Cameo Board, Tom Moore had come through his surgery with flying colors. It appeared that his spectacles had shielded him from the worst of the blast and that he could reasonably expect to regain binocular vision once the corneal transplant had healed. Jackie noted that the average wait-time for a donor cornea was around six weeks. Somewhere in Shenzhen, a factory worker had put an eye out.

I was back at Fee's before sunset. My godsons had upgraded my accommodations to hospital standards, even if it meant staying in the clean room above the lab. A hyperbaric chamber sat in one corner which, with Dr. Banerjee's blessing, I'd be sleeping in periodically to speed wound healing. The whole area had been scrubbed with bleach and then treated with a narrow spectrum of UV-C light which was used preemptively to kill a broad range of staph and MRSA pathogens and reduce the risk of surgical site infection. The triplets had offset the Neverland Ranch motif with man-cave touches like the heated massage chair placed in front of the wall-mounted

70-inch OLED display. A virtual reality headset sat unopened in its box on the coffee table, a small bag of candied ginger nearby. It turned out my forehead, stomach, and self-regard were still too tender for full-goggle VR.

The view out the unshaded window faced downhill and west toward the Pacific Ocean. Before storms, you could often see the foam in the distance as huge surf detonated just offshore. This evening the horizon was backlit a deep orange as day turned to night. Calm seas heralded fair weather. Fee trudged up the stairs to join me, a large dinner tray in hand.

"Hope you're hungry."

"Oh, man. Big time. Thanks."

Just as he set out the food his cellphone rang.

"Hello? Hey Art...Sure. I think his phone's on the fritz. Yeah. He's right here."

He handed me his mobile. It was my boss from the limo company calling to say that Arun Agrawal, CEO of Parsec, had been trying to get in touch with me for unstated reasons. He texted me his number and rushed off the line to dispatch another driver.

"That's weird."

Fee looked up from his poke bowl.

"What?"

"Have I ever told you about Arun Agrawal?"

"The Serpent of Search? Yeah. You've mentioned him."

"He's not really one to reach out to the rabble."

"Isn't he the CEO always in the know?"

I nodded.

"AKA the godfather of predictive analytics - among other things. The story goes that they tracked a smartphone traveling in a car being driven slower than usual - immediately following that user's medical exam - saved in his calendar - and sent him ads for membership in the Hemlock Society before he made it home."

"Sweet guy."

I tried the number from my boss. Agrawal picked up before I could hear a ring.

"Bill. Good of you to call. I hope you're convalescing nicely."

It was pointless guessing how he knew about my health and I didn't even try.

"What can I do for you, Mr. Agrawal?"

Despite seeing him frequently, we rarely spoke by phone. Like most passengers, he preferred SMS over voice for communication. And no side errand was too small to put in a text. But his desire to be served was subordinate to his demand for privacy, and to drive him was to know your place. There could be no mistaking gauffeur for confidant.

Which made what followed hard to believe. He wanted to buy me dinner. Tonight. In about 20 minutes. When I explained I was coastside and had already eaten, he insisted we get together over drinks at the Ritz-Carlton Half Moon Bay. I knew this was crazy, but, despite everything, I decided it was way too rich an offer to pass up. I'd waited outside in the foggy parking lot of the very same hotel for Agrawal too many times to count. Hardly back-breaking labor to be sure, but Fee understood my urge to gloat under the circumstances, and generously offered to drive me. I called and left a message for Sanjay, apprising him of my plans.

Parsec's *Avogadro* - widely known as the *Avo* or *A-Phone* - was the world's most popular smart device. It would never challenge the fetish devotion that Cameo Bambino users showered on their higher-priced and more elegantly executed mobile, but it was clutched in a lot more hands. Despite earning the lion's share of its revenue from search advertising, sales of Avo apps and licensing Avo software to a number of hardware manufacturers also brought billions of dollars into Parsec's coffers each quarter. But they wanted to hedge their bets even further against their leading-but-declining share of the ad market, a less usurious customer rate structure, and growing disenchantment with advertising in general. Add a patented grain of grotto green to their latest A-Phone and, when the sleepy Bambino went down for a nap, they could power through to rule the world.

Chapter 60

Fee dropped me off and waited in my usual spot near the caddy shack just off the first tee. The hotel, propped high on a bluff, boasted two spectacular oceanfront golf courses, including 18 holes of Scottish links, where staying guests were treated to a bagpipe solo at sunset, surely as part of the exchange program that sent the Beach Boys to St. Andrews.

I sat at a table in the bar. Sanjay got there before Agrawal and took the seat across from me. He didn't look happy.

"You do not want to deal with this guy."

"C'mon...when is a limo driver gonna get courted by two of the world's biggest tech moguls in the same week?"

"Do *not* let this go to your head. Arun will be playing the chip on your shoulder. He will inquire about your health, pretend he knows something about sports, and squeeze your arm just a little too long. Then.."

Arun Agrawal walked in and stood behind Sanjay. When I raised my eyes, conversation ceased. Sanjay looked crestfallen without looking around.

"Hello Arun."

"Sanjay."

Agrawal brushed past Singh, who remained seated, as I stood up to shake hands. He then sat in the chair between us and turned his head in my direction. Studying the bandages on my face, he frowned, showing concern.

"How are you healing?"

"Better every day, thanks."

"You look like you just went twelve rounds with Mike Tyson!"

He smiled and clutched my bicep. Sanjay leaned back and rolled his eyes.

I edged away slowly, and Agrawal broke contact.

"I'm in good hands."

"Doctor Banerjee is a fine physician. First-cabin credentials, that one."

He looked at me with a wry grin, expecting to see astonishment. I tried my best to deny him satisfaction and met his gaze with as flat an affect as I could muster. Agrawal suddenly turned toward Sanjay.

"Oh, BTW, the mean age is 51, and *no*."

Sanjay looked taken aback.

"I'm sorry?"

"*When does menopause start?*, and *Has anyone ever died from electrolysis?*"

Sanjay's eyes narrowed and he stared daggers back at Agrawal.

"Do you make house calls if I search really sensitive subjects? Like...I don't know...when exactly will Parsec be starting to log keystrokes for their Beijing overlords? You smell of sulfur, old friend."

He then took his feet and turned in my direction.

"Make no promises, Bill. And please call me."

◆◆◆

As Sanjay walked out of the bar, Agrawal's face slackened into a satyr's smile.

"Have you ordered? I thought we might take our drinks out on the terrace."

Agrawal lead me outside like he owned the place. We sat elbow-to-elbow in padded armchairs facing a star-lit sky, the thumping surf the only hint of the Pacific below. A waiter brought him a hard-to-spell single malt scotch and me a draft craft ale. The two of us sipped in slightly awkward silence until the only other person on the terrace repaired back indoors. We now had the fire pit to ourselves.

"They say that JFK delayed the embargo on Cuba for 24 hours so that he could bring in his own private stash before closing the door. Viva La Revolucion."

He reached into the inside pocket of his lightweight down vest and removed a lighter, a clipper, and two cigars. He trimmed and lit one for me and then one for himself. As he savored the rum-soaked tobacco with his eyes closed, I noticed a glint coming from something he'd placed on the fire pit's stone coping right in front of me. Shining like a chrome stogie was one of the core sample test tubes from Mrs. D's stolen Pelican case.

If I was right this was #11 of 12. Getting ahead of myself I wondered who had the last one.

"I believe the person who left it with me came by it dishonestly. And, in any event, didn't live long enough for us to negotiate in earnest."

Agrawal kept his gaze toward the fire. I waited a bit before responding.

"The truth is, it belonged to her mother. The authorities would have you believe otherwise. What do you make of it?"

"It changes the game. No question. How do you expect to manage all the attention?"

I shrugged. He continued.

"Let me paint the picture. Coltan mining in Congo, lithium in Bolivia, cable and peripheral manufacturing in Taiwan and Korea, power players world-wide funding profit and conflict from all-things-battery will gladly take a number to put your head on a pike if that green dust hits the market. I grew up playing cricket - not hot potato."

And with that, he stood up, patted me on the shoulder, and left me alone by the fire. For the first time in memory, I didn't feel like finishing my beer.

On my way back out through the lobby, the doorman, who I'd ducked on the way in, and who I had hoped only knew me by sight in my work clothes, and without bandages, pegged me instantly, looking like he'd love to frisk me for silverware. He ushered me past the bell captain's booth in a hurry, and with relief watched me climb into Fee's battered pickup.

◆◆◆

We barely made it out of the parking lot before two unmarked sedans swooped down on us - pinning the truck against the curb. Special Agent Li strode over to my lowered window.

"Good evening, Mr. Feeney."

She put out her hand - palm up. I didn't return the greeting.

"Hand it over."

"If you're referring to my property...I think I'll hold onto it. Thanks. And I think what you're doing here may actually be illegal."

"We believe you to be in possession of evidence critical to a murder investigation, an attempted murder investigation, and the sinking of a Panga vessel associated with the transportation of illegal narcotics. This lawful seizure is allowable under the asset forfeiture provision sanctioned by the Department of Justice. Hand it over and you're free to go."

Fee looked at me, a look of weary resignation on his face. I reached into my jacket pocket and turned the next-to-last core sample over to the FBI.

♦♦♦

"That son-of-a-bitch set you up! He knew the feds were watching the whole time!"

I'd phoned Sanjay from Fee's cell while in the truck. An incoming call beckoned.

"Sanjay...I'm gonna have to put you on hold. Sorry."

I cut my VC friend off and answered to Arun Agrawal's unctuous voice.

"Hello Bill. Apologies for the heavy hand at the side of the road. What's today's federale but mall security with marriage prospects? For the record, I did not alert them. But I did suspect we were being surveilled. Let's not let this interfere with a burgeoning partnership. Call me when you're ready to get really bloody rich."

He signed off and I took Sanjay off hold. Of course, he beat me to the punch.

"Arun?"

"Of course."

"What did he offer you?"

"He wasn't very specific."

"The world, Bill. He'll offer you the world. But he's going to hold onto the moon and the stars and the Middle Kingdom."

Enter China.

Search had been shut out of the People's Republic for a while now, but Parsec was the world leader in the R&D of artificial neural networks, among other things on Beijing's shopping list, and had a horizontally-integrated focus on a lot of what they called Long Shots in their financials. Sanjay believed that a mobile with perpetual charge would be impossibly attractive to a country intent on instituting a system of "social credits" to monitor and control it's 1.4 billion souls. Add a gently-censored search engine and a suite of free features from maps to email to telephony, and Parsec wouldn't be looking over their own shoulder anytime soon.

Chapter 61

An overnight in the hyperbaric chamber was music to my wounds. My godsons took shifts changing my dressings and generally keeping an eye on me, even fashioning a crude but effective intercom system to make it possible to converse without shouting through the clear plastic walls of the giant cylinder. After your ears stopped popping and you got used to the noise of the motor, it actually wasn't all that hard to fall asleep. They only kept me under pressure for a few hours at a spell, and I barely noticed the interruptions.

Upon awakening in the bed outside the chamber, I was greeted by Aaron Copland's *Fanfare for the Common Man* - the New York Philharmonic's stirring version piped into the clean room through the sound bar under the TV. The huge screen displayed a webpage titled USPTO PATENT FULL-TEXT AND IMAGE DATABASE, and under the title *Compact Solid State Long-Life Battery,* today's date, and a six-digit number, and just above the abstract, description, and drawings, was my name - last, first, and middle initial - listed as **Inventor**.

Cue the Milli Vanilli.

Across the room the broad door to the freight elevator slid open and out stepped all four Fainu'us. Fee brought me a breakfast plate and a glass of milk.

"Thanks for the...uh...ballyhoo."

"Like it or not, you the man now."

"The Einstein of energy storage."

"I stand but on the shoulders of giants."

"Truly, you are to innovation what Ireland is to space travel."

There was a lot of laughter and it took a while for me to realize how much the pain had subsided all over my body. Unlike Fee, I'm not all that stoic, and as much as I'd taken some lumps recently, I'd also brought my problems into my friends' home. My buddy almost died on his own boat as collateral damage. My godsons had been given the third degree by the FBI. I needed to give them all a break and start owning my own issues.

"I'm gonna go into the City today."

No one paid the least bit of attention to my announcement.

"And I'm gonna take a ride-share."

Fee looked over at me. All conversation stopped. Dean dropped the volume on the music.

"You're gonna what?"

"I gotta go into the City. Just for a coupla hours."

"You *are* looking a lot better.."

"That's probably against the infection control protocol.."

"..which you've already breached anyway...last night."

Brandon looked at his father, like it was his transgression.

"Let's call Jackie."

"I'll be fine. I'll be back before...if...she stops by this evening. She can yell at me then."

There was another stretch of silence, before Fee weighed in.

"It's your call. Not one of your better ones, but, hey. If you insist on going, I'll drive. I'm headin' up there anyway. Not to pry, but what's so important in the City?"

"I need to hash everything out with Carl Frost. He's not returning my calls."

"And even if he did...you don't have your old phone and number."

I nodded at Gilbert and continued.

"I appreciate the offer, Fee, but I'm good. And I'm sure you've got better things to do."

Fee rolled his eyes and scoffed.

"Get a grip, E-Z. I'm goin' with you. Discussion closed."

"I'm hoping to just *run into him* at the South Side. Lots of people around."

"Then I'll wait in the truck."

Dean tossed me a burner phone.

"Leave the line open."

Chapter 62

I ran my key card over the reader above the handle to the members entrance of the South Side Rowing Club and let myself in. The empty lobby was windowless and lit by a single overhead bulb said to have seen continuous duty since VJ-Day. Vintage photos of pioneering members covered the shiplap walls. Sturdy looking men of action - all the old shots were of men, before women were admitted in the 1970's - plied the waters of San Francisco Bay in rubber swim caps or beautifully-varnished rowboats, wearing the vigorous smiles of the mad, utterly ignoring the frigid, gray elements that engulfed one and all. Hale, hardy, hearty - tellers of tales tall and true - the early-birds of swimming and rowing portrayed here looked like types preternaturally disinclined toward traditional organization of any stripe. Even today, the South Side was a magnet for free spirits, famous for impromptu mischief and merriment, a place where rules were few, and the timid were exceptional: the amphibious equivalent of the Bull Moose Party.

Uncharacteristically, the place was dead. I'd never come at this hour on a weekday and supposed that this was the slack tide between the morning and evening rushes.

I padded through the clubhouse as quietly as possible and popped my head into the workout area, galley, and locker room. Not a soul to be seen. One of the showers dripped slowly on the other side of the sinks. A few tendrils of steam wafted from around the corner of the tiled wall.

I sat down on the bench dividing one bank of lockers from another and rehearsed my approach. A trail of puddles marked the cement floor - left footprints only - each sandwiched unevenly between two small ringed circles. The tall figure of Carl Frost showed up in water's reflection. I froze.

"Bill! What the hell, stranger! Have you gone sustaining?"

I looked up. He was off his crutches, wet hair combed, fully dressed, his prosthesis concealed beneath his slacks.

"What happened to your head?"

He approached slowly and I tried not to flinch.

"Janet Farr and friends tried to kill me. Maybe more than once. Thanks for the referral."

He stopped and looked genuinely perplexed.

"What?"

"Cut the crap, Carl. What's in all this for you?"

His face got a little red and he looked angry.

"I don't know what the hell you're talking about. Janet Farr's hardly had time to breathe, let alone try to kill you. She had twins a few days ago. I think she just got outta the hospital."

"Janet Farr? Had twins? You are so full of shit."

I stood up and he backed off almost imperceptibly, reaching deep into his coat pocket. He pulled out a phone, turned on the speaker, and dialed. After several rings, a woman whose voice I didn't recognize answered.

"Hello?"

"Janet, it's Carl Frost. First of all, congratulations!"

"Hey, thanks, Carl."

"So you were really eating for three all this time?"

"Can you believe it?! They missed the twin on the first ultrasound. So much for technology. Darren says maybe they faked the moon landing after all."

"And mom and babies are A-OK?"

"Roger that. Dad's freakin' out a little, though."

When they both stopped chuckling, Carl continued.

"Listen Janet, I'm sorry to bug you on your own time, but as your old trainer, I have to ask: I heard you might've lost your duty phone.."

There was a sigh on the other end of the line.

"Are you gonna bust my chops, too? I thought you were retired!"

"I don't mean to pile on.."

"I was headed to an OB appointment in a motor pool vehicle and I must've left it on the front seat. I didn't see it...you know...black on black and all that...and with all the commotion at the doctor's and everything...I..I just completely forgot all about it. Didn't report it missing for more than a week. Carney already told me he's put a note in my file."

"It happens. At least it wasn't a service weapon. I dodged that bullet...no pun intended...my rookie year. Finally found it myself after the longest 24 hours of my career."

"So Carl Frost is human after all."

"Congrats again, Janet. Tell Darren the offer's still open if he ever wants to join the South Side. Take care."

"Thanks Carl."

The call ended and Carl Frost gave me a wide-eyed, open-palm, I-told-you-so look. I was more than a little taken aback. But not quite ready to concede.

"So how do you explain her impersonator coming up with just the exact right identity to steal?"

"Didn't you call me yourself...from your own phone...to tell me about the bugs in your limo? I can remember referring you to Special Agent Janet Farr by name. Don't you think somebody could've been listening in on us? Jesus, Bill, how bad has this thing gotten?"

I owed him an apology and an explanation. He sat on the bench in front of me as I spilled my guts.

When I was through, Carl patted me on the back sympathetically. But he didn't offer to lobby or even contact Special Agent Michelle Li on my behalf, saying he'd only met her once, just before he put in for early retirement. He made a purely perfunctory request to be kept in the loop, as he headed out to the Red Cross for his daily shift as a volunteer. I couldn't blame him for being a little put off by my accusation. I'd acted badly.

♦♦♦

On my way to the truck to rejoin Fee, who'd been waiting patiently, monitoring the open line to my temporary cell phone, I almost bumped into Finbar, headed slowly toward the Club in his white bathrobe and fuzzy slippers - no doubt returning from a leisurely lunch at Fisherman's Wharf a few blocks away.

You wouldn't know it from his scrawny frame and tattered togs but for a really old guy on a fixed income, Fin had done pretty well for himself over the years. He swam regularly from the Club's beach, out of the cove, past the breakwater, and down along the waterfront by the heavily-touristed restaurants whose bay view locations were packed almost every day of the year with people from around the world.

Wearing only his swim cap and goggles, he'd dolphin-kick in a bawdy butterfly stroke back-and-forth, peekaboo in plain view of those paying top dollar for an authentic West Coast seafood experience. From the gray-green waters, the full moon would rise, usually chapped pink from the wind, causing children to squeal and their grownups to point and click, rounding out their vacations to zany California.

Alas, even "Only in San Francisco" had its limits, and when his antics began scaring away the beloved sea lions who'd gather around the pilings under the panoramic windows of the eateries above, some accommodation was necessary. To continue the gravy train of bottomless bowls of crab cioppino and lobster bisque, supplied to him gratis on a rotating basis by all the waterfront establishments on his route, he'd agreed to stay outside the buoy line beyond the naked eye. But he always made good on his threats when the soup wasn't hot enough, or the sourdough too stale, leveraging the local indulgence of free expression into a legendary lunchtime protection racket.

"Fin, how was the catch of the day?"

"Fresh, free, and I hope 18."

With terry cloth threatening to flap open any moment, one of the Greatest Generation shuffled past.

Chapter 63

"You're still good if we swing by the museum? I kinda promised I'd at least make an appearance."

"Of course."

We were driving west up and down San Francisco's hills in Fee's truck. Prior to her passing five years ago, his late wife Teuila, a gifted flower arranger, had been a mainstay in an annual event at the de Young Museum which paired tributes in bloom with paintings and sculptures in their permanent collection. The week-long *Bouquets to Art,* one of the biggest draws of any museum in California year after year, showcased the considerable talents of floral designers from the greater Bay Area. Traditional vases and custom vessels, limited only by the space in front of a partner piece, held horticultural reinterpretations of Impressionist oils, landscape watercolors, and Grecian marbles - life exuberantly imitating art.

Teulia had been as gentle and gracious a woman imaginable. Blunting the free testosterone at home with good humor, and its fragrant funk with her delicate arrangements of plumeria and hibiscus and gardenia had revealed a gifted eye for color and light and perspective, every bit the equal of the celebrated artists whose works in more enduring media hung from the de Young's walls.

The usual traffic flow through the galleries had clotted around each arrangement on the first floor of the museum. This was intended to be a high-friction exhibit, and unlike other times of the year, cell phone photography was encouraged. Contemplating a still-life or re-sketching a nude from an unobstructed viewing bench would have to wait until the petals dropped and the throng moved on. Today's Bouquets was an unapologetically crowd-pleasing mash-up of a show. What had started out in Teuila's time as a genuinely sublime feast for the senses had become, some local purists would say, just another easy dopamine hit, like lending the Mona Lisa to the Cheesecake Factory or binge-listening Liberace during *Shark Week*.

Fee, flip-flopping across the polished wood floors, was greeted warmly by at least one person in each gallery we visited. He hugged women, men, and decline-to-state with equal affection. As confusing contemporary gender identification, expression, and fluidity can be at the human level, it's nothing compared with the mind-boggling botanical gang bang among flowering plants when pollen is crossed. More than once, Teuila had quietly declined special "Best in Show" recognition because, like her husband, she believed judgment best left to the Lord.

"Arrrgh!"

"This stupid thing!"

"What the hell?"

"Did yours die too?"

All around us, people were staring furiously at their phones. Tapping, shaking, pushing any and all buttons, powering off and on - it seemed as though half the population in our particular gallery were suddenly holding dark screens in their angry hands.

"Wait...wait.."

"Here we go."

"Whew!"

The same blank displays blinked back to life, and log-in windows beckoned one and all to look front-and-center so their devices could recognize them.

"It's me. Yes, it's really me! C'mon! Open up!"

Everyone affected seemed to be having the same problem. Fee's face too went unrecognized by his phone. He tried the six-digit numerical passcode workaround to no avail. Curiously, a slightly smaller cohort of attendees continued snapping pictures of the featured attractions with their early-version Bambinos - without interruption. The murmurs among the Avo crowd would quickly turn to full-throated howls of indignation.

Just like that, Fee and every other Avo owner within shouting distance was greeted by a ransomware demand in bold block font:

TAKE YOUR CLOTHES OFF AND TRY AGAIN

"What the hell?"

"No freaking way!"

"Picked a great year to quit working out!"

There were squeals, and cursing, and some laughter, and a lot of oblivious people toting Bambinos traipsing through the halls untroubled.

All at once, people rushed the restrooms, jamming stalls and blocking changing tables until there was no room for privacy. Out in the public spaces, more modest patrons disrobed desperately behind carvings of skimpy nymphs and bulwarks of baby's breath. Others dropped their inhibitions and clothes in wrinkled puddles where they stood. In the overflowing lobby, a matronly security guard stepped down from her Segway, stripped off her uniform, reorganized her breasts, and flashed her phone with the nonchalance of a newborn. Now-alert Bambino photographers recorded the whole thing.

♦♦♦

Fee and I waded past people in various stages of undress on the way down to the underground garage. We climbed into his truck. He stared straight ahead through the windshield at the concrete wall eight feet away.

"Do you think we can ever...unsee all that?"

"Deep breaths. Deep breaths. C'mon...Nice and slow.."

He rubbed his eyes and shook his head.

"It's gonna be OK, Fee. Really."

My friend finally keyed the ignition. I continued.

"You gotta hand it to Tom Moore. Looks like his people have a sense of humor after all."

"You think Cameo's behind this?", he asked.

"Dunno. But I'll bet, privately at least, they blame Parsec for the buggy Bambino the other day. Tit for tat. Or, could be a false flag...By the way, if you want to open your phone, I'll avert my gaze.."

"Nobody likes a smartass, E-Z. Besides, it's working fine now."

"So...maybe the hack was one-and-done. Point made."

"What point is that?"

He had me there.

"But whoever's behind it sure scraped up a lot of lucrative data, if they're inclined to monetize," I pontificated.

"Sounds like a dumb way to go about blackmailing today's crowd if you ask me. Good luck trying to body-shame people around here. You saw what I saw. Kinda like the last days of Rome...with fleece."

"Yeah, but.."

"Besides, viewers'll lose interest in the time it takes to get your clothes back on. What's his name - the Principle of Uncertainty guy?"

"Heisenberg?"

"As soon as your GIF or JIF or whatever it's called is trending, everybody's already looking at something else. 'What's for dessert?' - before you even touch your dinner. Augment this. Virtual that. Avatars with syphilis but millennials still living at home. I heard more people now watch other people open packages on YouTube than know where babies come from."

The gate arm to the parking lot lifted and we pulled out into street traffic.

"Did someone miss his walk with Trudy this morning?"

Chapter 64

Jackie Banerjee, M.D. was waiting for us in Fee's driveway when we got back from the City. Eyes narrowed and arms crossed, she glared at me as I stepped out of the truck.

"Hi Jackie."

She didn't reply right away. I'd thought she might be stopping by a little later. From her blue scrubs it appeared she'd come straight from work.

"Your early discharge came with certain stipulations."

"Sorry, Doc."

Fee sounded genuinely contrite, but I wasn't getting off the hook that easy.

"Enabled or not, he's a big boy. Let's have a look at your grafts. And then your butt's back in that hyperbaric chamber, Mister."

She turned and led the way.

"You can't be serious."

"As a MRSA infection. Besides, plenty of girls find a man living in a barn on a farm in a cylinder under negative pressure irresistible. Maybe you could hook up with someone in an iron lung."

From the front porch my godsons roared with laughter.

This wasn't exactly the bedside manner I'd been secretly hoping for. Or, in truth, maybe it was.

♦♦♦

To my regret but not surprise, the house call didn't last long. Jackie examined my wounds, seemed satisfied that they were healing well, and waited until the boys had me locked and loaded back into my chamber before she left a little abruptly. I'm sure she didn't appreciate me ignoring her instructions to self-quarantine until medically out of the woods, especially since she was looking after me off the clock in her limited free time. And she didn't let on exactly, but it seemed like maybe she'd had a rough day at the hospital. That said, I think we left on good terms: she smiled and waved up at me from the driveway before getting in her car.

I lay back and watched 90 minutes of TV news: local, world, network, cable - switching back and forth from hard hitting to human interest (emphasis on the latter) - with the remote the Fainu'us had left with me inside the clear plastic tube. Per Fee's prediction, the world-wide kerfuffle over the pervy hack on all Parsec-branded smart phones had already been demoted to back burner status. There were more pressing developments. To the consternation of everybody, North Korea had quite suddenly resumed underground nuclear testing. To the relief of her pet tortoise, a sturdy woman in Poland had turned an astonishing 123 years old. To the surprise of no one, scientists in Bolivia had discovered a gene for shyness in the gut bacteria of shepherds.

The triplets eventually let me out for dinner. Everyone called it an early night, with Fee and the boys planning to head out on the water before dawn to set and retrieve two boatloads of crab pots.

Chapter 65

The Fainu'us made it back from their work day shortly after noon. Unlike my morning of indolence, theirs had been quite fruitful. One of their pickup beds was laden with a small saltwater tank filled with live Dungeness crab. They'd already sold most of their take in Princeton harbor, straight off the sterns of *Lucky Duck* and *Lucky Duck II.*

Dungeness crab are said to prefer muddy shallows to sandy deeps while they claw and tear at anything dead or alive - including each other. True bottom-feeders, they're as ugly as they are uncongenial. They *scuttle.* But by some strange alchemy, debris turns to delicacy beneath their shells. Garbage in - ambrosia out. Theirs is quite possibly the sweetest meat in the sea.

I joined my friends in the dining room for an evening feed. Tuckered out from their early morning, they were quieter than usual. Five guys cracking crab around a table is plenty loud enough. After a lot of slurping and gulping, they debriefed their day.

"Hey, Pop, you hear Whole Foods is selling at 12 bucks a pound?"

Fee looked up from his plate and, still chewing, nodded approvingly.

"Not bad."

"This season could pencil out big time."

"Pay for the overhauls, maybe."

"Did you tell Bill about the frogman?"

Fee shook his head, swallowed, wiped his mouth with his napkin, and faced me.

"The *Lady Anne*...remember Anson Silva?"

The name came back to me.

"From high school. Played flanker."

"He's got a boat too. Anyway, he was spooling in his pots not a quarter-mile from us, when he starts screaming like he's got a man overboard or something. Harley was actually closest to him, checking licenses and rigging and whatnot, anyway, a human corpse comes up with his crabs.."

"..not inside the cage with 'em.."

"..but somehow tangled up in the line.."

"They said it looked like he'd been dead for a while."

"But here's the thing, he's rigged up in full high-end SCUBA gear. Heavy wetsuit, wearing mask and fins, with air still in his tanks."

"And get this, according to Harley, who called the Coast Guard, the guy'd been using a Chinese-made closed-circuit rebreather."

"No bubbles."

I must have looked puzzled.

"Military-issue gear. Not sold anywhere in North America."

It was still a small world down at the harbor and Fee and I had been classmates with several other local fisherman along with Harley, the district Fish & Wildlife warden. I was as curious as everyone else.

"Any ideas on what a Chinese navy diver might've been doing in U.S. waters? Anything out there worth the trouble? How deep is it anyway?"

Gilbert went first.

"We were only over about a hundred feet of ocean. But those kinds of regulators can be used to dive shallow or deep. They allow for a lot more bottom time."

"And a lot less time in decompression."

"So he might've come out of a submarine?"

"Roger that."

"We weren't all that far from the old waste drums our navy dumped in the fifties and sixties."

"Almost fifty thousand of 'em - filled with varying levels of radioactive material. Scattered over more than 500 square miles of continental shelf and slope."

"Most sunk pretty deep, but some are only down about 300 feet or so. The surveys done by the government have been pretty spotty."

"There's even an old aircraft carrier down there - from test days at the Bikini Atoll. Decommissioned and deliberately sunk. Out of sight, out of mind."

"Every few years they test our catch for harmful levels of radiation. So far, only traces in deep species like Dover sole."

"Not much to go on."

Dean squinted in thought, before weighing in again.

"You guys think he could've floated down from Point Arena?"

His brothers were uncharacteristically quiet for a brief moment of reflection.

"We're talking about 150-160 miles…"

"..with the Cali current flowing north-south.."

"..definitely works direction-wise.."

"..average speed about 4 knots this time of year.."

"..he makes it down here in a day and a-half.."

"Round numbers here, Brandy.."

"Sure. That could definitely work."

"Submarine insertion off Manchester at Point Arena - they'd have hard ears on the cable."

"What exactly's at Point Arena?"

"It's the main fiber landing for trans-Pacific communications."

"Our internet connection to Asia and the world."

Chapter 66

I spent what remained of the evening tucked in my tube for what turned out to be my last hyperbaric therapy session. Jackie had stopped by to help me pass the time - the Fainu'us cooking her up the last of the crab. Tonight I made sure to let her do more of the talking. In my mind, hers was a vocation that juggled life and death in a real high stakes human drama set against a beeping backdrop of heroic interventions. Of course, she was having none of it and steadfast in rejecting any attribution of nobility to her work. She gracefully changed the subject to her family's three-generation quest for assimilation into America's heartland.

"When we were kids, my Dad - over my very vegetarian Hindu mother's strong objections - thought he'd take us hunting - like real red-blooded Minnesotans - and tried to stash our new outfits under our bunk beds. 'Quick! Hide the camo!' he yelled when he saw Mom coming up the driveway. 'Right after we revive the duck, Dad.' My sister still uses that in her voicemail greeting."

Headlights shone suddenly in the window, accompanied by the sound of gravel crackling under the weight of two cars approaching up the driveway. Fee appeared in silhouette to challenge the driver of the first vehicle before tapping his phone. Mine rang a few seconds later.

"You accepting visitors? Arun Agrawal and Tom Moore are here to see you."

"You've got to be kidding. They came together?"

He lowered his voice to a whisper.

"Separate cars. But each drove himself. You gonna call Sanjay?"

"Great minds. Thanks. Send 'em up, I guess. You're welcome to join."

"I'm good. But you gotta tell me everything in the morning."

He hung up and I'd just finished texting Sanjay Singh when the broad doors to the freight elevator opened and out stepped the two most powerful people in the Silicon Valley.

♦♦♦

Both men assessed the strange setup in front of them in ways consistent with their personalities: Tom held his poker face as Arun's registered bemusement. The Parsec boss addressed Jackie first.

"Doctor Banerjee, your reputation precedes you."

I couldn't help myself.

"So you don't actually know each other."

Jackie glanced at me sideways in lieu of an elbow to the ribs. I made the introductions, my amplified voice still a bit hollow from inside the chamber.

"Jackie, this is Arun Agrawal and Tom Moore."

She shook hands with both men and gathered up her plate and silverware in preparation to leave. Agrawal grinned at me as I lay back on my little pillow. He came closer and tapped lightly on the plexiglass.

"Overall, how would you rate your experience with Airbnb?"

I ignored him and addressed Jackie.

"You're welcome to stay, you know."

She looked at her watch.

"Your godsons will let you out in about thirty-five minutes. I'll be by again tomorrow."

"Thanks for everything. See you then."

Jackie stepped onto the elevator, the doors shutting behind her. Tom adjusted his eye patch before speaking.

"We think your battery is beyond the proof-of-concept stage and ready for integration into the system architecture of both the Cameo and Parsec mobile platforms. Arun and I.."

He looked over toward Agrawal, who nodded portentously, and then continued in his own voice.

"..believe the time is right for us to go forward, together, in developing the proprietary solution stack software to best exploit the full market potential of your patent."

My phone rang inside the chamber. It was Sanjay, asking to be put on speakerphone. Turning up the volume, I held it next to the intercom.

"Tom and Arun, this is Sanjay. Please tell me you both just happened to be in the same neighborhood..."

Arun just smiled. Tom raised his voice in greeting his fellow Board member.

"Hello, Sanjay."

Sanjay cut to the chase.

"If Boeing and Airbus showed up together at the doorstep of the guy who just solved turbulence, suspicions would be warranted. Bill, again, whatever you do, please keep your ink in your pen. I'm sorry, but this has collusion written all over it."

There followed a silence that I broke with a question.

"On a personal note, Tom...um...how is your eye coming along?"

Moore nodded a little bashfully before responding.

"Thanks. The doctors expect recovery to pre-incident baseline acuity. I was quite fortunate under the circumstances. The explosion turned out to be more of a noise-maker than a serious fragmentation event."

"Does the FBI know who was behind it?"

"They have not shared any information."

"Do you suspect anyone in particular?"

Arun shifted uncomfortably in the chair he'd taken.

"Our people are working in parallel with the authorities."

The quiet was unsettling. After a very long pause, Tom Moore continued.

"We've ruled out peer competitors."

Arun's shoulders slumped slightly in relief. I decided to test the temperature on Parsec's side.

"Arun...the worldwide ransomware hack...the so-called 'birthday suit reboot'.."

Tom Moore tensed visibly. Arun put his fears to rest.

"We've patched the hole in the back door and are confident an attack like the other day's can never happen again. We utterly reject any suggestion that Cameo was involved."

Sanjay chortled over the phone.

"So...where are you two magnanimous gentlemen proposing to do battery fabrication? QC testing? Installation? I'm gonna go with...China."

Arun was adamant.

"They have the deepest experience with scale, bar none. Together, we would, of course, be working closely with them every step of the way. There really is nowhere else to consider."

Tom nodded in agreement. Sanjay kept on the offensive.

"And Huawei and Baidu are just going to let you guys waltz onto their home field and let you run up the score? Whatever deal you've struck with Beijing, Inc. will never please the European courts, let alone pass the sniff test in Washington. Unless you both plan on reincorporating in Vanuatu."

Moore and Agrawal both looked down at their shoes. For a long time no one said a word. Sanjay eventually broke the hush from over the phone.

"Crickets? Really? Wow. Bill, my advice is, get a good night's sleep, and either call me in the morning, or renounce your citizenship and seek asylum in the Chinese Consulate."

♦♦♦

Mercifully the multi-leveled awkwardness of my meeting with the two titans of tech ended with their departure about 30 minutes after Sanjay hung up the phone and just as the boys finished releasing me from the pressure pod. The parting was amicable, I think, and we pledged to keep the lines of communication open. They made me an offer as we walked slowly out to their cars.

"Name your price."

I'd declined their initial tender to buy the battery patent outright. Their counter proposed a lucrative licensing arrangement - contingent upon their control over the processes of manufacture, testing, and assembly. Writing the bespoke code for the operating system would be entirely their responsibility and the development expense borne by them exclusively.

So, for Parsec and Cameo, and maybe me as well, it was looking like China or bust.

Chapter 67

Unrefreshed, I called Sanjay second thing in the morning.

"Are you leaning one way or another?"

"Their offer was exceedingly generous."

"Your patent is exceedingly valuable."

"I just got off the phone with the SBA."

"Excuse me?"

"Small Business Administration. Their loan terms are quite favorable."

"What!? I will *not* hold your beer and watch this! If you insist on starting your very own battery business, then let's figure out how much you'll need and I'll spot you the angel funds. Done."

"If this all goes to hell.."

"..you'd rather be on the hook to the SBA forever than have me offset the one-time loss against my capital gains? What do they *teach* people in the Humanities? Compared to you, my wife's ficus is Chairman of the Fed."

I briefly considered Sanjay's offer. It wasn't a hard decision. I had no collateral to show the SBA and could barely bootstrap my own groceries. Fear of letting my friends down was getting in the way of moving forward.

"I haven't asked them, but I think my godsons might also want to invest. They expressed interest back when Mrs. DeLong was still alive. I'll feel terrible if they come out on the short end of this whole thing.."

"That's why it's called *risk* capital. And give the boys some credit. They're young, but they've already been around the block a few times. Do you want me to broach the subject with them?"

"I can let them know you're interested. You'd be OK having partners in the deal?"

"Of course. If anyone's earned the right, it's the Fainu'us. We could start with a pari passu seniority seed round and a 1X liquidation preference. If the boys want in, we'll draw up a term sheet for you to look over. This thing's a bit of a different animal without the ability to do a defensible pre-money valuation, but for the cap table, right now, I'm thinking the money should only take 10% - leaving you with 90% equity - undiluted. We'll do this all again in English if you still want to move ahead. Your call."

We ended our conversation and I walked over to touch base with Fee, who was alone in his office, filing fuel invoices. I wanted to ask for his blessing, as it were, before speaking with the boys. We both knew they were perfectly capable of making their own decisions, but I think he appreciated the heads-up.

"They'd be really disappointed if you didn't ask them."

The triplets were on the speakerphone with Sanjay, working up a budget, thirty seconds after I walked out of the lab.

♦♦♦

On my way upstairs, my burner phone buzzed with an incoming SMS. Filling the screen from bezel-to-bezel, a rolled copy of today's Salt Lake Tribune clenched in her jaws, fur matted and ribs showing - but piercing blue eyes very much alive - was Gwennie, the coy-dog, in a photo close-up. A caption scroll read:

The Airstrip @ Montezuma Creek -
Tomorrow - ALONE

But hadn't I heard the rifle shot? She'd survived?! My shock quickly mixed with anger at the anonymous abductor behind the camera. At least there was proof-of-life. Apparently.

I ran my phone back downstairs to the lab and interrupted the boys in the middle of their brainstorm with Sanjay. They must've read the distress on my face, as they politely cut their phone conference short. Without delay, they examined the photo for authenticity. Less than an hour later they reported no evidence of image manipulation. I started packing.

Before heading out, I sat down again with my godsons. Using a template molded from one of my lower molars and then 3D printed as a hollow porcelain cap - including a mercury amalgam filling both for effect and to shield against any scan search for electronics - they glued a miniature GPS tracker powered by a few grains from the green grotto under the new crown and fastened it all over my existing tooth. It was only fitting that I be the first test subject of an implanted battery now bearing my name.

They then asked me to pick a fixed physical address near the airstrip where they would overnight a parcel. I could only think of the abandoned auto tire store where I'd first met

Gwennie. Finding the street number on the internet took less than five minutes. The undisclosed contents of the package weren't yet ready for "deployment", in triplet-speak, but I was cryptically advised to keep an eye toward the sky.

♦♦♦

The argument with Fee was as heated as I can ever remember. He insisted that he and the boys tag along. I flat-out refused. Brandon, Dean, and Gilbert eventually persuaded their dad that the forces compelling my presence in Montezuma Creek likely had the resources to identify and interrupt any guardian angels at any point along the way. The boys doubled down on rigging my personal vehicle with video and audio capture, satellite and 4G locators, both emergency position-indicating radio and personal locator beacons, and even my initials and DOB written in giant font on the roof of my car in infrared ink - visible only via specialized overhead camera. But all these measures could be defeated as simply as separating driver from car. Plus, the EPIRB distress call defaulted to summoning the nearest cavalry - and the FBI already had me in their sights with dubious motive.

The threat to kill the coy-dog was implicit. Fee stressed tactfully that her life was not worth mine. On paper, no question. But he hadn't had the privilege. In any event, someone was now close to breaking this whole saga wide open and I didn't intend to sit it out three states away like a pigeon under glass.

Chapter 68

The drive to Montezuma Creek took just shy of 15 hours, which was only an hour or two longer than flying from SFO to Salt Lake City and driving the rest of the way, by the time you accounted for traffic getting to the airport, trying to snag a stand-by seat on a last-minute flight, security checks, and the predictable rigamarole at the rental car counter in Utah. I pulled into the empty parking lot outside the deserted tire store at about 3:30 am, reclined my seat, and tried to catch a few winks before heading over to the airstrip. The time on the road had passed quickly, as I hatched and scrapped plan after plan. It looked like I'd be forced to improvise - historically not my strong suit.

A few years ago at the wedding reception of a high school classmate with whom I'd only recently resumed a tepid friendship, a staid affair with a string quartet and a strict dress code held in the ancestral home of the bride, whose family had acquired vast tracts of California ranchland via the system of Spanish Land Grants in the 1700's, I accidentally dropped my spoon into my water glass during the lull prior to the eagerly-anticipated toasts by the best man, maid of honor, and father of the bride. As a hush fell and all eyes turned to me, I stood, nervous and unprepared, and croaked a short and safe tribute in my best eighth grade Español: "Wishing You Health, Wealth, and Happiness, and Time to Enjoy Them", which, when out of practice, sounds exactly like "May Your Lifeless Plantain Grow Happy in Time". I'm not that good under pressure.

♦♦♦

I woke to the noise of a FedEx truck squeaking to a stop in front of the tire store. The driver heaved and slid a large cube-shaped package next to Gwennie's old water spout. He bounced back up into the cab, released the parking brake, and rolled away as the sun peeked over the eastern mesa.

I was squinting at the forbidding BIOHAZARD sticker on the side of the box, when something inside began to move. A whirring circular blade emerged and cut through the thick packing tape, the top flaps, and down each corner, dropping all four panels of cardboard flat on the ground before retracting like a transformer toy into the center dome of the quadcopter that then assembled itself by unfolding its four blade arms. Without warmup or noise, the drone rose vertically and flew toward my car. It hovered over the windshield just long enough to dip its rotor booms, and zoomed off in a blur. I've got to get those kids a ham.

It was time to scout out the situation at the meeting point. In the dark, I hadn't noticed the long freight train stopped on the single track now blocking my view of the dirt runway. I left the protection of my vehicle and headed over on foot.

The rail cars, all ore carriers by the looks of them, appeared empty, and stretched as far as I could see; the engine and caboose both well beyond my line of sight. I climbed carefully over the coupling between two cars and faced what used to be the airstrip.

On the other side of the windsock was an idling herd of Brobdingnagian-scale earth-moving machines: dump trucks and bulldozers, giant augers and excavators, even a huge tracked steam shovel, arranged as if staging outside an open pit mine. Parked in front of this mega lineup, Mrs. DeLong's pickup looked like Andorra facing off against the Red Army. Forget subtlety. This was a brute force operation.

Approaching the familiar 4x4 with more than a little trepidation, I tried to keep my shoulders back and gait steady. Walking the gauntlet of ten-foot tall tires, I could only make out dim forms behind the windscreens up in the cabs of the gathered fleet. The heads all wore ball caps; the faces: sunglasses and beards. All cut from the same cloth: "contractors" you might see on the ground in places like Helmand Province and the Sunni Triangle. Nation builders, I told myself. Maybe Montezuma Creek was springing for a new runway. Maybe Trudy can fly.

By the tailgate of the pickup, a tall man in coveralls, his face covered by sunglasses and a ski mask, held a computer tablet in one hand and a dog leash in the other. Slightly behind him, head up, but lying on the weedy gravel, was a canine muzzled with duct tape. I stopped about ten feet away.

"Gwennie?"

The skinny coy-dog hopped to her feet. All three of them. She was missing one of her forelegs. I felt sick.

"What happened to her?", I demanded of the faceless form.

In response came the sound of his finger tapping and then tracing over the touchscreen display on his device. When he was through, he held up the computer slate.

SHOT BY RANCHER. PROBABLY CHEWED OFF WOUNDED LEG. AFTER ALL SHE DID FOR YOU.

"You gotta take that tape off. How's she supposed to.."

I moved toward her. He easily stiff-armed my advance and went back to his slate.

GET IN THE TRUCK. YOU'RE DRIVING. YOU KNOW THE WAY.

"I don't think so."

The tall man stiffened.

"I..I mean, know the way." I stammered.

GET HER ON BOARD. OR SHE DIES HERE AND NOW.

He used his leash hand to show me the stainless steel .45 automatic pistol just inside his front cargo pocket. Without delay, I boosted Gwennie into the front passenger's seat and slid behind the wheel as our mute host climbed behind me into the crew cab. Good thing I'd thought to bring the key. Iceberg eyes looked over at me as I started the engine. She shook her head just once and then stared straight ahead out the windshield. This was not going to be like old times.

♦♦♦

"She'll do a lot better without that tape."

I'd barely made it into the first narrows before realizing I was already lost. Every other arroyo and mesa looked exactly the same.

SHE BITES ME AND I PUT ONE BEHIND HER EAR

I nodded and then braked long enough to pull the duct tape off her snout as gently as I could. She squeezed her eyes shut a few times but didn't make a sound. We continued deeper into the wilderness of rock.

In the rearview mirror, just over the shoulder of our captor, I saw what looked like a drone following us - maybe a hundred yards behind. With the front windows part-way down, it was now close enough to hear the faint buzz of its rotors.

With only my single trip here to go on and Gwennie on strike, we made it to Mrs. DeLong's trailer above the dry wash in about 90 minutes. I made several wrong turns into box canyons and dead-end trails along the way, but somehow managed to blunder back to the main path each time. Silent throughout, but carefully plotting GPS coordinates along our route, our captor had tapped me on the shoulder on two occasions, each time before getting out of the truck to take photos and digital measurements of the widths of particularly narrow passages.

Who *are* these guys? The drivers back on the airstrip were right out of Central Casting; almost parodies of the modern-day mercenary. White, ex-military, as American as mom and apple pie. If mom made her crust with C-4. The big mime in the back seat was a tougher nut to profile. Deep pockets, long reach, logistical chops - who has the kind of throw-weight to roll in a *train*? Some sort of state actor was my guess. Although Cameo and Parsec might be on that short list too.

The three of us stood in front of the 4x4 facing the trailer. Our keeper motioned toward the heavily-reinforced front door. Making a hard landing with the support of only one foreleg, Gwennie lay down on the gravel and stared ahead stoically. I produced the carbon fiber key from my pocket, walked up the steps, and opened the lock. The masked man gestured for me to enter first while the buzzing drone hovered conspicuously high overhead. No doubt his friendlies on the other end of that joystick.

Inside, he pointed to the couch. I sat as instructed while he searched the space from room to room, methodically and exhaustively; pushing up ceiling tiles and using an electric screwdriver to remove the fan vents in the bathroom and the range hood in the kitchen. If he was angry at finding nothing that interested him, he didn't let on. Rather than ransacking the place, he neatly returned it to the way I'd found it on my first visit. He retrieved his tablet from the coffee table and tapped out another command.

TAKE ME TO THE MOTHER LODE

♦ ♦ ♦

Gwennie had made it clear from the outset today that she wasn't playing ball and continued to stare stubbornly out the windshield. Panic began its cold creep up my spine. I was driving blind now, steering the pickup over a torturous landscape that threatened to roll us at any turn. The guy with the gun banged his head on the side window and grunted his displeasure. As he continued to slosh around in the back seat,

I concentrated on keeping at least two tires in contact with terra firma through the nastier dips and bends.

I was completely lost. And without a plan. And unlike the loyal coy-dog, I'd cough up the location of the green grotto without hesitation, if I could only remember the way. The gas tank still read ¾ full, and driving it dry would only postpone the reckoning.

At the bottom of a drainage I high-centered the truck on a tall fin of sandstone. Teetering side-to-side with no rubber touching the ground, the rear seat passenger shouldered open his door and timed a clumsy jump onto the slick rock below. He hobbled on landing, but steadied himself and gestured in broad, angry sweeps of his arm for us to get out of the cab.

Gwennie, unfazed by the rough ride, let me lift her over to my side, out the door, and down to the ground, as the truck's tires continued to spin slowly, their treads grabbing only air. Again, we faced the slate.

YOU DON'T SEEM TO BE TAKING THIS SERIOUSLY

He put the tablet down on a table-sized rock and pulled the gun out of his pocket. As he racked the slide, Gwennie growled. Maybe without her handicap, she could've made it in time. But like she was, he was too far away, and I grabbed her leash as she lunged for him, swinging her around in mid-air like a rodeo calf. She landed hard on her good side. As I reached to check on her, from somewhere overhead I heard a thundering, familiar voice.

"Slowly lower the pistol," Dean demanded.

Looking up at our captor, I saw a bold red dot marking the center of his chest, just over the heart. He saw it too.

"Now press the magazine release button with your left ring finger," Gilbert continued.

As the gunman and I craned our heads toward the drone loitering silently less than forty feet above, Gwennie exploited our moment of inattention to yank the leash from my hand and launch her hobbled self at the man with the pistol, knocking him off his feet. As the weapon flew from his grasp, she sunk her fangs deep into his leg, shaking her head violently from side-to-side. Without crying out at all, he simply grabbed her by the scruff of the neck and tossed her away like a plush toy into a creosote bush. As he scrambled for his .45 I saw the flash from the tracer round. Then came the ***BOOM***. The gun simply disappeared from his grasp. Satisfied that he still had a hand, he raised them both in surrender.

This time, it was Brandon's disembodied voice that blared through the drone's bullhorn attachment.

"With your left hand, remove your sunglasses. With your right, take off the mask. Throw each to the side, and lay face down on the ground. Then place your hands.."

Another ***BOOM***.

The captor hadn't had time to comply with any of Brandon's orders before a second, larger drone - the platform shadowing us earlier - fired on the first. Both humans and one coy-dog stared slack-jawed as, like airborne dreadnoughts, the Fainu'us' whisper copter traded muzzle blasts with the noisier bird. Both choppers missed in the initial exchange and quickly fled to the cover of opposite canyons.

I finally looked down to see Gwennie, head tilted, still looking up at the retreating drones. But the masked man was gone.

Chapter 69

Eager to put daylight between ourselves and our mysteriously-vanished captor, and with Gwennie's renewed cooperation, we made it back to the familiar dry wash on foot in not too much more time than it had taken us to get stuck in the truck. She bristled when I tried to give her a hand over some of the steeper sections, and hopped along slowly but capably without a hint of complaint or self-pity.

Approaching the trailer, we saw right away someone had been here just before us. The gravel around the water faucet out front was freshly damp. Locked outside without the key, I started to fill Gwennie's water bowl as quickly and quietly as I could, hoping we'd go unnoticed in case our abductor was inside loading one of the long guns from Mrs. D's closet. Before I could top off the empty canteen I'd salvaged from the stranded 4x4, the shadow of the helicopter was over us.

This was the real deal - a full-size HH-60 Pave Hawk with **FBI** painted in bold on the tail. It descended rapidly, the buffeting from its rotors enough to keep us rooted where we stood. A crewman in a green jumpsuit and visored helmet grabbed the back of my arm and urged me toward the open door of the cabin. I pulled free, grabbed Gwennie, and climbed onto the aircraft. The co-pilot offered me a pair of noise-cancelling headphones which I put on while cupping my palms over the coy-dog's ears. The flight back to the airstrip took less than fifteen minutes.

After letting us off, the chopper immediately took to the air again in a deafening whirlwind. Wearing sunglasses, and what looked to be a tailored FBI windbreaker, Special Agent Michelle Li stood waiting by the orange windsock, the downdraft whipping her toner-black hair around her head until the aircraft shrank from view.

"Mr. Feeney."

She greeted me with a thin smile, every hair already back in place, as I continued to untangle the comb-over from around my ear.

"Agent Li."

I gripped Gwennie's leash a little tighter. Looking around, I couldn't help but notice that the huge array of trucks prepositioned on the runway had been deserted, with no drivers in sight.

"It got mighty quiet around here all of a sudden," I remarked.

"They've all been cited and released. The cost of doing business for a contractor. There's an even chance we may re-hire most of them back ourselves if they don't already have next gigs lined up."

"Who were they working for before you showed up?," I asked.

"Red Sandstone, LLC. AKA The People's Republic of China. They typically get paid through an intermediary, which gives all parties deniability. So, in fairness, they might not even have known who was signing their checks. Do you have any idea how badly Beijing wants your battery?"

I shook my head. Looking over Li's shoulder it was now clear she wasn't exactly alone. Four tan machine gun-mounted Humvees were parked between the freight train and the landing strip. I quickly lost count of helmeted heads leaning against the vehicles as she answered her own question.

"Enough to nudge their client state to resume underground nuclear testing."

"What? You're serious?"

"We have it on good authority the Chinese have acquired your twelfth core sample. They'd really prefer to get their hands on your substrate in bulk as a proven concept, but believe North Korea might just have the right geology to source a competitive battery. You didn't think this was merely another provocation by the Hermit Kingdom?"

I gestured at the earth-moving armada all around us.

"And you're just gonna let all this slide? It seems pretty hostile to me, if not a downright act of war.."

"Nothing...and I mean *nothing*...is to upset our crucial trade negotiations with China. We look the other way and pretend nothing happened. Actually, that's where you come in."

"I'm afraid to ask."

"We now know that Elizabeth DeLong, for no consideration, and for reasons that remain unclear, some 18 months ago deeded more than 30,000 acres of nearby land here in Utah to you, her occasional limo driver, via a transfer formalized under a canopy of shade better known as the great State of Nevada. Don't take this the wrong way, but, why you?"

"No idea. I am pretty punctual, I guess."

She smirked. I shrugged.

"That's all I got. Believe me, this baffles me as much as anyone. Listen, can I tell you about the guy who held us at gunpoint? Before your chopper picked us up?"

"Do you have a description?"

"He was wearing a mask. And sunglasses. But white, by the color of his hands. Never said a word, just tapped out his demands on his tablet. But he...or somebody...sent me a ransom note...to my email here.."

I turned on my phone and opened my email account. There was no sign of the message.

"It's not here. Can they do that?"

"Hack your email? A cockatoo with Bluetooth just ordered crackers and a locksmith from its cage."

I spread my arms broadly.

"This whole...attempted...excavation...He had to have been the ringleader. Probably a little on the tall side to be Chinese."

"OK. How tall? Build? What was he wearing?"

"About 6-5, 6-6. Medium frame. Coveralls. Blue coveralls."

"Tell you what, just make a mental note of anything distinguishing about him you remember...posture...gait... did...did...he have labored breathing.."

"You're not gonna look, are you?"

"Bigger themes at play here. For what it's worth, I actually believe you about your abduction. The guy didn't have to be Chinese. Let's just agree that would be dumb and a little obvious. Throw a rock in any direction and you'll hit a Western proxy greedy enough to do their bidding. It turns my stomach, but that's what it is. In your case, it's gotta be no blood, no foul, I'm afraid."

She paused for a moment, as if trying to read my mind, before continuing.

"Now you wanna ask me, why me? There is nothing *inscrutable* about my loyalties, if that's where you're headed."

"Huh? I'm headed home, unless the U.S. government has some other idea."

"Speak of the devil...your land here, all rights and claims to any mineral resources, and all improvements hereupon, pursuant to the Defense Production Act of 1950, are now effectively under the joint control and authorization of the United States Departments of Energy and Defense. The corrected amendment to title will be made *in camera,* and will not require your assent."

"On what grounds are you expropriating the...my... property?"

"Think of it as an eminent domain action in the interests of public safety and national security. The residual radiation represents a local health hazard. More significantly, Elizabeth DeLong, and her assign - you - came into possession of the source material forming the plenary basis of your battery patent, illegally."

"How so?"

"Please, Mr. Feeney."

"My attorney.."

"..will have time to file an injunction. But he'll come to see the futility and counsel you against it. In 1968, DeLong's missing paramour, with treasonous intent, stole critical government property before the ink on his discharge was dry. You have no standing to enjoy the spoils of his treachery. Period."

"But he died in Germany on a training mission while on active duty. I read the obituary."

"Are you familiar with Project Green Light?"

Struck dumb, I stared at her with my mouth open.

YOU'VE GOT THE GREEN LIGHT.

Somehow, she didn't read my surprise.

"Look it up online and fill in the fibs. By the way, full disclosure to the U.S. Patent Office might compromise sensitive information about the nature of the attendant security breach and is never going to happen. So, you'll still have that shingle to hang alongside your I-peaked-in-high-school diploma."

"Wow."

"Sorry. This job definitely doesn't help, but I was told early on as a child that I lacked sensitivity. Ironically, by a piano teacher who denied the Holocaust. Ah…"

Her cell phone pinged. She looked down at the screen and muttered smugly.

"Multiple offers. No contingencies. Drive safely, Mr. Feeney."

She pirouetted 180 degrees, and walked away.

Chapter 70

Gwennie was a much more affable co-pilot on the long drive home to the Bay Area. Her cold shoulder on our excursion with the kidnapper had apparently only signaled her resolve to resist his demands to reveal the location of the green grotto. She now actually seemed excited about the next chapter in her life, eagerly looking out the windshield at new landscapes, and munching chips and pork rinds like a two-legged road warrior. And I could swear she pointed right with her snout toward an exit with a gas station seconds before the low fuel indicator chimed. Maybe she was one of those animals who could pick stocks or predict earthquakes.

That flight of fancy jogged my memory about the Fainu'us' inquiry into the USGS archives and the long-forgotten temblor of 1971 just outside Montezuma Creek. Agent Li had coyly suggested that Elizabeth DeLong's "paramour" had outlived his own obituary, practically scoffing at the idea that he'd died in 1968, as reported. Project Green Light, I learned from a cursory online search from my phone, was a highly-classified program begun during the Cold War that planned for small teams of elite American commandos to infiltrate behind enemy lines with portable atomic explosives intended to wreak asymmetrical havoc when the shooting started. Staff Sergeant Raymond Doubletree had served in the U.S. Army's Special Forces - one of the elite units from whose numbers Green Light operators were selected. The FBI's clear accusation was that Doubletree had stolen critical government property. The unspoken implication was that that property was a backpack nuke, and that its detonation, by intent or accident, had triggered the green gravy train.

I wondered what Doubletree was up to in the years between his "death" in a training exercise in Germany, as reported by *Stars and Stripes,* and the blast that caused the earthquake in Utah three years later. One thing was for sure: prim and proper Mrs. D had a thing for bad boys. Or at least one.

The triplets had texted twice and left three voicemails. I pulled off the road as Gwennie slept, called to allay their concerns about my welfare, told them I was on the way home and would give a full report upon return. The rest of our debrief was made via video, the boys forwarding me a secure link showing, all from an on-board camera, first, the dogfight having gone their way, with their drone downing its larger adversary; second, their robot claw attachment scavenging and retrieving wreckage from the vanquished UAV for forensic analysis; and finally the whisper-copter returning to the abandoned tire store, touching down in the middle of the splayed-out FedEx box, swapping the scary BIOHAZARD label for a call tag, retracting its rotor booms, and taping up the corners and top flaps, *from the inside.*

I then reached out to Sanjay Singh, who got Jay Montague out of a meeting and onto our three-way call. The lawyer said he would immediately file a motion to request a stay to delay the seizure of property by the feds, but he was quite downbeat about my long-term prospects to keep them off the land. We set up an in-person meeting for tomorrow.

Rather than continue over the Coast Range to the Fainu'us', I decided to cut the trip a little short and crash at my own place for the first time in a while. I let Fee know in a text I hoped he wouldn't see until after daybreak. Gwennie hobbled up the stairs to my apartment and fell sound asleep at the foot of my bed before I'd finished brushing my teeth.

Chapter 71

The first stop in the mid-morning was a local veterinary clinic. Even without an appointment they were able to squeeze us in to see a tech and finally a vet after only a short wait. I suspected Gwennie's unusual pedigree might have piqued the interest of the staff who bumped her toward the head of the line. They gave her a short physical and a couple of catch-up vaccinations. Not surprisingly, she had an infection at the site of her stump and would need what was described as fairly straight-forward surgical debridement of necrotic tissue. I patted her head as they put her under and then went out to the car and caught up with the Fainu'us on the phone in the time it took perform the operation. The vet let me be there when they woke her up. She looked a little dazed by the overhead fluorescent light at first but eventually turned toward me and licked my hand. Probably just the anesthesia talking, but cheap sentiment or not, it brought tears to my eyes.

Gwennie had much the same reaction when she first laid eyes on Trudy in her pen at Fee's farm. In retrospect, she may have gotten the wrong idea. Never, we guessed, had she seen and smelled anything quite so scrumptious in the wild. I walked the coy-dog over to the thin gap in the fence.

Trudy bounded over like the big-boned gal at the cotillion who knocks over the punchbowl on the way to greet her new friend. As Gwennie was sizing her up, Trudy planted a big sloppy kiss right on her snout. The coy-dog stiffened and her hackles appeared. But the hog wouldn't be deterred and continued to demonstrate her affection. Sensing impending violence, I reached to pull Gwennie back by the scruff, only to watch her tail begin to wag.

"Are we live-streaming this?", asked Gilbert.

"Lions and lambs...There's hope for humanity!", declared Fee.

"Disabled..", noted Brandon.

"..morbidly obese..", remarked Dean.

"..inter-species! Bi-curious! This is fetish gold! Keep rolling!"

"She's gonna blow up our channel!"

"No pronouns!"

I stuck around a while longer to make sure Gwennie was adjusting to her strange new surroundings. By the time I left she was fast asleep in the dry corner of the pen, her head on Trudy's snout, rising and falling with each snuffle.

Chapter 72

If you were looking for discretion, the Rosewood Sand Hill would not be your go-to place. A low-rise luxury hotel located on a gentle slope below an off-ramp at the intersection of Interstate 280 and Sand Hill Road, it looks out at the oak-studded foothills of the Santa Cruz Mountains over some of the most expensive office space in America. In a digitally distributed world, mostly of their making, venture capital firms continue to pay through the nose for the privilege to keep a physical presence on the broad asphalt artery above Stanford. Exotic sports cars idle their days like trophy wives taking the sun in the well-watched parking lots up and down the hill. The hotel's restaurant, and adjacent library & bar, are strictly see and be seen. You come here to make a splash. I'm not sure what Sanjay was thinking.

Jay Montague and Sanjay were waiting for me at a faux low-key table next to a lit fireplace in the corner of the bar. Neither had yet ordered. A waitress approached.

"Gentlemen?"

"Bill?" Sanjay waited for me to order a beer. Jay had a single-malt. Sanjay, a Coke. The VC continued, maybe a little louder than necessary.

"What do you get when you take Adderall with Viagra?"

Jay and I shrugged.

"An erection that remembers your anniversary."

Our waitress fumbled her tray of empty glasses on her way back to the bar. Sanjay was playing the room, cooling rumors before they started. You never knew who might be listening. He continued at a much more conversational volume.

"Jay's motion I told you about should keep the feds off the land for at least 90 days."

Jay elaborated.

"But they've already countersued to prevent any hasty exploitation of the resource on your part pending a decision in the 10th Circuit. The case is theirs to lose. Our only chance lies in their fear of open court. But even if you get to keep the property, doing anything productive with it may prove impossible. The CFIUS sitting today is probably the toughest we've seen in decades."

I had to ask Jay to explain.

"CFIUS?"

"Committee of Foreign Investment in the United States. Members from Justice, State, Defense, Commerce, Energy, and Homeland Security, led by Treasury. Started by Gerald Ford out of fear of Japanese investment in American companies involved in key sectors - mostly electronics, manufacturing, and energy. Today it's almost all about the Chinese, with the Saudis a distant second. Anyway, the Committee examines proposed takeover bids, joint ventures, minority stake funding, now even real estate deals near military bases. Anything seen as a potential threat to national security is considered. They convene in secret and report directly to the President. It's either an unaccountable protectionist racket or a sensitive tool to safeguard our industrial base from malign overseas control. Or maybe both."

"Wow."

"We don't know if the Committee has discussed your interests yet. Your case is not an exact fit with their mission per se, but they're rarely shy about making recommendations - usually to keep home-grown strategic assets reliably air-gapped away from any overseas supply chains. The BIS...sorry for the alphabet soup...Bureau of Industry and Security, which is part of Commerce, manages any proactive or remedial measures involving export controls and the like. Meanwhile, the FBI has already made an informal request asking about the exact location of the resource on your property."

"What do you advise?"

"I haven't responded. I think silence is the best strategy at the moment."

I nodded back at Jay. Despite his best efforts to hide it, Sanjay looked a little crestfallen. He finished swirling the ice in his glass and looked right at me. This time, he spoke just above a whisper.

"They're not likely to threaten the patent. So that's something. How are you doing for money?"

"I'm OK."

He went on.

"Your Cameo shares are still way under water."

I nodded and then continued.

"The stipend from Mrs. D gave me a little cushion."

Sanjay and Jay both nodded quietly. I went on.

"But I'll be calling my boss in the morning."

Chapter 73

As fate would have it, my first pickup was Sanjay, headed to the airport.

"Morning, Bill."

"Morning, Mr. Si...Sanjay."

Old habits are hard to break. He raised an eyebrow but didn't rib me as he might have ordinarily. We traveled in silence for several long minutes. I knew he'd crack first.

"How are you doing?"

"No complaints. It's not like I had time to get used to the idea and develop a taste for falconry or something."

"Indulge me a small tale. My grandfather was a poor man. Even by the humble standards of India. And almost perversely proud of it. My stoic grandmother played along for years, cooking up any sorry scraps he might bring home as food for the family. But when he insisted that dandruff was a condiment, she snapped. And actually left him. A very big deal there. What I'm saying here is, don't be too proud of it."

I nodded slowly before replying.

"Point made and taken."

"I hope you don't feel insulted."

"No. No. I was just wondering...."

He leaned forward almost diffidently toward the back of my seat.

"Yes?"

"When did they translate the Brothers Grimm into Punjabi?"

He snorted a surprised laugh.

"You bastard! I thought the Irish were prone to the maudlin."

"The day is still young."

I dropped him at SJC and did the rounds between SFO and the South Bay almost on autopilot. By early evening, I'd driven ten separate people and covered more than three hundred miles, only deadheading two trips. I knew every passenger and his or her predilections, and beyond the pleasantries and polite concern about my bandaged forehead, was able to keep the chatter to a minimum. The day was oddly relaxing, and I couldn't remember a thing anyone had said in the car the whole time.

Fee called to make sure I was still on-board for our long-planned treasure hunt with Trudy. Of course I'd forgotten, but didn't let on. This was to be the big shakedown before her eventual run at the elusive black winter truffle, and he wanted to be reassured that she'd let bygones be bygones. Risking a small fortune to a potentially vindictive omnivore was to be avoided. In Italy, a man could retire on the proceeds of a single white Alba variety. Fee kept a close eye on the commodity prices and knew exactly the premium a prime Périgord black could fetch these days at some of the better restaurants in the Bay Area - almost a thousand dollars a pound. Truffles cultivated locally in California and, like fish, sold fresh, were now commanding top dollar. Through Harley, our old classmate and the local Fish & Wildlife warden, Fee had learned that an illegal pot farm busted, burned, and then replanted with native white oak saplings, now had all the trappings of a first-rate truffle habitat. He wouldn't divulge the location other than to say that it was on public land. Fee had narrowed down the likely spots to a manageable few.

For logistical reasons - we were less likely to get caught under a new moon - tonight was the night for our dry run under the stars. Legend had it that the good citizens of Half Moon Bay had buried a time capsule in the narrow patch of lawn in front of the old clock tower on the corner in front of the dry goods store on Main Street in 1906, three months before the devastating San Francisco earthquake. Untold keepsakes and valuables awaited. My plan to ask Jackie Banerjee out for a proper meal would have to be postponed. I'd promised my oldest friend, and the Fainu'us had welcomed Gwennie into their barnyard brood with open, if somewhat mercenary arms.

Chapter 74

On this foggy, moonless night, Fee and I drove down the hill into town with Trudy and Gwennie, already inseparable, behind us in the bed of the pickup. The boys had opted out of our adventure, sharing an apathy toward "old timey" things like rooting around for mementoes from prehistory. It was late, and the few restaurants and bars on Main Street were now closed.

We pulled off into a gravel parking lot behind the feed and grain store and got out, Fee dropping the tailgate and sliding out a long piece of 2 x 6 lumber for Trudy to brave. She hoofed it down the ramp, bowing the wood with every mincing little step, and cooperated without protest when Fee put her in her harness. We'd rummaged up an old dog leash from the back of the barn for Gwennie, who was happy to get the same treatment as her new bestie. Fee grabbed the shovels, handed me mine, and we headed on tiptoes toward the old clock tower.

We'd intentionally left the metal detector back at the farm. Fee had been preparing Trudy by familiarizing her with the smell of nickel and other corrosion-resistant alloys commonly used to construct and line mugs, boxes, and other containers in the early 1900's, several samples of which he'd scavenged from flea markets up and down the coast. While the existence of the local time capsule was one of the worst-kept secrets in town, interest had faded along with the underwhelming public reception surrounding the disinterment of similar troves in communities nearby. Antique collectibles were one thing, but nobody cared about a rotten bottle stopper and some yellowed want ads from a bygone era. Besides, the exact whereabouts of the capsule were unknown. Fee was working a hunch he'd had for years, after overhearing the ramblings of an old timer his late wife Teuila had taken care of in his dying days.

Despite Gwennie having only had an introductory training session with old metals back at the farm, the second set of nostrils paid off almost immediately. Just behind the old clock tower, in a fortuitously situated spot alongside a flower bed well-hidden from the casual passer-by, the pig and coy-dog, starting from different directions, combed the earth in a grid pattern until they stood fixed, one after the other, over the exact same spot. As legend had the time capsule buried in front of the tower, we were circumspect, but had felt a thorough search of the little plaza was warranted. Thinking this couldn't possibly be this easy, we pulled the two animals off the scent and tried out front. After only cursory sniffs over the small grass strip, the pair retreated around back, practically nose-diving in unison over the same spot as before. Sometimes you just get lucky, I guess.

We tied the animals to a concrete garbage can on the sidewalk and started digging as quietly as we could. The flower bed was well-watered and the dirt soft. In less than twenty minutes we were able to hollow out a two-foot square hole about a yard deep before Fee's shovel blade tinked against something solid and would go no deeper. His next dig met similar resistance and made the same noise. Eyes now adjusted, I could see my buddy's wide grin in the darkness. Without a word, he gave a hopeful fist pump, handed me his shovel, and dropped down on his knees. Leaning into the hole, he turned on his pen light.

Looking down over his shoulder, I could make out the top of a metal box as he brushed the dirt off the lid. He did the rest of the extrication with a tablespoon, carefully lifting a rectangular container the size of a small sewing machine up out of the hole to ground level.

Fee quickly turned off his flashlight at a sound we couldn't identify. We hunkered down and kept our breaths shallow for what seemed like ages. Satisfied that it was nothing, Fee turned his light back on. I took a flathead screwdriver from my jacket pocket and handed it over, thinking my friend should do the honors. He nodded and passed me the flashlight.

The box was of metal construction, probably an alloy from back in the day, and the exterior appeared to be in remarkably good condition. The two hinges and hasp were intact and there was no lock to open, but the lid was stuck fast. Fortunately, the dirt in the threads of the fastening screws came off easily, and Fee was eventually able to pry the lid off without even damaging the finish.

Something inside reflected off the narrow beam of the pen light. As Fee lowered his hand into the box, he gasped as something jostled his opposite shoulder, knocking him onto his side. Startled myself, I dropped the light into the open hole. The light stuck handle-side down in the soft earth and shone directly up out of the pit into Trudy's twitching pink snout.

"How the hell did she get loose?", Fee whispered.

"I have no idea."

I reached down and retrieved the light as Fee stood up and looked around for the end of Trudy's leash. The giant pig stood staring into the open time capsule. I made my way over to the concrete trash can to look for Gwennie, who was lying down on the sidewalk, he head resting angelically on her front paw. I patted her and went back to the clock tower.

Fee was struggling to pull Trudy away from the hole. She was sitting on her hind haunches like a dog, but a dog with a very rounded rear end. As Fee tugged on the lead to her harness, she rolled over like a giant pink cherub onto her side - and there she stubbornly remained. With too much mass to move, he simply dropped the leash with his own snort of disgust, and returned his attention to the metal box.

The first thing Fee removed was a sealed glass jar containing a few coins and a ribboned medal which were packed tightly under a scroll of parchment and a heavyweight paper envelope. Our breathing grew faster as he cut through the protective wax seal and popped off the metal cap. He reached in and unrolled the scroll, then motioned at me impatiently to redirect the narrow flashlight beam.

The document was a formal proclamation that the Ocean Shore Railway had completed the last section of track serving Half Moon Bay's new *Spanishtown* depot. We both knew the railway connecting San Francisco to the north with Santa Cruz to the south would fall prey to the great earthquake only a few months later. The floridly verbose optimism on the scroll was both sad and amusing. Fee rolled it back up and removed the envelope. He pulled open the flap and removed what looked like a baseball card.

A tall set of ears bounded out of the flower bed in front of us, and Fee and I flinched. Out on the sidewalk, Gwennie, who had somehow slipped her leash, bolted toward the jackrabbit faster than three legs had any right to move. I stood up just as the coy-dog pounced on the bunny and crashed into the patch of petunias under the tower. Before Fee could react, Trudy poked her snout past his hand, grabbed the card, and headed toward the street at a full sprint.

The rest is almost too painful to recount. The time capsule contained few curios and only a modest taste of local history: the railway scroll, a handful of U.S. coins minted in 1906, a military medal stamped the same year commemorating the commission of the USS Pompano, an early supply vessel sailed by the U.S. Navy nowhere near Pacific waters, and a pristine, one-of-a-kind, 1906 Honus Wagner trading card, with an estimated worth at auction of roughly 5 million dollars. Having bided her time, and not one to forgive and forget, Trudy gulped down the legendary shortstop's prized paper likeness with a defiant burp, as I clung to Fee's knees to keep him from strangling her in the middle of Main Street.

Chapter 75

Despite what the scale said, Fee was a lightweight when it came to alcohol; he'd probably had two drinks in his entire life. The debacle under the clocktower drove him to the mini-mart where we bought two 40-ounce cans of malt liquor. I'd called ahead, and by the time we made it back to the farm the boys had formed a picket line to keep their dad from harming their cash sow. I returned her and Gwennie to their pen while Fee, can of brew in hand, trudged disconsolately upstairs to his room in the main house. I headed back over the hill to my place and quickly gave up trying to drink myself to sleep as the recurring image of Trudy's payback kept bringing suds out my nose.

My morning went much the same as yesterday's - steady and predictable. I was starting to get used to getting my old life back. My boss was talking about replacing his fleet with Teslas. Broaching the subject with me at all usually meant his mind was already made up. Questions about charging logistics and downtime optimization and range anxiety all fell away when he explained exactly how much he'd been paying for gasoline over the past several years. Add to that the attractive low maintenance of electric vehicles, the undimmed geek cachet, and the differentiation from most competitors' rides, and I knew it was a done deal. Not a word about climate change. Economics was the real "settled" science in the Silicon Valley.

Already in San Francisco between jobs, and in desperate need of a swim, I found a metered spot on the street big enough and safe enough to accommodate the Town Car. Having beaten the parking odds, I was happy to walk the twenty minutes through Chinatown, North Beach, and Fisherman's Wharf to Aquatic Park. Few neighborhoods in the City are exempt from the well-worn insults of street life, but on the bay side, at least the turds hide the needles.

On my back alley shortcut behind a dim sum place, I walked past the opened screen door to the kitchen and nodded at the chef leaning on a dumpster taking a smoke break. Two steps later I stopped and turned around, finally registering the familiar face inside. I peeked through the pots and pans at a tall Caucasian guy sitting sideways at the back counter: Carl Frost - not eating - but speaking animatedly to an Asian man, also framed in profile. I watched them for only a few seconds before the chef coughed and I continued on my way to the South Side Rowing Club.

♦♦♦

"Hey Fin...Did you know Carl could speak Mandarin?"

"It's gotta be easier than Cantonese."

"You speak Cantonese?!"

Looking like a dissolute nun, he nodded from underneath the bath towel cowled over his head. He continued.

"Met number two in Hong Kong."

"How many times have you been married?"

Even speaking in a loud voice in the tight confines of the steam bath he didn't hear me.

"She had a sister. Could hardly tell one from the other."

"Were they twins?"

"They were Chinese."

Fin was once booted out of assisted living for demanding an open-carry wing. But I was just enough of a San Franciscan to make this a teachable moment in sensitivity.

"Fin, you ever think maybe they might have trouble telling *us* apart?"

He frowned and looked at me like I should be out netting butterflies.

"If the Eskimos have a hundred names for snow, and the Irish have a thousand names for drunk, then the Chinese must have a billion four for doppelganger."

I put my towel over my head in defeat. Fin and I sat across from one another in silence for a few minutes.

"You hear Carl's gettin' a new leg?"

I was startled by the question.

"What?"

"The old one looks all chewed up or somethin'."

I felt the blood draining from my head.

"Did he say what happened?"

"Didn't ask. Only got a quick peek before he pulled his pants on after his swim this morning. But I heard him talkin' on his phone about insurance covering the new one."

There was another lag in the conversation. My mind was reeling when Fin uncharacteristically asked me a follow-up question.

"How long you known him...Carl?"

"I dunno...goin' on three, four years, I guess."

"A real international man of mystery, that guy."

"Whaddya mean?"

"Two FBI agents stopped me on the street on my way back from lunch at Tarantino's today. Askin' about him."

"What did they want to know?"

"How often I saw him, any change in his schedule...that kinda thing. Didn't take long. And you know all this stuff about him volunteering at the Red Cross, right?"

I gulped, nodded, and he continued.

"I was down there the other day tryin' to give blood, and asked around for him. Nobody'd seen him in months. But I practically ran into him right outside the Chinese Consulate. Acted like he was headed to Mass at St. Mary's down the block."

It was all coming together: the mask, the tablet slate, the Chinese connections, the stoic silence when Gwennie sank her fangs into the tall man's leg. He'd been unflappable when I'd accused him about Special Agent Farr, but Carl Frost was no longer who he pretended to be. The FBI was now onto one of their own.

I debated sharing my deductions with an already suspicious Fin, who was already headed in another direction.

"Cute nurses down there at the Red Cross."

"Did they take your blood?"

"Said I needed a note from my doctor. Even after all their personal questions. 'Have you ever taken money or drugs for sex?' What is this, Make-A-Wish for seniors?"

"Fin...uh...about Carl.."

"I got it, kid."

Chapter 76

The SFO - Peninsula run with my next passenger went unremarkably. I was getting back in the groove, a good thing considering the tenuous nature of the whole battery project. Sanjay called and did his best to buck me up, but without much new from Jay to report. As caustic and coldly analytical as Singh could be, VC's often needed to mix the Kool-Aid themselves if their teams had any chance at success. Tellingly, the exuberance in his voice was gone today.

While waiting on the last point-to-point transfer of my shift outside a well-camouflaged plastic surgicenter in Palo Alto, I texted Jackie Banerjee and asked if she was free for dinner some evening this week. To my delight and maybe a little surprise, she said she was. As we finished arranging the details around our schedules, my customer appeared discreetly from behind a row of dense hedges and waited next to the rear passenger compartment. I got out of the car in a hurry and opened the door. With her broad-brimmed flowered hat and saucer-sized sunglasses, the lip enhancement made her look like a grouper trolling the Kentucky Derby. I drove delicately over to the Ritz-Carlton Half Moon Bay in a little less than an hour and, after dropping off, thought I'd check up on Fee.

I could hear the boys carrying on from outside the barn. After saying hi to Gwennie and Trudy, I stepped through the open door. My godsons were seated shoulder-to-shoulder at three separate computer workstations, their backs to me.

"Speaking of causation...let's put our hands together, close our eyes, and pull any finger not your own. Ready? On three."

"Randomized and double blind. I like it."

"Don't touch me."

"Why are we doing this?"

"It might spark parasympathetic flatus across the clonal network."

"How?"

"The troika reflex."

"The elusive triple axel of epigenomics?"

"The stuff...of Nobel. Only observed previously in one matched pair from Latvia. Known juicers. One.."

"Don't do it, Uso! His farts have antlers!"

"In the interest of science? For posterity? *The Fainu'u Conjecture*! Two.."

"No! Uso! No!"

"Three.."

BRAP.

Pfffft.

Pfffft.

"Proof of concept!"

"Jeez, Gilly! What did you eat?! The freakin' Donner Party?"

Stone-faced, Fee walked right by me into the lab.

"You're three grown men still making noises in your pants. The only way this could've gone better is if you were still conjoined."

He left the room, shoulders slumped.

"Well that was mean-spirited."

"He didn't have to go all Pago Pago on us."

I followed Fee back to the main house. He conspicuously averted his gaze from the pig pen as we passed by without a word.

♦♦♦

We sat across from one another in facing sofas in front of the fireplace. He stared up at the ceiling for a very long couple of minutes. I broke the silence gingerly.

"Pouting doesn't become you, Fee. Really. Makes you look like a hippo with a goiter. But not my call. That 'Honus' is on you."

Feeling pretty droll, I chortled at myself.

He glared at me.

"You are such an a-hole."

"The s's being silent between *still friends*?"

He shook his head, broke open a grin, and snickered. Whew.

Chapter 77

Over the next two days I settled back into my job almost as if nothing out of the ordinary had ever happened over the past few weeks. I didn't hear anything from Sanjay or Jay and had largely resigned myself to a full-time return to a mid-life of livery, recently punctuated by an almost indescribably surreal, sometimes painful, but never dull escapade deep into worlds I could've scarcely imagined. Understanding that I'd done nothing to deserve to live the adventure in the first place made it a little easier to let go of the tantalizing idea of having control over an almost immeasurable material fortune. Some things are just not meant to be. Mrs. DeLong had set me up, so to speak, eighteen months before my well-intentioned but bumbling intervention after her heart stopped in the back of the limo. Her lawyer, Thomas Lippincott, had clearly done some kind of background check on her behalf, but I really don't think she saw something there that others didn't. So why me? As sad as it sounds, probably because she'd had nobody else to turn to.

Tonight, Jackie Banerjee and I were heading out on our first official date: dinner at a seafood place we both knew about but neither had tried. It overlooked the crashing waves of Montara Beach, one of the wildest, most picturesque shorelines anywhere. If the air and water were a tad warmer, the fog less persistent, and the riptides a little less grabby, Montara might be the Bondi Beach of North America. I could only hope she was even half as stoked about dinner with me as I was with her.

I'd had an early start at work - first pickup in Marin County at 4 am - and finished up a little past noon - more than enough time for a dip and steam at the South Side. I was still working on my strategy for confronting Carl Frost again, if I ran into him, and had decided to play it cool until my ducks were more aligned. He was a formidably shrewd and ruthless man, as quick a thinker as I've ever met, and I knew the only gun to bring to the showdown better be smoking.

♦♦♦

There was a black-and-white police car and an obviously unmarked government sedan double-parked in front of the club. The front door, usually key card-restricted, was propped open. A little uneasy, I walked inside. On the way to the locker room I heard some talking, two men and a woman - a familiar voice. In front of Carl Frost's open locker stood Special Agent Michelle Li alongside uniformed officers from both the SFPD and SFFD. Peeking down the narrow hallway out the rear window I could make out the diagonal red stripe on the bow of the small Coast Guard search and rescue craft usually berthed on the Sausalito-side of the Golden Gate Bridge. All conversation ceased. I broke the quiet.

"Agent Li."

I could make out what presumably was Carl's new prosthetic leg under the shirt and pants hanging in the locker. A brown loafer was still attached to the hard plastic "foot". I continued.

"Did...something happen to Carl?"

Li exhaled loudly through her nostrils.

"What do you know about it?"

"Nothing. What's going on?"

"When was the last time you were here at the South Side?"

"A few days ago. Tuesday afternoon."

"And you're sure not since Tuesday?"

"Yeah. Why?"

"You haven't heard? Carl Frost hasn't been seen since a training swim early yesterday morning."

I felt dizzy and the need to sit down. Steadying myself and keeping my feet, I said the first thing that came to mind.

"Probably practicing for another Alcatraz crossing. He did it all the time. Did you talk to any of the Sunrisers?"

The Sunrisers were a particularly hardy clique within the club that swam regularly at and around dawn. Sometimes before. The lights of the City would twinkle as they'd merrily splash in the ink-dark waters of the Bay. Way out of my comfort zone. She ignored my question.

"Did Carl Frost make it a habit to swim alone?"

"I don't think so. I mean I'm sure he has. But probably stays inside the breakwater if he does. I've heard of early birds grabbing a buddy or two and going out in two's and three's. But I usually swim in the afternoon."

Following Agent Li's lead, the cop and the fireman glared at me.

"I'm going to need an hour-by-hour record of your whereabouts since Tuesday. Names and contact information of each and every person you spent time with. And you're to stay put in the Bay Area until further notice for follow-up questioning. Your phone.."

I handed over my cell and stared at her, dumbstruck. As usual, she got the last word.

"You might've left this to professionals."

She cut me off like I wasn't even standing there, and returned to examining Carl's locker. The police officer and firefighter brushed past me without speaking. I've never needed a swim more in my life and changed into my trunks in the bathroom.

♦♦♦

I can't even remember my time in the water, but by the time I returned, Carl's locker was closed and the room was empty. The Coast Guard vessel had chugged away as I made it back to the beach, and the cars out front were gone. Trudging to the steam room, I passed by a couple of regulars sitting on barstools drinking coffee in the mess. They just shook their heads in bewilderment when I looked at them. Carl Frost was most likely the strongest open water swimmer in Northern California. To lose him to the Bay was almost inconceivable.

The steam was thick as tule fog as I sat down across from Fin, who nodded at me somberly. We were alone. Neither of us said anything, nor probably knew what to say. As the feeling returned to my cold limbs and the sweat started to bead and roll down my chest, I stood up and reached for the glass door. Fin's voice wafted out of the vapor.

"If the sharks don't have him, he'll be past the Farallones by now."

I stopped in my tracks and turned in his direction. All I could make out through the mist was his wizened right shoulder, now marked by a single tattoo - the five-starred red flag of the People's Republic of China. With a black X through the center.

Chapter 78

The Tesla X was a dream to drive. Mostly. It accelerates like a laser, has a substantial feel while underway, corners unexpectedly well, and runs quiet. The SUV is laden with sensors that actuate comfort and safety features before you even register the need. To the electromechanically disinclined like me, it's a sleek black box - a thinking man's car that does all the thinking for you.

Passengers, livery's bread-and-butter, either love or hate the falcon wing doors. The back seat's not as plush as the Town Car, and people regularly comment on the road noise - ironically more noticeable in the complete absence of engine racket. The unaccustomed quiet can combine with the seamless shifting of torque-on-demand to produce a kind of disequilibrium caused by a *lack* of sensory input. According to a neuroscientist who prefers the Lincoln, the cerebellum may be waiting for balance cues that never arrive. The jury's still very much out on the customer experience.

I was between pickups at a charging station near the San Mateo Bridge off of Highway 101. The wait to get on a tap had been about 20 minutes and I was halfway through the 40 minute charge. It's definitely not as easy as topping off a tank of gas and hopping back on the road. The timing required to keep the current flowing between hard-out passenger pickups exacerbates the vagaries of freeway traffic and planes landing early or late. And there were only so many charging stations and docks. I'd barely had a month behind the new wheel and was already seeking coping mechanisms for range anxiety. Time off's usually the best medicine, but mental health days are strictly on your own dime. Not many drivers take long weekends, but quite a few could use a good 72-hour hold.

On the good side, a job's a job, Jackie Banerjee has been able to ignore my snoring, and I'd accounted to Michelle Li's grudging satisfaction that I'd been nowhere the South Side Rowing Club prior to Carl Frost's disappearance. No remains had been recovered in the weeks since. Fin hasn't mentioned Carl again.

I'd had plenty of time to mull over the events since finding the bugs in the Town Car and the cascade of craziness that followed. There remained plenty of unsolved mysteries, but for me the most puzzling was the fate of Staff Sergeant Raymond Doubletree. The official explanation of his accidental death in Germany didn't hold water. And the idea that he'd been vaporized by the stolen bomb in Utah meant he'd successfully avoided human contact for three whole years after the printing of his phony obituary. I concluded that I stood a better chance of winning the Lotto or getting struck by lightning than learning how he really met his end.

My phone rang. It was Sanjay Singh, who I'd driven three or four times now to the airport without any further mention of our grand battery scheme. He'd mostly talked business on the phone. Our conversations had been cordial but stilted, and I'd starting calling him Mr. Singh again. He hadn't suggested I do otherwise.

"Are you sitting down?"

He sounded excited.

"That's my default, yes."

"All my investments in AI have tanked. Cars drive themselves into lamp posts just like we do and my Roomba's now taken to drinking out of the toilet. I think I may have contracted Mad Cow from my wife and my little girl's probably sequencing her genome with the gym teacher as we speak. The seas are rising and California now officially has more sunny days than Mercury."

"Did you need a ride somewhere?"

"What was the name of your Navajo friend in that little town with the mothballed ordnance plant?"

"Chimney Flat. Um...um...Lee...Lee Thomas. Once a Marine. Always a Marine."

"Do you have his contact information?"

"No. But I could probably track him down. Why?"

"I had Jay Montague order a survey of your property the feds seized."

"Why?'

"A hunch. OK. A Hail Mary. Guess what?"

"What?"

"The feds won in court and they're taking all your land in Utah."

"Uh, yeah. That's what we figured."

"But the force of the explosion caused a strike-slip across the border. The green grotto's been on Navajo land since 1971."

Silence on both ends. Sanjay eventually went on.

"Will you make the introductions with Lee Thomas? Tell him...my other Indian name is *Lunches With Laptop.* And you'll need to give proper notice to your boss this time."

I TRUST YOU'LL DO THE RIGHT THING.